SUDDEN STOP

He was the one person who would turn her luck around. He was the man with the happily ever after. She stared at his face and that beautiful smile. Dear God, here was a kindhearted man. Isabel felt so lucky to have known him, if only for a moment. Then, without realizing, she blinked, and the moment was gone. The lights flickered, and everything went black.

Roadblock
Blind Curve

by

Neil Prior

Copyright © 2015 Neil Prior

ISBN-13: 978-0692371572
ISBN-10: 0692371575

For Irene: *mi amor, mi vida, mi luz*

Chapter *1*

1972. ISABEL ESPINOSA sat on her patchwork quilt and reached to her Pioneer turntable. She spun her new Miles Davis album and set the cartridge needle to the opening track of *On the Corner*. She hoped that an hour of soothing jazz might ease her racing mind. She hoped that the complex chords and trademark improv might take her to a faraway place and allow her a small distraction from the chaos of last week. She hoped that a moment of peace might balance a long war of mother and daughter words.

To Isabel, a short escape from San Jose, California seemed like a simple wish, but in the back of her mind, she sensed that nothing was simple anymore. She sensed that her entire life was about to unravel and the real chaos was set to start. At seventeen years old, she believed that she had lived long enough to trust her feelings. At seventeen, she thought she knew it all. Truth was; her life had barely started.

Halfway through the A-side of the album, Isabel shuddered. The steady base and repeated riffs did nothing to help her anxiety. The bizarre mix of sax, bongos, and electric piano seemed more of a post-production traffic jam. It grated her nerves and made her clench her already-tight spine. *On the Corner* proved to be a definite waste of her twelve dollars. Why didn't she listen to the reviews of her friends? Why didn't she save her money for the Monterey Jazz Festival?

Roberta Flack, Thelonious Monk, Herbie Hancock; they played some good music. Those were the people who could touch her soul.

They were the artists who could make her forget her day to day problems. And right now, she desperately wanted to forget. She wanted nothing more than to set aside any hint of drama and move forward to a clean slate—or at least the illusion of a fresh start.

Grudgingly, she slid the album into its splashy yellow cover and put it next to her bed. She felt disappointed and deceived, frustrated and disheartened. She lamented her now-empty wallet and felt a headache coming on strong. Then—to her dismay—came the flip side.

Her mother, Charlene, bellowed from the hallway. More noise to reckon with, Isabel cringed at Charlene's nasal, strident, accented Spanish voice and bemoaned being too poor to afford a decent headset. Too late to duck under the covers, she felt the knots in her back tighten. She felt her temples throb. She braced for another lecture on the evils of men and music and the temptations of a young woman's body. Isabel yanked her waist-long black hair to the side and fell back to her pillow.

"I can hear that trash halfway down the hallway," Charlene said as she burst through the bedroom door without knocking. She had her dark brown hair pulled back with a rubber band, clearly showing the wrinkles on her cheeks and the scowl on her face. She waved her arm like a short and skinny traffic cop. "It's like you don't try to hide it anymore."

"It's not trash, Mom. It's just bad music."

"*Sex* music is what I would call it. He bought the album for you, didn't he?"

"No one bought it for me. I paid for it myself, and I'm already sorry."

"Even worse that *you* bought it. That's what you play to get him in the mood—and you in trouble. How many times do I have to tell you; you know what it does to a man."

"Trouble?" Isabel muttered, immediately regretting she had said it aloud.

"You know what I mean," Charlene said sharply. "Trouble; like in getting pregnant and having babies you can't afford. Trouble; like in leaving the house and living alone. And I do mean alone because no man in his right mind is going to have a Mexican seventeen-year-old for a mother. You should know that. No man is going to stick around after the fun is over. You'll be on the streets and homeless before you know it. You'll be exactly where you deserve."

"Because of one album? I don't think so. I bought it because I like his music—or *used to* like it."

"Whose music?"

"Miles."

"Miles?" Charlene sneered. "That's what, the name of the boyfriend or the band?"

"There's no boyfriend." Isabel crossed her arms.

"Yes, there is. And the sooner you give me his name, the sooner we can move on."

"Move on to what? More of the same? How is that going to help? Like I told you; I don't know anything about sex music. I don't know anything about a boyfriend. But then, according to you, I don't know nothing about nothing."

Isabel abruptly stood, snagged her purse, and made her way to the bedroom door. She carefully avoided a face to face confrontation with Charlene. But as she passed into the hallway, she picked up the scent of fresh tomato salsa. That meant lunch was on the menu; pork gorditas, Spanish rice, and refried beans. Although she felt tempted to stay for the food, she had no intention of ruining a good meal with a bad argument. She quickened her pace to the front door.

"Don't talk to me like that," Charlene growled as she caught up from behind. "Don't you ever use that tone. *Conozco bien tus trucos. Y tu padre—conozco bien todas las mentiras.*"

"Okay, I have no idea what you're saying, and you know what; I don't care. I know I'm a good daughter, and you can't tell me otherwise. If you don't believe me; that's not my fault. I can only do so much. I can only tell you the truth and stand back. It's not worth the aggravation to argue."

"You won't argue, because you can't. And you don't have to know what I'm saying. The house rules are clear in any language. Follow them, and you'll be fine."

Isabel shuddered. "You and your rules. I'm sorry, Mom, you can't control me for the rest of your life—or the rest of *mine*. That's not going to happen. I will *never* let it happen."

Charlene set her hand to her hip. "Where do you think you're going?"

"Out."

"Where?"

"For a walk," Isabel snapped. "Maybe to Cathie's house. Maybe somewhere else. I don't know."

"Go ahead," Charlene said, folding her arms across her chest. "No money, no car, no job, and it's Saturday."

"Saturday?"

"I know your schedule to the minute. It's always the same— boyfriend or not. Today; you'll be home for lunch. I guarantee it. You'll eat what I'm making then leave for the rest of the day. Only difference; this time, when you get home, your gimme-your-love record will be gone. Total trash; that's what it is."

"It's a moot point," Isabel said, softening her tone. "You won't be hearing the album again—or any music for that matter. I'm ready to give up on jazz. I'm ready to give up on a lot of things."

"You know I'm right," Charlene said. "I usually am."

"Yes, Mom. So I've heard."

Isabel stomped out the front door. She latched and locked the screen door behind. Suddenly, Charlene's one-story tract home seemed barely bigger than a closet, barely roomy enough for a struggling middle-class family. It would've been so much easier if Isabel had had an ally in the immediate family; someone to talk to, someone to confide in, someone with a hint of common sense. As it was, this middle child felt in the middle of a large void.

As she hurried along the sidewalks of the neighboring streets, Isabel brooded about the family spotlight always beaming in her direction.

She had an older sister, Ruby; tall, pretty, perpetually smiling. She had moved out of the house and moved on with her life as a telephone operator. Good for her; she got her act together. But nowadays, Ruby had little time to talk, even less time for big-sister advice. When Isabel went looking for support, Ruby was often nowhere to be found.

Randy—the much younger brother—struggled in grade school, kept busy with junior football, and savored his collection of Hot Wheels cars. He had little kid problems of his own and couldn't care less about girls or young women. Essentially, Randy stayed out of the picture, and for the most part, he stayed out of trouble.

Leo was the father. He spent most of the days driving trucks and most of the nights playing cards. Short, thin, balding, and frowning; he seemed far from a powerful patriarch. He rarely intervened with family affairs and never dispensed fatherly advice; to Randy, to Isabel, or to anyone. Leo seemed a father by genetics only. To Isabel, this family of five hardly seemed a family at all.

Thank God for cousin Cathie. Even though Cathie was ten years older, she and Isabel had developed a special bond. Shared dreams, a sympathetic listener, and a passion for jazz and mango iced tea; Cathie was about the best friend that Isabel could hope for. And she lived nearby. That meant no begging for the Chevy Impala and no long reports of, "I did this, and Cathie did that."

Cathie, to her credit, had found a good man; Grant. She married him and settled down to raise a family. According to Charlene, Cathie would've been the perfect daughter. Perhaps so.

Isabel glanced up at the clear October sky and took in a deep breath. The warm sunshine fell on her face as she inhaled the scent of butterfly bush that drifted from a nearby garden. The fragrance took her back to an easier age of morning walks to grade school and weekend picnics at Almaden Lake. She had no worries back then. She had no troubles; except getting her hands on the newest Barbie. The simple pleasures seemed worthwhile.

She slowed her walk to appreciate a few minutes of calm. She welcomed a nerve-settling respite that seemed little more than a nap in the eye of a hurricane. Isabel sighed. Trouble was always one step behind. Worries; one step ahead. On the horizon; a major storm was brewing, and there was no way to avoid it.

Despite Charlene's incessant ranting about men and jazz, despite her interminable rules about her house, car, and budget, Isabel realized that all of that paled compared to what lay ahead. She struggled to find the best words and the best time to inform her mother that their lives were about to be changed. She had procrastinated as long as she could, but time had run out. Her dilemma had a fast-approaching deadline. Now, only one issue remained. Even so, the remaining task seemed insurmountable; how could she possibly tell her mother that she was engaged to be married in six weeks?

Chapter *2*

ISABEL TRUDGED UP the winding, oak dotted street to Cathie's house. Already, she felt a million miles from Charlene's house and a world away from a neighborhood of chain-link fences, cars on cinder blocks, front yards in disrepair, and people who just didn't care.

She saw Cathie's MGB in the driveway and realized that Cathie was home. Immediately, she felt safe. The garden of azaleas, the cool shade of a crape myrtle tree, and the ladybug-adorned sign that said 'Welcome Friends' felt truly inviting.

She passed through the gate of the white picket fence, latched it behind then lingered. Why couldn't this be her home? Why couldn't her own family be so cordial? Perhaps one day, if she made a family of her own, she would find her slice of paradise. Isabel ran her finger along her shoulder. She could barely feel the gold necklace that lay beneath her burgundy, boat neck sweater. She could easily feel her mood shift from despair to glimmer of hope.

Out of habit, she glanced at the street. There was no hint of Charlene or anyone who would spread gossip to Charlene. With one step closer to a safe and friendly house, Isabel pulled at her gold necklace until she withdrew the diamond ring that dangled at the end. The one-and-a-half carat, brilliant cut, flawless diamond sparkled. She couldn't help but smile. In six weeks, she would marry the man of her dreams and begin a promising new life.

As if harboring a sixth sense, Cathie swung open the front door and grinned at Isabel. "I've seen that look before," she said. "Head in the clouds, feet off the ground. You'd better come in before you get swept away."

Isabel laughed. "Just thinking ahead. There's no harm in that."

"Well, I'm thinking biscuits in the backyard. And lucky for you, I've got plenty." Cathie held the door open. "I had a hunch that you might come over."

"Hardly a hunch. It's more like the usual Saturday morning; I mind my business, my mom intrudes, I get upset, and we go our separate ways. Since Mom rarely leaves the house, I have to go somewhere. Usually, I wind up here. You don't mind?"

"Honey, you're always welcome. I promise; I won't get upset."

Isabel nodded. As she walked in, she hoped that Cathie's calmness would be contagious. They seemed to be off to a good start. Cathie, especially today, seemed to exude a special glow. No surprise. Here she was; over eight months pregnant and looking more wholesome than a model from a country life magazine. Her long dark hair shimmered with a natural henna frosting. Her perfectly oval face glowed from a natural blush. And why disturb her perfect five-foot-five height with another inch of heels? At twenty-seven years, Cathie had finally discovered that her God-given features needed no help from Revlon.

She ushered Isabel through the kitchen, snagged a tall glass, and then led her to the backyard deck.

Immediately, the refreshing scent of a lemon tree and fresh-cut lemons took Isabel one step farther from Charlene's house and one step closer to sanity. Finally, she could hear herself think. Her mind felt totally blank, and that feeling was surely welcomed. She lingered against the railing and soaked in the country ambience. Nothing at Charlene's house could give her a fraction of the peace and quiet.

"You can have my entire savings account if you would adopt me." Isabel sighed when Cathie poured a glass of mango iced tea.

"Wonderful, now what would I do with twenty-four dollars?"

"Consider it a down payment on rent. Short-term rent, that is. I'd like a nice place to stay for about six weeks. Then after that; no worries."

Cathie pulled out a chair and sat. Isabel did the same.

"What did you fight about now?" Cathie's eyes widened. "You told your mom about Ross, didn't you? I thought I heard fireworks, but it could've been you guys."

"You're kidding? No, maybe someday I'll work up the nerve and tell Mom. But not today. She doesn't know I'm dating him, and that's how I prefer it."

Cathie glowered at her cousin. "You know that you have to tell her sooner or later. And sooner is usually better."

"I'm not sure about that. I could send her a postcard. You know, from the Chapel of the Chimes in Tahoe. 'Hugs and kisses, Mom; from Ross and Isabel Hutten.' First she'd say, 'Who on earth is this?' In a couple hours, she'd figure it out. *Then* she would scream All Mighty and start throwing my clothes on the porch. Yeah, no question about it."

"A mother's love; so many ways to show it." Cathie smirked and set down her glass. "Seriously, Isabel, let me tell you that mothers have a way. They have a way of provoking you no matter where you live. You think it's bad now; try living with guilt the rest of your life. That's her best weapon. Charlene doesn't have to say a word; not a single word. No screaming, no yelling. Nothing. There's the irony; she would be totally silent, but she would make you miserable, totally miserable."

Isabel sucked the lemon at the end of her fork. How could life get any more bitter? Deep down, she knew that Cathie was right.

Running away was not the answer. To get that perfect storybook ending, Isabel had to include a loving mother, an adoring father, and a husband to satisfy every possible whim. Unfortunately, that perfect ending seemed an elusive dream. At the moment, she simply had a fiancée, a ring, and a whole lot of promises.

Ross, at least, showed promise of giving her chapter one of the fairytale romance. If the past three months had set a pattern, the next twenty years would be nothing short of ideal. Ross was Isabel's first love, and it didn't take her long to realize that he was the answer to her often-forgotten prayers. She had spent most of the summer at Cathie's house, and Ross, strangely, had done the same. He was a good friend of Grant's, and soon, he wanted to be more than good friends with Isabel.

He proposed, and she said, "Fine." Quick, easy, and romantic; that was exactly how it should've been done.

"Are you listening?" Cathie touched Isabel's hand and snapped her out of her daydream. "I said you are the luckiest woman on earth."

"How's that?"

"I mean, ignoring your mom for the moment—and, yes, there could be issues—I'm talking about you and Ross. Honestly, Isabel, when it comes to men, you do have a gift."

"He is cute; I've been told."

Cathie rolled her eyes, but Isabel easily acknowledged her understatement. Yes, Ross was cute. He was also tall, trim, and muscular. He had bright blue eyes and sandy blond hair. The hot autumn weekends had tanned his water skiing body to the perfect shade of California bronze. He was more gorgeous than cute, but details didn't matter. Isabel loved him as he was. Plus the fact that he had a new Corvette, a new house, and a fast-track career made Ross a pretty-good catch.

"And he's kind of smart," Cathie said.

"Definitely smart; almost a doctor, I would say."

Cathie laughed. "There's nothing *almost* about it. A resident *is* a doctor, and people are going to call him that whether he's at a free clinic in East San Jose or a hospital in Stanford."

"Regardless, I'll call him 'Ross.' Dr. Hutton is too pretentious; except once on the invite; our wedding, that is."

"No, pretentious would be; Dr. Ross Hutton—Stanford *psychologist*—and Isabel Espinosa request the honor of your presence. Château Nouvelle, Lake Tahoe, California. Beluga caviar and Dom Perignon will be served. This will be the wedding of the year."

"Just because it's true does not mean I have to advertise it."

"I don't see why not," Cathie said. "You hide your ring. You don't tell your mother. You downplay the fact that Ross is a doctor. That's exactly the opposite of what most women would do. But then, maybe that's your blessing; you're not like most women we know. And I think Ross understands. Grant said it, and I agree; you are *both* special. You were meant for each other."

Special? Isabel wondered. What was so special about a middle-class, San Jose high school girl who had no car, no close-knit family, and no prospects for a career except a handful of dreams? 'Ordinary' would be a better word; ordinary with an occasional streak of good luck.

That was fine; Isabel had no problem with being average. And she had no problem recognizing good fortune when it passed her way. She appreciated good luck and welcomed it. She stayed hopeful; if somehow that luck carried forward, then someday, she might be special. Until then, ordinary and average would be fine.

However, she did have one personality quirk that set her apart from the other women of her day. While her trendy and cutting-edge friends dabbled in polyester pantsuits and suede miniskirts, Isabel stuck to the classics. She preferred comfortable jeans, a cool linen top, shoes with a one-inch heel, and a floppy hat to keep away the sun. True fashion was timeless. Simple was better.

Of course, when she found a comfortable theme, she stayed with it. Her notion of simple and timeless went well beyond clothing. In the back of her mind, she believed that she was born to the wrong era and the wrong place. Arguably, that one belief could have been true, especially these days; with her imagination in overdrive. Isabel spent countless hours at night envisioning a more innocent era. She saw herself in a Hollywood fantasy.

Romantic movies of the 1940s and 50s fascinated her, almost to the point of obsession. Real men like Gary Cooper and Henry Fonda ruled the big screen. They had big hearts and big attitude. They were self-assured and self-reliant. They were good men. And back then, classy, beautiful women like Audrey Hepburn and Grace Kelly struggled through heartache and circumstance to stumble onto a happy ending. No doubt, they were real women. Contrived or not, those old movie plots tugged at Isabel's heart like a voice from a faraway home.

But then, Victorian Europe—England and France, London and Paris—seemed like a second, albeit imaginary, home. Tea in the afternoon, croissants, scones, and Devonshire cream sounded quaint and appealing. It seemed elegant and stylish. Isabel daydreamed herself into that life. She pictured a romantic getaway in a long-ago time or a faraway place. No troubles, no pain. Only a strong man at her side. That would be ideal.

These days, she felt impatient to turn her fantasy into a long-overdue reality. She couldn't wait to visit an English tearoom or a Parisian café in real life. She couldn't wait for a one-way ticket out of San Jose.

Isabel yearned for the bygone years, and whether it helped or hindered, she had picked up some truly old-fashioned notions about men, love, and family. In no uncertain terms, she made those notions clear to any man she met; no sex until marriage, no marriage without passion, no family without everlasting love. It seemed a miracle that she had any man at all.

"Isabel?" Cathie tapped her hand. "Your mind's wandering again."

"Sorry," she said. "I'm just thinking ahead."

"Anyway, my point is; Grant's a great husband. He can design a computer while you fry a potato, but he is not a doctor, and he will never be one. I would say that you're very lucky to have Ross, but ..."

"But what?"

"I think that Ross is the lucky one. He's getting the better of this deal; I'll tell you that. He sure seems happy. Grant saw him yesterday, and his eyes lit up when he talked about the wedding. 'The sooner, the better,' is what he said."

"Not soon enough," Isabel said. "That's why I want to talk to Ross."

"You talked about a June wedding, right? And with your mom helping or not, we'll get it done. The dress, the flowers, the catering, the smoked salmon and caviar; I remember that from your list."

"And *pâté foie gras*," Isabel said. "And Napa Valley chardonnay; even though I'm too young to drink it ... technically."

"The flowers—I'm not worried about. We can do that at the last minute, especially with Esteban. He's got a crush on you, of course— like most of the guys at the flower mart."

"I know."

"If we start now," Cathie said, "it's an easy wedding. We'll make it a day to remember for the rest of your life. How's that?"

"Well," Isabel said, hesitantly, "that's why I want to talk to you and Ross. You both can help."

Cathie topped off her iced tea and dropped in another lemon slice. She gave a slight scowl. "I've seen that look before. You're scheming, and you know that it never turns out well."

"Come on, Cathie, hear me out. I'm on a mission. It's a simple assignment; just tell me how to get out the house and get married in a month and a half. That's it. It shouldn't be that hard."

"Would that be the morning of your birthday or the afternoon?"

"It doesn't matter," she said. "I'll be in the eighteen-to-twenty-five age bracket. Legally, I can do it at midnight—which is not a bad idea."

"Ethically, you should do it in June—which is a better idea. And tell you mother as soon as you can, because that's what really matters. Family first; then a wedding plan."

"No," Isabel said. "What would happen first is; my mother would have a fit. Then she would throw me out of the house. Then, like you said, she wouldn't speak to me for the rest of her life. It's a control thing, nothing more. I think I'll wait until the week of the wedding. If she throws me out then, I can stay here. Yes, no, maybe so?"

Isabel grinned. She slipped the engagement ring off her necklace and slid it onto her finger. She stretched her hand and let the facets sparkle in the sunlight. The dancing beams seemed mesmerizing—almost blinding—as a symbol of hope and soon-to-be-fulfilled dreams. She thought that six weeks would not be soon enough. Two people in love, two people agreeing to a life together; a small head-start only made sense. The details could easily be worked out.

"What's the point in waiting?" Isabel asked. "Ross and me; we both understand the meaning of 'until death do we part.' Whether we take our vows in December or eight months from now; our words will mean the same. Our love will be as strong."

"The only difference," Cathie said, "eight months from now, you won't be in high school; and you *may* not have your mother nagging you. She may even look forward to the wedding."

"Now who's dreaming? Cathie, I know my mother. The happier I get, the more miserable she becomes. We balance out to one barely functional family. No, I think it's best that Ross and I do it and move on. Then the question becomes; if I don't hear Mom's angry voice, is she really that dreadful?"

Cathie chuckled then reached behind to a stack of magazines and catalogs. She pulled out a *Bride* magazine, plopped it in front of Isabel, and flipped to a dog-eared page.

"Now, this is a beautiful dress." She slid her finger along the image of a white satin, strapless gown. "It's inexpensive and off the rack. Basic and stylish, huh? But if you prefer, Ross could certainly pay for a custom gown—any style."

"Off the rack is fine," Isabel said. "If it's not perfect, you and I will make it so. I mean, Ross is marrying me and not the dress. And I'm not perfect by a long shot. Thankfully, Ross is fine with that. The dress should be the least of our worries."

"Sweet Isabel. So much to learn; so little time."

Isabel laughed. "I'm not that naïve, am I?"

"If you say so." Cathie placed another magazine on the table. "But regardless, we have a lot of work ahead. Let's get started."

Isabel sipped her iced tea and relaxed. Planning a wedding didn't seem like work in the least. Excitement and anticipation grew with every page turned. It seemed a perfect way to spend a lazy Saturday morning. Only one thing could top off a day like this. She stood and passed Cathie the last of the honeymoon destination brochures.

"One last favor," Isabel said.

"What is it?" Cathie said.

"Can I borrow your car?"

"To see Ross, I assume."

"We have the dress picked out. We have the flowers and the venue. The only detail we don't have is the date. I'm not going to push for six weeks ... probably. But a winter ceremony in Tahoe does sound romantic. Everything white; dresses, flowers, the entire landscape. New beginnings; like a Hallmark card. That would be a nice compromise, you think?"

"Maybe so," Cathie said. "But one word of advice; whatever you do, do not use the word, 'ultimatum.' Do not hint of it. Do not even think about it. Trust me, men hate to be pressured—good cause or not. You've got a good thing going. Don't mess with it."

"I think I know Ross by now, and I think I know how to handle men. Well, I can handle *one* man; and that's face to face, calm, self-assured, irresistible brown eyes. How could he say 'no?' "

Cathie shrugged then passed Isabel the keys to the MGB.

"I'll call you from Ross's house," Isabel said. "If I start squealing, you know we have a date."

She said, "So long" to Cathie. Then she bounced out the front door and smiled at the MGB. Of course, she would smile at any car other than a '65 Impala. Red, fast, and sporty. Top down, clean and sleek. With the MGB, Isabel knew how to make an impression. She thought for a moment; with the top up, she would keep her hair in place and keep away the windblown look. But with the open air and sun on her face, she always felt her confidence surge, and she felt energized. Confidence would be good, she believed. So no question; the MGB top stayed down.

Isabel plopped onto the driver's seat and checked her purse. From a hidden pocket in her wallet, she withdrew Ross's house key and set it beside her. She thought ahead to another welcoming house, and she couldn't wait to get there. When she switched on the ignition, the MGB engine purred like a happy tomcat. Isabel didn't know the horsepower and didn't care. A new car and a diamond ring made her feel like a princess; in control and in demand.

She cranked up the radio as *Long Cool Woman (in a black dress)* came on the air. It seemed the perfect background music to ease her into a perfect day. She slipped the car into gear, drove the back streets and avenues, and let her long hair flow with the breeze. A million dollars could not have made her happier.

Within minutes, she pulled in Ross's driveway. Isabel shut down the engine and let the calm and quiet return. She took a deep breath and looked ahead. Ross's two-story, Tudor style house seemed more elegant and more inviting than usual. *Ross's house?* She corrected herself. *No, in a few months it'll be our house, our little getaway.*

She grabbed the house key, stepped out of the car, and straightened her sweater. She ran a brush through her hair and did a last check in the MGB's side-view mirror. Looking good and feeling great, she eased her way to the front door. Ross had parked his Corvette in the driveway, and that meant he had called it an early day at the hospital. *This should be a good surprise.* It was well worth skipping lunch at her mother's house.

She knocked on the front door but heard nothing but the soothing sounds of a Donny Hathaway album. That always put him in a good mood—which would be a good start for their discussion. She slid the key into the lock and opened the door. Ross was nowhere near, but from the other room, *What's Going On* blared. Isabel wondered the same.

"Hi, honey. Your sweetheart's home," she sang out playfully. She felt so much at home. She felt like a wife—a doctor's wife—coming to relax after a stressful visit with her mother. She heard a voice from the upstairs bedroom. Obviously, Ross was on the phone with a patient or another doctor from the hospital.

Maybe this was not the best time to interrupt or the best place to talk about the wedding. Nevertheless, she climbed the stairs for a quick 'hello.' Isabel had only seen the bedroom on her first tour of Ross's house. She said that her next tour of the bedroom would be when they got married.

"Honey, it's me," she called out as she climbed the stairs. Again, it felt strange. Ross never had sounded like this before. She couldn't tell if he was laughing or crying. And what kind of patient was he treating on the phone? Isabel swung the door wide open and found out.

Oh God, it was a nurse. Rather, it must have been a nurse, looking at those white heels that she wore. White heels and nothing else. She was flat on her back, and she had nowhere to run. The woman squealed, and Isabel just about died.

Ross didn't know what was going on; he kept doing whatever he pleased. All Isabel could do was stand there and stare.

The nurse jabbed Ross in the shoulder and yelled, "Turn around. Turn around!"

Finally, Ross got the hint. He yanked at the satin sheet and spun to face Isabel. "Oh God. Oh God," he squeaked.

Isabel desperately wanted to scream, but there was no air left in her lungs. Her heart and head had totally shut down. Everything froze while her memory burned with that one searing image; two lovers in a king-size bed of deceit.

Ross stood then stumbled with the sheet wrapped around his waist and ankles. He sure didn't look like a fast-track psychologist. He was little more than a fumbling teenager caught in the act.

"It's not what you think," he whined like a pathetic dog.

How stupid did he think she was? How blind did she have to be? Isabel slammed the door closed, bounded down the stairs, and raced out the front door. She scrambled to the MGB, climbed in, and shoved the key into the ignition.

"Please start. Please start. Please start."

The engine mercifully jumped to life. She escaped out the driveway with one final look at Ross's cheating dog face. "Never, never again," she cried.

Chapter 3

"I DON'T CARE. Send it registered or send it insured. Just send it so it never comes back." Isabel paid her five bucks at the Post Office and mailed away her life, her future, and her one chance to escape her cold, dysfunctional home. She stuffed the envelope with the engagement ring; just the ring and nothing else. There was no note, no regrets, and no turning back. Goodbye forever.

The clerk tossed the package like a piece of third-class mail, and when it hit the bottom of the canvas bin, so did Isabel's heart. She had trusted Ross and loved him dearly. She had loved him so much that she was willing to spend the rest of her life with him—and only him. Was it so much to expect the same from Ross?

They had had one argument, maybe two, during the three months they had dated, but that was simply no reason for Ross to behave as he did. How long had he been cheating? A day? A week? The entire three months? The very thought tore her apart. How could he share his dreams and his pain with her during the day and open up his black satin sheets for his lover at night?

For the next week, Isabel did little more than go to school, sulk at Cathie's house, and hang up on Ross.

All Cathie had was, "I'm sorry. I didn't know."

All Ross had was, "I can explain," or 'Give me a chance."

Isabel would have no part of it. No explanation, no apology, no groveling could ever erase the hurt she carried. Just the sound of

Ross's voice grated on her like the squealing brakes of her father's truck. Ross wrote letters—care of Cathie's house—but Isabel tore them up, unread. She flushed them down the toilet. Could be her life was headed there too. Could be that Charlene had spoken the truth.

"All men are scum. They'd just as soon rape you as buy you dinner." That was the gospel according to Saint Charlene.

Unsolicited opinions and personal anecdotes; Charlene had a million each, and she had no qualms about doling them out. Isabel got yet another reminder of her hopeless situation when, on a careless Saturday morning, she unintentionally set a paperback romance onto the kitchen counter.

"What's this?" Charlene scowled, fingering the cover. "Ski instructor and some young, pretty, white girl. Yeah, well, how about you look in the mirror? You're hurting yourself when you read this. Men like that won't give you a second look unless they want something in return."

"You can't say that. Every man is different. Someday, I'll marry a man just like him," Isabel cried. "Someday. I don't care how long it takes. I'll wait until he shows up."

"You think you know everything, don't you? I waited for years, and you know what; nobody showed up for me. I was like you when I was a kid, but with one big difference; I knew where I stood. I knew that I was poor. I knew I was Mexican. I never went shopping for something I couldn't afford."

"I'm not like you, Mom, and I'm not going to argue. So don't try to get me upset."

"You know I'm right." Charlene gave a smug little grin.

Isabel ran to her room. Her mother was dead wrong. How could she claim to know about men? Charlene had dated five or six men, all told, and she wound up marrying a truck driver for God's sake. How on earth did that qualify her as an expert? She might have been right about men like Ross, but that was coincidence. Ross was despicable, no question. Because of him, Isabel felt emotionally devastated and physically ill. Her stomach, head, heart—everything hurt. The best summer of her life had become the worst chapter ever. Inevitably, she sank into a dark, loveless abyss.

The only thing that kept her moving; high school classes and her mother banging on the bedroom door every morning. For now, it was oatmeal for breakfast and sloppy joes for lunch. No chance for pâté de foie gras or scones with Devonshire cream. No chance for real romance or an escape from an ordinary life.

Isabel realized that eventually the stark reality of senior-year classes would help her recover. Sooner or later, she would start to move on. Slowly and thankfully, she took her mind off Ross and focused on a good education—or San Jose high school, as it were.

When November came, she decided that a trip to the Eastridge Mall and a new school outfit might nudge her away from her lingering doldrums. A new Kay Unger dress might lift her spirits enough to enjoy long periods of California history, algebra, and English comp. Some new Birkenstock sandals might distract her from the torment of a broken heart or the annoyance of a nagging mother.

Isabel changed into her jeans and comfortable blouse. She grabbed her purse and went looking for the keys to the Impala.

"Mom, I need to borrow the car."

"Where are you going?" Charlene asked.

"To the mall; to buy clothes for school."

"When are you coming back?"

"An hour or so," Isabel said.

"Who's going with you?"

"I'll swing by and pick up Colette. Is that okay?"

Charlene wrung out a dish rag in the kitchen sink. She glanced through the front window then looked at Isabel. "Colette's a good kid. She had a good job at the market and a good boyfriend—Pepino. Not pregnant and not in debt. Take the afternoon if you want. I trust her, and I don't need the car."

"Thank you."

"Oh, and one more thing." Charlene stared at Isabel's white top. "You don't have to flaunt your chest like that. And those jeans; they'll rip if you bend over. Wear something that fits."

"These clothes are fine. I know what fashion is."

"Then I know you won't get the car. Change your clothes or you don't go."

Isabel grumbled, but she knew a lost cause. She retreated to her room and slipped into a gray sweatshirt and baggy pants. She put her fashions back into the drawer. Maybe her entire love life belonged in the same place.

She stomped through the living room, snatched the keys to the Impala, and dared her mother to say a word. Charlene kept silent and kept her eyes on the TV. She stared at a repeat episode of *Bewitched* and seemed plenty happy in her make-believe world.

Isabel walked out the front door and stepped into the car. As soon as she turned on the ignition, she pushed the button to her favorite station. Her stress disappeared when Johnny Nash came on with *I Can See Clearly Now*. She tapped her fingers on the steering wheel. Old car, old clothes, no money. She still had music to make her smile, and hopefully Colette could keep her smiling. Isabel swung by her house to pick her up.

Colette bounded down the porch of her parents' house. She was a bit older than Isabel and a bit shorter, but Colette, with her tight jeans and camisole tank top, was definitely more stylish.

"You look great," Isabel said as Colette eased onto the passenger seat. "How come you couldn't stop by my house? If Mom saw how you looked, she might have changed her mind about this." She yanked at her sweatshirt.

"I have a reputation to uphold. If I had shown up at your house, you can bet I'd look just like you." Colette spoke with the hint of a Spanish accent while she excitedly poked at Isabel's sleeve and laughed. She settled back then snapped off the radio. "And I have a reputation with you."

"How's that?" Isabel asked.

"You're my girlfriend. We support each other. We got each other's back."

"At the risk of sounding like Mom, just tell me; what are you up to?" She merged into traffic and caught Capitol Expressway for the shortest route to the mall. She glanced at Colette and caught her smiling.

"No, it's more like; what can I do for you?"

"Pardon?"

Colette softened her tone. "It's been weeks now, and you're still moping around. I think it's time to put an end to it. And boy, do I have a plan."

"*My* plan is fine," Isabel said. "If I wait long enough, Ross will fade away. Patience will do it ... and a new dress and purse. That's it. Right now, I don't want to talk about him—or think about him. Just point me to the Halston aisle. I can still daydream."

"I agree; talking about Ross is *not* going to make it better."

"Good. We agree."

"That's why we got to do a little action." Colette waved at the cross street ahead. "Turn left."

Isabel turned down the block but had to ask, "This is not the way to the mall. Where exactly are you taking me?"

"We are going for payback. Pure and simple retaliation."

"What? No way. Trust me, Colette, I've moved on. I don't need to get even with anyone. I've accepted what happened as one of those god-awful truths. It's pretty clear; Ross and I were never meant to be. Someday, I'll meet the right man. But for now, I just want to go shopping. Is that okay?"

Colette scowled. "No, it is not okay. Isabel, listen. I've broken up with a dozen men—boys really—and I've found one common truth; no one messes with me or my friends and skates away scot-free. That's a given. It's never happened to me, and it's *not* going to happen to you. Sit back and relax. Watch and learn."

"Okay, fine." Isabel gave up on the argument. Better to sit through a short diversion than risk a weekend headache. She followed Colette's directions up King Road. "Where are we going?" she asked.

"There's a flower shop ahead," Colette said. "I've got the bouquet picked out, and it's ready for delivery."

"Delivery? Where?"

"To the other woman, of course."

"What?" Isabel said harshly. "I want to kill the other woman. Why would I send her flowers?"

"Here's the lesson; a little suspicion goes a long way. We send the roses with a note; 'Thanks for last night.' She calls Ross to thank him, and that's when the trouble starts. He gets confused, and after a while, *she* gets confused. Bottom line; they both get suspicious. Without trust, you can't have love. And without love, there's nowhere to go but down. Sounds good, huh?"

Isabel squirmed. She didn't agree with Colette's plan, and she bristled at the notion of getting even. But arguing with Colette seemed like a futile effort. It seemed a waste of energy and good money. Nevertheless, she went along for the ride—if only to close the door on the darkest days of her life.

"I paid for the flowers," Colette said, "and I'll send them, but I don't know where she works."

Isabel thought back to the incident at Ross's house. She recalled Ross's long-ago mention of his nurse and her name. Now, she easily made the connection. Now, she didn't mind sharing it. She told Colette the address of the clinic, and Colette wrote it on a scrap of paper.

"Double-park in front," Colette said, pointing at the flower shop. "In and out should take twenty seconds and *then* we head for the mall."

Isabel looked ahead for a legal parking spot but saw none. Traffic was light so she dropped off Colette by the entrance. She told her, "Once around the block should do it. I'd rather not park in the street."

Colette nodded then disappeared into the shop.

Isabel tapped on the gas, eager to move—but not quite fast enough. From behind, she heard the sharp squeal of skidding tires. A moment later; Bam! Hit in the bumper by a distracted driver. Barely a nudge on the monster Impala, but with no restraint, her head swung like a bowling ball on a stick.

Almost immediately, she felt the effects of a whiplash; stabbing pain in the neck, pulsating ache in her shoulders, sudden ringing in her ears. Her temples throbbed when she turned side to side. She knew that it was bound to get worse.

Colette rushed to the window. "My God! Are you okay?"

Isabel blinked then muttered, "I'm not sure."

"Forget the mall," Colette said. "We're getting you to the hospital." She carefully urged Isabel out of her seat and to the passenger's side.

The distraught driver approached. The young man kept his eyes wide and his voice calm. He waved his insurance card and license. "I'm sorry," he said. "I'll do whatever it takes to make it straight. I didn't mean to hurt you."

He passed the documents to Colette, and she wrote down the information.

Another apologetic man, Isabel griped. Sincere or not, it didn't matter. Now was not the time to quarrel. "Let the insurance company deal with it. I've got better things to do." She sent the man back to his truck.

Much later, as Isabel sat in the treatment room at San Jose General, she looked at herself in the mirror and groaned. A ten-dollar wardrobe, a twenty-dollar neck brace. It hurt to say anything more than, "How long do I have to wear this?"

Every thought of romance and revenge—on doctors, truck drivers, anyone—totally vanished from her mind. She had two goals on her mind and nothing else; survive the 'I told you so' of her mother and make it through the coming weeks of school. Isabel dreaded what lay ahead.

One small consolation; Colette popped into the treatment room and plopped down a dozen roses to Isabel's side. The gift card read; "The best times are yet to be."

Isabel wasn't so sure.

Chapter 4

IT BECAME her first lesson in medical therapy; neck injuries do not heal overnight or in a week. And by Thanksgiving, Isabel was wondering if her neck would ever heal. She had missed almost a month of school on doctor's orders; confined at home with a prescription of bed rest, peace, and quiet. If she wanted to get well, that meant no stress; physical or emotional.

So, she had a problem. The rest of her body begged her to get up and go dancing, but as soon as she stood, the stabbing pain told her that she was going nowhere, except back to bed and under the covers. There were some days—too many to count—when the pain became so great, she couldn't lift her head off the pillow. Those days had to be the worst. Every little noise in the house flew through the plasterboard walls and focused on her suffering ears.

Charlene, whether she knew it or not, kept piling on the stress. She turned up the volume to the Mexican soap operas. She argued with Leo when he came home for lunch. She complained about him when he left. She griped about anything and everything; from the kids on the block to that clumsy daughter of hers in the back room. What therapy? This place was totally insane.

Nevertheless, the world still revolved. If Isabel wanted to graduate with the rest of her class, she had to commit to her studies. She had to finish every piece of assigned homework; algebra, history,

English, and economics. With every lesson, she had to hustle to keep from falling behind.

Fortunately, she had a tutor who made house calls. That small blessing kept her in touch with the real world. Unfortunately, the tutor was a young woman who often bragged about her late-night dates with older college men and the incredible fun she had.

"Think of it as motivation to get well," the woman said. "Sooner or later, you have to leave home."

"Dear Lord, I hope it's sooner. I'm so afraid that I'll never leave home."

Saturday night parties with men, music, and innocent high school mischief; that was part of the outside world that Isabel missed. That was the one view she became desperate to see. Last year—with Charlene always on guard—it had been a rare treat to steal away and be with anyone with a hint of sophistication. Nowadays, it would be a rare treat to stand anywhere and not wince at the near-constant pain.

At this point, she didn't need to kiss a man, or hug him, or run her fingers through his hair. It would be great to sit and talk with any guy who was cute and blond and didn't scream when his tortillas came late. It would be fine to take it slow and steady. Isabel preferred it that way. After that nasty experience with Ross, she understood what could happen when a woman rushed to commit her heart and her passion. She realized that fast and easy could not guarantee a forever bond.

But hope was not lost. Soon, she would be eighteen years old, and that meant it was time for a little heart to heart chat with Charlene. It was time to see if, after four years of begging and pleading, Isabel would be allowed to see guys free and clear; without harassment and abuse. If Charlene faithfully kept her word, then it was easily a matter of working out the details, such as; could Isabel bring men into the living room, did Leo have to see them first, did she have to show records of vaccination, birth certificates, or criminal background checks?

It was a cool December morning when Isabel wandered to the washing machine and cornered her mother with a new proposition.

"Mom, I've been thinking. My birthday's coming up. You know what that means." Isabel fluffed and folded a bath towel while Charlene stuffed the washer with a pile of her husband's boxers.

She went on, "I can go on my first date, right? I know we talked about this before, but I thought I could make it easy. How about this … There's a party at Colette's house, and there might be some guys there. Okay? I told her I could stay for a couple hours at the most. You know, because of my neck and the meds. But if one of the fellas wants to drive me home, I said it would be okay with you. Right, Mom? I mean, that's what we agreed, isn't it?"

Heavy, heavy sigh. Charlene dropped the lid to the washer with a bang and picked up a set of dry towels. "Your father and me talked about that."

"And?"

"I don't know. Your father says you're behind in your schoolwork, so how can you talk about dating?"

"I'm getting help; you know that. I'm doing the assignments and getting the grades. Everything's fine."

"Let me finish. He doesn't think you're ready. And I think if you go out, you're gonna mess up your neck worse. And *then* what about school? This is your last year. You can't take any more chances. Think about school first *then* worry about men."

Isabel felt a knot in her stomach. She had a sickening feeling that had nothing to do with the accident. "So, what are you saying? I can't go out until my neck heals. Is that it?"

"Your father says you shouldn't go out until you graduate."

"I can't believe it," she said harshly. "He can't go back on his word. Not after what I've been through."

"Yeah, well, I have to agree with him. I think you should wait."

"Graduation is over six months away! You promised me, Mom. You said when I turned eighteen—"

"Look at you. You're in no shape to go out. Those pills make you dizzy, like you're half-drunk. You want some man to see you like that?"

"I know what I'm doing. I wouldn't even get close to a man like that. I just wouldn't."

"Honestly, if you didn't mess yourself up, then you wouldn't have this problem."

"The accident was not my fault." Isabel scowled and crossed her arms.

"I didn't say it was. But I am saying you gotta be careful. You can wait six months. It's not the end of the world."

"We had an agreement."

"That was *before* you got hurt." Charlene picked up the pile of frayed bath towels and headed for the hallway closet. For her, the topic was officially closed, discussion over. She turned her back on Isabel and stacked the towels according to color; as if beige and taupe had become number one priority. As if laundry meant more than love.

Isabel cried. What was the point of fighting? It was like butting heads with an unmovable object. Forget about the party. Forget about men. As far as she was concerned, her dating life had just died.

For much of the winter, she went into hibernation. Isabel had no energy to take on Charlene *and* a new boyfriend. Sneaking around with a man was out of the question. It was too dangerous and not worth the risk. The neck brace had slowed her to a hobble, and she had to be fast and agile to dodge the old woman's suspicions and avoid a slap on the face.

By early March, however, days became brighter. Isabel had returned to school and did her best to get her life back to normal. Her health improved but not nearly fast enough. Every day became a battle to look and feel good. Every day became a balance between painkillers and pain. Frustrating. It had been over four months since the accident, and she was still hurting and still without a date.

Something had to be done. So in the spirit of working top issues first, Isabel decided to meet some men. A clear head, she rationalized, could be found later. With her priorities set, she didn't need to wait long for an ally.

"Party," Colette said when she heard of Isabel's dilemma. "And you're in luck. I have one lined up for Saturday night."

"Luck?" Isabel said. "I remember the last party we went to. What was it, a year ago? And what was his name? Kevin? He worked at a shop, delivering flowers. His only ambition was to work the morning shift."

"Kevin was a nice guy. He'll make someone a nice husband someday. You wait and see."

"Maybe so," Isabel said, lowering her voice and scooting under the bed covers. "But tell me more about Saturday night."

"Like what?"

"Like where it is, for starters."

"It's off-campus," Colette said. "Near San Jose State. You know what that means; college men and lots of them. Upperclassmen, graduate students. Freshmen; if you want. Take your pick. You like smart men, don't you? I'll guarantee you'll find one."

"Tempting, but it might be too much, too soon. I was hoping for something more tame—like an after-church picnic."

"Church?" Colette laughed. "Seriously, if you want to meet some real men, you need to expand your horizons. Go to college and spread your wings, huh?"

"I want to say, 'yes,' but I've got my mom to reckon with."

"The party's nearby," Colette said. "We can arrive and depart in three hours. I won't go alone, and I won't go without you. How's that? And regarding your mom, I can deal with her. You told me yourself; she trusts me."

Isabel wanted to say, "I'll think about it," but the words came out, "All right, I'll go … But I'm just going to watch the guys and listen to the music. An icebreaker, so to speak."

"What do you mean, watch? You don't go a candy store to look at the wrappers. You have to participate. You have to gorge yourself to appreciate it." Of course, Colette believed that binging and purging applied to men as well as food.

"When?" Isabel asked.

"Saturday, eight o'clock. I'll pick you up."

Isabel shrugged. She had nothing to lose and only her sanity to gain. Any party—good or bad—sounded better than sitting at home, listening to Charlene and Leo argue about who was in charge of the toilet seat.

To her relief, Saturday quickly arrived. In the morning, she picked up some new pills; a muscle relaxant to speed her recovery and reduce her light-headed feeling. If that was true, she could throw out her neck collar by the end of the month and return to a normal existence. Isabel felt thrilled. After an impossibly long confinement, she finally felt free to celebrate. Almost free.

Eight o'clock came, and she invoked her standard ruse. "Mom, I'm going to Aunt Carol's house. Colette's picking me up, and I'll be back in three hours."

She strolled through the living room in baggy jeans and a dirty old sweatshirt. She slipped her J. C. Penny satchel over her shoulder and bounced out the door. She sighed when she stopped at the front porch. One of these days, Charlene would get smart. One of these days, Charlene was bound to find out. At least it wasn't tonight.

Colette, promptly on schedule, pulled into the driveway. Isabel hopped into the '69 Dodge Dart and waited for Colette to ease into traffic. Then she reached into her bag for her short-heel shoes. She set the shoes aside. She next pulled off her old sweatshirt, revealing a lavender blouse. She wiggled free of her baggy jeans, preferring the look and feel of her black, cotton twill pants. The only apparel she didn't change was her stunningly white, neck collar. She put it on and adjusted the fit.

"You still wearing that?" Colette scowled. "Not so chic, is it?"

"Next week is the last," Isabel said, fingering the collar. "Friday, it comes off. I don't care what the doctor says. Until then, I am not going to chance it." At the red light, she propped a mirror on the dashboard and put on the final touches; blush, mascara, lipstick, eyeliner—just like the old days. She had almost forgotten how glamorous Revlon could make her feel.

When they arrived at the off-campus Victorian, the party had already shifted to third gear. Parked by the house was an eclectic mix of BMWs, Volkswagens, and Camaros. Inside the house seemed elbow to elbow with men straight from a GQ spread; camel hair jackets, Florsheim shoes, polo neck shirts. Bell bottoms, floral shirts, and platform shoes had apparently been banned.

It was obviously an older and more sophisticated crowd than both Isabel and Colette had been accustomed to. The women at the party matched the ambience; Gucci or Louis Vuitton handbags, designer skirts, stylish tops. It seemed a high-maintenance group— men and women alike.

Elton John blared from a stereo in the corner while one couple, oblivious to the rhythm, slow danced to their own beat. Isabel took a quick count; more men than women, and more attractive than the other kind. *This could be entertaining or fun.*

Colette had her own numbers. "I'm guessing thirty-two men, twenty-two women. I'd say those are pretty good odds."

"Stay close to me," Isabel said. "These new pills are making my head spin."

"Stick to the punch and keep away from the booze. You're foggy enough."

"Believe me, Colette, a clear head is my only goal."

Almost immediately, a young man approached. He held two glasses of wild cherry punch. "Hey, you two; no loitering in the lobby. There's plenty of room inside. I'm Steward—your host of this little soirée. First let me say; if you need anything, anything at all; snap your fingers, and I'll come running. That's a promise. Oh, and by the way, don't worry about the drinks. If your glass is ever empty, I have standing orders to shoot the bartender."

"Well, what's one more homicide?" Isabel grabbed the glass and downed the drink. Immediately, another young man raced to her side and filled the glass to the brim.

As Steward and his friend retreated to the bar, Isabel turned to Colette and smiled. "I have a feeling; this will be one party I'll never forget. Thanks for the invite."

Isabel mingled the best she could—with and without Colette at her side. Once again, it felt good to be in the company of men. Even so, she believed that this get-together was simply a warm-up for parties to come. She realized that her neck collar flashed like a neon sign; disabled, slow, and fragile. It was a handicap anywhere and especially a drawback at a function like this. But then, so what?

She felt her confidence surge. She had no fear of rejection and no sense of intimidation. After all, what man in his right mind would date such a frail and pathetic invalid? With nothing to lose and a party to enjoy, she freed herself to talk about anything and everything; French impressionistic art, religious freedom in Spain, jazz ensembles of the 1960s, the sad state of men in California. Soon, she began to work the audience, and they began to listen.

"Wow, what happened to you?" The men began with the same line.

"Skiing accident," she told them at first. Then it became skydiving, rock climbing, full contact karate, or whatever else came to mind.

"You're an adventurous woman," Steward said. "A lot of women claim to be one, but in reality, few are."

"I don't know if I'm adventurous," Isabel said. "But I do have a passion for life. I realize that there are risks involved in *everything* we do. From buying flowers on a street corner to flying a plane; nothing is totally safe, and few things are inherently dangerous. Rather like men, I suppose. Each one presents a new challenge." She winked and grabbed herself another glass of punch.

She smiled. It had been months since she had felt this good and almost a year since she enjoyed a party. As the hours flew by, Isabel must have smiled at every man who glanced her way. She said hello to any man who didn't stare at her collar. She said thank you to each genuine compliment. Toward the end of the evening, as her curfew approached, she grabbed one last chance to sharpen her wit.

She felt obliged to share a parting word with those guys in the other room; the ones who swilled Cabernet Sauvignon by the fireplace and boasted of their latest conquests. Contemptuous brats, they were; especially that prima donna in the middle. Isabel trusted her instincts and despised him in a moment. His Vandyke mustache, the horn-rimmed glasses, the receding hair, and protruding lips; here was another self-taught, arrogant snob from the university. The man puffed on his pipe and blew the acrid smoke overhead. He seemed to fall in love with his own words.

"... and so I divulged to her, after the moment had passed, that it was indeed not a genuine climax, but merely a cathartic release related to my appointment to the board of regents. She was devastated, I'm sorry to say."

There was a round of laughter from everyone but Isabel. She had her own punch line to add. "So, her only choice was to put on her Freudian slip and leave."

More laughter, but it quickly died. The Vandyke peered over his glasses and offered a condescending grin. "What's this? A heckler in the crowd? Oh, I see. An underclassman. Or should I say underclass woman?" He chomped on the stem of his pipe and raised an eyebrow.

Isabel placed her hands on her hips. "The only thing that's *under* here is an ego trip that's obviously underway."

The man shot back, "I'm sensing hostility here—or envy, if you know what I mean."

"No, what you're sensing is your resentment toward women; probably extending back to your lack of breastfeeding as a child. First of many deprivations, I'm sure." Isabel snickered and quickly added, "Now stick that in your phallic symbol and smoke it."

"Respect; where has it gone?" The man jerked the pipe from his mouth and fumbled for a response. But it was too late. The room went silent except for a sole male voice laughing in the background.

Colette hustled close and yanked at Isabel's sleeve. "Hate to tell you this," she whispered. "They've spiked the punch, and I do believe you're affected."

Some warning. Isabel had been sipping the punch for most of the night. No wonder the room became a blur of Teds and Toms and Samuels and who knows who. Isabel and Colette quickly and quietly left the party with barely a "So long and thank you" to Steward. It was fun while it lasted.

When Isabel finally arrived home, she didn't remember a thing about the party except that she had enjoyed herself, and it sure felt great to be out of the house on a Saturday night. She thanked Colette for being a good friend and pressed her to find another college party—without the spiked punch.

"I'll do what I can," Colette said.

Monday morning sparked a rebirth of Isabel's spirit. She easily walked without the collar, and for the most part, the pain in her neck had vanished. Finally, her life had returned to normal. At last, she looked forward to the same old routine.

A clear head led to optimism, and that optimism carried her until Thursday. Then confusion took over. On that afternoon, she walked home from school to a strange message.

"Some man named Drake called for you," Charlene said as Isabel walked through the living room.

"Who?"

"Drake."

"Drake who?"

"How do I know?" Charlene snarled. "I'm not your secretary."

Isabel searched her head for that name but came up blank. A phone number would've helped, but he didn't leave one.

And Colette; she didn't have a clue. "Salesman," she said when Isabel called. "Car insurance or magazines."

"Probably so; and I don't need either." Isabel hung up and went on with her chores. She cleaned her room. She folded her clothes and ironed a blouse.

A half hour later, the living room phone rang.

"Isabel?" the man asked.

"Yes," she answered with some hesitation.

"Hi, I'm Drake Phillips. We talked a few nights ago. At Steward Holsten's party. Remember?"

Isabel dragged the phone's long cord to her bedroom and locked the door. She spoke in a low voice. "To be honest, I talked to a lot of men at that place. I don't remember any one person in particular."

"Do you remember Alex? I was with him most of the night."

"Nope. Name's not familiar."

"Then how about this; I'll tell you what we talked about. Then you tell me if it rings a bell."

"I'll listen," she said, "but no guarantees."

"How about this for starters. We talked about your whiplash and the accident. I said your settlement was much too small. You should've asked for more. And we talked about the fire in Santa Cruz last month. And let's see ... oh, yeah, you mentioned that famine in East Africa."

"Could be," Isabel said. "But I talked to everyone about that. Sorry to say, your name is still not familiar."

"Fair enough. But how about this; do you recall agreeing to go out with me, like on a date?"

"No, I don't recall. I mean, *that* I would've remembered. Besides, we weren't properly introduced."

"Oh, but we were—by Alex. Sound familiar now?"

"No, sorry. I don't know any Alex."

"Boy, that's going to make it tough to sweep you off your feet; if I can't see you again."

"No one said it would be easy." Isabel felt intrigued but cautious. "You see, I have one rule about men; if I don't know them, I don't date them. It's simpler that way. And safer. I wish it were otherwise, but ..." She faded then dangled her finger over the disconnect.

"No, wait. I'll make it as safe as you want. Give me a chance on the phone. I'll tell you whatever you need."

"Like what?"

"I'll tell you my story in three minutes or less."

"Then go for it," she said. "Clock's ticking."

Drake took a deep breath and held the phone close. "Okay, I can tell you I go to Stanford. I can tell you that I'm a third-year law student. I've got a GPA of 4.0, and that means I have no problems with my classes or keeping up grades."

Isabel had heard that story before. "You take a lot of Mick classes, huh?"

"Take what?"

"Mickey Mouse. You know, like the legal tactics of Abraham Lincoln."

"At Stanford?" Drake laughed. "No, the easiest class I have now is criminal law. And I've got a twenty-page synopsis to write by next Friday. Of course, what helps is a photographic memory. I can read a book once and never go back."

"That's handy," she said, skeptically. "If that's the case, then you can tell me what I wore that night."

"Come on, that's too easy. But if you insist ..." Another deep breath and Drake came back. "You had black shoes with open toes and three straps on top. You had black pants and a lavender top. You wore a heart-shaped pendant with four garnets and two diamonds. Am I correct?"

"Not bad. Not bad. The necklace has *five* garnets. But still, that's almost impressive."

"Almost, huh? What would it take to *definitely* impress you?"

"You tell me; tell me something about yourself that a woman might like. And make sure you keep it clean."

"I can do that," Drake said. "Let's talk about romance. Women love romance, yes? Tell me if you would like sailing the San Francisco Bay on a cool summer night, sipping Bordeaux and relaxing to the beat of a good jazz band."

"Jazz is good."

"I thought so. But if you don't like sailing, I've got a pilot's license. Think about it; a day in Tahoe with blackjack, roulette, or anything you want. Or Mendocino. You know, fly up for an afternoon and tour the art galleries and gift shops."

"Well, Drake, that sounds, uh, that sounds not bad." Isabel pulled her hair back and stretched out her legs. "But what *else* do you have?"

Drake sighed but came back enthusiastic. "Let's see. I've got a black belt in karate—got that a few years ago along with plenty of trophies. I'm in great physical shape, and what else? Oh yeah, I've been to Europe. I've got stories to share about that if you'd like to hear."

Was this guy for real? Could be. Isabel wasn't sure if Drake was a common braggart or someone with a genuine story to tell. But she was curious enough to open the door a little further and explore the possibilities. *Carefully open the door*, she told herself. She had gone so long without a man, and a voice told her to watch out for this one. She had to play it safe.

"I'm sorry, Drake, I have to go now. My mother wants the phone."

"Can I call you back?" Drake asked quickly, with a desperate voice.

"Maybe tomorrow."

She gave him the number to her own phone, hung up, and then stared at the sunrise painting on the far wall. Drake, he called himself. But who was this stranger, why was he calling, and what did he know about *her*? Could it be that he was telling her the truth? Oh God, what if he was. Her intuition told her that this man followed a fast life, even faster than Ross's. How could she possibly keep up; if she wanted?

Isabel went to her drawer and fished out her heart-shaped pendant, trying to recall one memory, one conversation of that Saturday night. She noted nothing except one little item. Drake's memory was spot-on; the fifth garnet of the pendant was missing.

Chapter 5

THE NEXT NIGHT, Isabel locked herself in her room and watched the phone. She wanted no distractions to get in her way. She had placed her bet and rolled the dice. If Drake was the winning number, she would be there, waiting to collect her prize. And how could he be anything but the classic white knight; what with that soft, seductive voice, his dreams of romance, and his perfect attention to detail. It was as if he had stepped straight from a novel. Only in this case, she hoped it was true. Finally, the pieces fell together; her grades, her health, and now her love life. All would be heaven *if* he called again.

At seven thirty, the phone rang. It was Drake.

"Great, you're home." His voice carried a smile. "It rang four times. I thought maybe you were out."

"Nope. Just doing my homework."

"Let me guess; *Elements of Psychoanalysis.*"

"Try *Algebra*," Isabel said. "You know, if a train leaves Chicago at sixty miles an hour, and another one arrives in Denver, then how old is the conductor's wife?"

"That doesn't make sense," Drake said.

"None of these problems do."

"No, that's not what I meant." Drake hesitated then went on, "Let me, uh, let me ask you this outright."

"Okay."

"Isabel, exactly how old are you?"

"How old am I? I suppose I can tell you. I turned eighteen about three months ago."

"Oh God." Drake laughed. "I can't believe how far off-track I was."

"Pardon?"

"I don't know where I got the idea. But for some reason, I thought you were a junior at State." Drake laughed again.

"I wish I were. Then I wouldn't have to do these problems."

"Sorry," Drake said. "I didn't mean to laugh. But you certainly project an older image."

"I'll take that as a compliment."

"It was offered as one. So, uh, Isabel, exactly *where* do you go to school?"

She thought for a moment. Somehow, Drake had secured Charlene's phone number, but that was about it. He didn't know where she lived or where she went to school. So far, it was safe. But then, what difference did it make? She was much too young for a man like that. This had to be their last call.

"If you must know," Isabel said, "I'm a senior in high school; San Jose. Is that a problem for you?"

"No, no, of course not. Simply curious." Drake went silent as though he had already said too much.

"If you say so," she quickly said. "Now you tell me—if I can be bold—how old are you?"

"That's a valid question. Let's call it twenty-five years; a shade older than yourself."

"Yeah, right. I already know where you go to school, but come to think of it, I have no idea what you look like. You tell me you're twenty-five, but how do I know? You could be some thirty-year-old codger who happens to have a young voice."

"Fair point. You want to know what I look like." Drake paused as if checking a mirror. "I could tell you that I'm six-foot-one with a slim build—athletic, you might say. I've got medium length, wavy blond hair. How's that so far? I could tell you that my blue eyes would make you melt in a blizzard. But to make you a believer, you have to see 'em in person. And I thought tomorrow night—"

"Oh, I'm sure that you've got the prettiest eyes, Drake. But I'm sorry. If we haven't been introduced, then we can't possibly meet."

"I understand. But what harm is a cup of coffee? We could meet at a restaurant and take it from there."

"I wish I could say, 'yes,' but I can't. It's one of these unwritten laws that I have." Isabel tried her best to sound sincere.

"Ah, but Isabel; as an attorney, I can tell you that unwritten laws have the most exceptions. No one would complain if—"

"Ah, but Drake, you're not an attorney … yet. And this particular law has no exception."

"Then tell me; would you object if I called you again?"

"No, as a matter of record, I might enjoy it," she said confidently. Feeling courageous, she gave Drake a few more clues about her family and friends. But even so, she was adamant. As their call drew to an end; no introduction, no date.

After reluctantly agreeing to her terms, Drake called the next night and nearly every night after that. Whenever they talked, Isabel discovered more about Drake and his life; pampered as she believed it to be. Regrettably, she learned few details about *his* family and friends. But that was fine; at this point, it didn't make sense to delve into trivia.

However, she did learn that his father was a corporate attorney who worked nine to five in San Francisco. He rarely took vacations and thoroughly enjoyed his job. Hard work and all business; that summed up the father in a few words or less. He was ambitious, confident, and talented—much like the son.

Drake's mother, on the other hand, seemed to be the stay-at-home type; content to socialize among friends and maintain their humble house in San Francisco. She worked hard in her garden and loved to shop in the city. "Charming and loving; like most mothers," he said. "No complaints."

Beyond a snippet here and there, Drake rarely mentioned his family. Somehow that seemed strange—but acceptable for now. After all, they had plenty else to chat about.

Every night, they shared a new topic. If Drake wasn't boasting about his school or his genius-level IQ of 160, then he carried on about his sports; skiing, kayaking, skydiving, scuba diving. He claimed expertise in those sports and a working knowledge of a dozen others.

"Football?" Drake said. "No, I don't play it anymore, but I've been to the past five super bowls. Seats on the fifty-yard line, of course. Race cars? Not myself, but if you want meet a Lemans or Indianapolis driver, let me know."

Isabel quivered. Was Drake fast or was he dangerous? Or was he, in the worst possible case, a volatile mixture of both? She saw herself in a moth and flame story, and she worried about that. Even so, she flew a little closer. Finally, after a month of Drake's tireless groveling, Isabel gave in. She agreed to meet him for a quick meal in the middle of the day at a public spot.

She explained the situation over the phone. "I've told you how my parents are. I told you I'm not allowed to date until I graduate. We can talk. We can have lunch. And if it works out, we might be friends. But don't ask for something you're not going to get."

Isabel flashed back to her relationship with Ross. She reminded herself; take no chances and take it slow.

"I understand," Drake said. "That's not a problem."

"I'll meet you tomorrow," she said. "After school; for a half-hour at Burger King."

"Wow! That's not quite what I imagined."

"My second choice," she said, "was Burger King for *ten minutes*."

"Then it's a date," he said. "A half-hour will be fine. I'll buy."

"And just because I agreed to see you, we can still walk away; no obligations. Yes?"

"I'm sure it won't come to that."

The next day, Isabel asked for and got permission to drive the family Impala to school. "Doctor's appointment," she said to Charlene. *Possibly a new boyfriend*, she meant. And enough stress to make her sick. Her last class would end around noon. She figured one o'clock to meet Drake.

Dress and act casually, she told herself in front of her closet. This was not a blind date. It was no more than a friendly lunch with someone she had met at a party—or allegedly met. Isabel picked out a cool cotton blouse and her favorite white slacks. This sure felt like a date.

In California History class, she kept her eyes on the clock. She wished it to slow down or speed up; she couldn't decide. Although it seemed like forever, inevitably, 12:30 came. She had no intention of backing out. Isabel hurried across the high school parking lot, started the old car, and headed straight for Burger King. That funny feeling in her stomach wasn't hunger or the muscle relaxant. She was nervous in a good way; like the anticipation of Christmas morning.

Shortly, she arrived at the restaurant. She saw a black Camaro, probably Drake's, on one side of the lot. She parked on the far side, believing it to be safer. Then, like a quiz show contestant, she went to the door and scanned through the glass into the lobby. She looked for her prize. *Please don't make it a consolation prize.*

Then it happened. Drake opened the door and held it. He had blond hair and piercing blue eyes. He stood six-foot-one and had muscles in the right places. No, he didn't look familiar, but God, he was gorgeous. He had dressed in casual, gray slacks and a powder blue shirt—custom tailored to a perfect fit. The body matched the voice, and in a second, Isabel knew that she was in for the ride of her life.

"Hi, Isabel," Drake said with a disarming smile. He lightly shook her hand then released.

"Hi, Drake," she answered musically and stepped inside.

"I took the liberty of ordering for us," he said. "I hope you don't mind."

"Not in the least."

"Your order, sir," said the kid behind the counter.

"Do you have a table for us, sir?" Isabel said, grinning.

Drake led her to a booth in the corner. "I was hoping that you would show. Not that I was worried, mind you. I knew that sooner or later, your curiosity would catch up. So, tell me; now, do you remember?" While they sat, he gave her a clear view.

Isabel studied Drake's face, actually looking for flaws and scars. But when she found none, she said, "Sorry. Are you sure we went to the same party?"

"Positive. You were there with a brunette, about your height."

"Colette," Isabel said.

"Possibly, I never got her name."

Isabel realized a question that she had missed from the start. "But if you don't know her, how did you get *my* name and number?"

"I asked a friend who asked a friend who knew Colette. You know how it goes."

"Do people always do what you say?"

Drake nodded. "People I know, well, they volunteer. I rarely have to ask. Like you; you volunteered to come here, didn't you?"

"Is that what you call it? I thought it was more like begging and pleading on your part."

"*Comme ci, comme ca.*" He smiled. "And now we are together."

Isabel returned his smile. She nearly kicked herself for waiting an entire month to meet this incredible man. Quickly, the burgers and fries disappeared. But they lingered in the booth, sipping Cokes, gazing at each other, and talking about everything and nothing at all.

"Sorry to say, Drake, we can't stay the whole afternoon. They're bound to throw us out." Isabel searched her mind for a better idea. "So I'll make it easy, like a walk in the park."

Drake widened his eyes. "Pardon?"

"Literally. If you have time, we can drive to Hellyer Park. Weather like this is made for walking ... or feeding the ducks. Take your choice. That is, if you don't have classes."

"Nope, no classes until Monday," he said. "We can take my car if you want. I'll drop you off on the way back."

"Better yet, I'll meet you there." *Slow*, she reminded herself. *Take it nice and slow.*

"I understand," Drake said. "I'll follow you anywhere."

"Then let's go."

They drove to the park in separate cars and parked by the hard strip of sand that Isabel called a beach. She couldn't have ordered a more perfect setting for a budding romance; wandering Mallard ducks, new blossoms on the cottonwood trees, a cloudless sky, and barely enough breeze to nudge the dandelions. There were no weekend crowds and no screaming families. The park seemed vacant except for Isabel and Drake.

They strolled along the water's edge, and gradually, with her encouragement, Drake lowered his guard and revealed his past.

"You know, you never did tell me." Isabel slowed her pace and turned to face him.

"Tell you what?"

"Why law school? Why not medical school, or engineering, or accounting?"

Drake showed a half-grin as if he had been asked that question before. "Would you believe I was twelve years old, and I saw Perry Mason on TV? I said, 'that's me; that's what I want to be.' A lawyer; rich, famous, and respected."

"At twelve?" She raised an eyebrow.

"Or I can tell you that it was my father's choice. He's been in law since, well, since forever. Born in Harvard, raised at Stanford; that's what I've heard. It seems natural that I carry the flag for yet another generation." Drake picked up the pace and Isabel matched him.

"But I'll tell you this; my father has a valid point. If you have the right set of contacts, the right combination of friends, you can achieve any goal. People—personal relationships—are the true source of power. You'll never find that sitting behind a desk."

Isabel nodded. "That's what it takes to be a lawyer? Go to Stanford, learn some law, and make some friends?"

"Basically, yes."

The wind shifted, and Drake's cologne became discernible. What was that scent? Subtle and foreign. Not only did Drake look and dress like a million dollars, he smelled heavenly. He was going to be a great lawyer someday.

"I wish I had better luck with friends." Isabel stared at the lake.

"Would that be men or women?"

"Take a guess."

"It has to be a man," Drake said.

Isabel shrugged. Ross Hutten was the snake that flashed through her mind.

"Big dreams," Drake said, "and then disappointment. That's more common than you think. Want to talk about it?"

"Nope. Rather not. You see, Drake, some memories are best when they're buried forever. Sometimes, that's the only way to move on."

"Unfortunately, it hardly ever works like that."

"You've been there before, I assume. Care to talk about it?" she asked as a dare.

"If you care to listen, I might share a story or two."

"Sure, why not? As you said, people are important. I'd like to know who has or *had* influence on you." Isabel gulped. She was curious but also a tad jealous. Even so, to ignore Drake's past would make her blind to their real future. She had to find out. She had to understand as much as she could.

"Tell me about her," she said, assuming that his story was about a woman.

"Okay, but remember; you asked for it." Drake took in uneasy breaths and stared at the far shore. He blinked, shuffled his feet, and sighed. "Her name was Lisa. First let me say, you don't have to worry. It's entirely finished. A hundred percent over. She was my first love, I'll admit. Hard to believe that I was willing to commit my life to her. We were this close to being married; or so I thought. I lived in a dream."

When Drake took on a faraway look, Isabel coaxed him on. "What happened?"

He picked up a pebble and tossed it into the water. When the ripples reached the shore, he spoke in a soft voice. "I thought it was a good plan; disappear for a while and take a summer class. I'd come back then we'd get engaged. Then we would get married and have a couple kids. You know how it goes. Somehow, I thought that Lisa would go along with the plan. Destiny—how can you fight it?

"So, I get back to California, and my old classmate, my old pal, Suji, says he's got a problem. Now, here's the good part; he pulls me aside—I'm straight off the plane almost—and he tells me that Lisa is pregnant. And guess what, I'm not the father; *he* is. I couldn't believe it. That two-faced little creep, I could've ripped his heart out."

Drake glanced at Isabel as she raised an eyebrow. He quickly added, "Metaphorically speaking, that is."

"Let me guess," Isabel said. "Lisa said it was a huge mistake. She did it once in a moment of weakness, and she begged you to take her back." She recalled Ross's pitiful letters and the stacks of phony regrets.

"Not even close. It seems that whenever I was gone for more than a weekend, Suji stepped in to warm her sheets. Yeah, well, what are friends for? Funny thing is; Lisa had no regrets about the whole affair. She said she rather liked the idea of sleeping with two men."

"That's sick. At least you won't see him or her again."

Drake agreed. "Until that point, I had owed him plenty of favors. None of that matters now. I figure we're just about even."

"How many favors and friends do you have left?"

"Could be too many of both." He grimaced and then followed with a polite smile. "Except for Berringer; the one friend I unconditionally trust. My roommate, my go-to man when it counts. I have no worries about him."

"And you don't have to worry about me," Isabel said. "I can barely manage one man at a time."

"Speaking of which," Drake said, "for the record; would call this our first date?"

"I'm not going to call *anything* a date until I graduate."

"I suppose I can wait." He sighed. "But you have to tell me this."

"What's that?"

"If you've never dated, then who's this other guy you mentioned?"

"Oh, I'm sorry, Drake. You know it's bad form to bring up old relations, especially on our first, uh, get-together."

"*Touché, mon Cher.*" Drake smiled and Isabel blushed.

Shortly after their first get-together, Isabel relaxed in her room and stared at the dots in the ceiling. Without a doubt, she was in love or infatuation; she didn't know which. She truly didn't care. That face of his; it had to come straight from heaven. What right did Drake have to look that good? Perfect teeth. Perfect smile.

She wondered; why would someone like that be smiling at someone like her? Good question, but Isabel decided to set it aside as long as she could. For the rest of the day, she replayed their encounter; reliving every moment and caressing each memory like a priceless jewel.

Finally, she had a real man to talk to—at least for the afternoons during the week and before curfew on the weekends. But how long would Drake tolerate all those rules and restrictions? Isabel had made it clear; no dating for the next two months. Not even a simple kiss or a token embrace. First, they had to be friends *then* possibly romance.

Drake remained a mystery. He was almost too good to be true. He was experienced. He had a good line and a perfect pitch. Was he real, or was it an act? Isabel knew that she had to be careful. If she had a Ferrari on her hands, she wanted to stay in first gear as long as she could.

The next afternoon, they met at the park. Again, they walked and talked among the carpets of dandelions. They dreamt about tomorrow. They planned for the next day and the day after that. And for the next two months, each rendezvous became a copy of the first; two hours in the afternoon, three days a week.

Once in a while, a stranger would walk into that park in San Jose and catch a glimpse of a young couple holding hands in the dark shadows of the oak trees. Even a stranger would call them a couple. Even a stranger could see the love that was undeniably growing.

During that spring, Isabel and Drake had little more than carefree afternoons in the warm San Jose sun. They made no mention of quick and easy sex. They had no expectations beyond a close friendship. Isabel did not have—and did not want—the power to ask for more. At times, she worried that her simple demands would put at risk the chance for a lifetime of love. At times, she felt totally naïve. There was no doubt that she was too naïve to realize that forbidden love could be the world's most powerful aphrodisiac.

Chapter *6*

GRADUATION. For Isabel, it meant much more than the end of high school. It became a moment of renaissance—of rebirth—because on that day, she would officially nullify Charlene's no-dating rule and kiss goodbye to the three-month, purely platonic, love at first sight relationship with Drake.

Now if she could only make it through the graduation ceremony itself. Over three hundred diplomas to pass out. Over three hundred "Congratulations on your great achievement." Isabel wished for one achievement; her family to sit through the process without three hundred complaints.

Charlene, Leo, Ruby, and Randy sat patiently, hidden in the bleachers of the San Jose Fairgrounds. It was a perfect June night to end four years of high school servitude. It was a perfect evening for new beginnings.

Isabel glanced at Colette, who struggled with the zipper of her white gown and giggled as she did in sixth grade. How did she ever make it this far? Isabel had studied hard, played fair, and finished in the upper ten percent of her class. As for Colette; it was none of the above.

Colette never made the grades, but she did make and hold onto friends. And for that, Isabel felt envy. Isabel had hundreds of classmates but hardly a friend. She searched the crowd beside her and saw little more than nameless faces and casual acquaintances. Whose high school was this anyway? Where were the memories? Where were the good times she was supposed to have had? They sure weren't around here. They sure had nothing to do with high school.

But no need to dwell on the past; Isabel believed that most of her memories lay ahead. Party tonight, followed by summer vacation, college in the fall, and then the rest of her years with Drake. It was not a bad plan for someone who couldn't decide what to wear to graduation.

Nonetheless, to make sure that Drake remembered the night, she had picked out a new pink chiffon dress that was guaranteed to arouse the passions of any healthy, red-blooded California man—especially Drake. Just how would he feel; kissing a beautiful *and* educated woman? In a couple hours, Isabel would find out, and no one, including the warden Charlene Espinosa could stop her.

The long-awaited miracle had finally happened. Charlene had given a reluctant okay to a night out with the girls, knowing that a few of the new-graduate guys would be available for rides, escorts, or other guy functions, such as dancing, kissing, or holding hands in the dark. Charlene's sole request; come home at a reasonable hour.

"No problem," Isabel said.

Isabel had her own terms and conditions to apply to her new guy; dates were to end by midnight, no meeting the parents, no stopping by the house. If Charlene ever found out the truth about Drake, she would invoke the eleventh and final commandment; Thou shall torment thy daughter for the rest of her natural life. Drake was too old; he drove a fast car; and he had way too much money and time on his hands. Charlene would never approve—if she ever found out.

After the ceremony, the family squeezed through the crowd and found Isabel. Charlene—dressed in a soft, flowery print—proved that stylish clothes and a new hairdo could highlight the best in any woman. She looked pretty. It seemed a shame that Isabel rarely saw this side of her mother. The scent of Christian Dior seemed a vast improvement over the pungent odor of Dawn dishwasher soap.

Charlene smiled and said she was proud. That was sweet. And when Charlene embraced; that was the best memory so far. Isabel nearly cried.

Leo himself; he seemed overly tense by the surrounding noise and activity. Like Charlene, he hated crowds. He tried for a hug, but it came off as unnatural and forced; much like that brown, corduroy jacket he wore. It seemed a token gesture, but Isabel nevertheless gave a sincere, "Thank you."

Then she added, "Sorry, I can't stay and talk. I've got a graduation party and I'm already late." She pushed the family for last-minute photos and then chased them to the parking lot. "Tomorrow, we'll celebrate. We'll have barbecue ribs and corn on the cob. How's that sound?"

"You have fun," Charlene said. "Don't worry about us."

With a slight twinge of guilt, Isabel watched the taillights of the old Chevy disappear into the dust of the Fairgrounds parking lot. "See you later." She waved. She held her smile as long as she could. Ruby and Randy waved from the back seat. Then they were gone.

Isabel, feeling safe again, raced to Drake, nearly tripping on her flowing white robe. "Did you see me?" she squealed. "Did you see me graduate?"

A moment later, she was caught up in Drake's arms. Her heart pounded and not from the short sprint across the field. His arms felt so incredibly good. She reached around his waist and allowed her hands to slide up the muscles of his back. Why did she wait so long for a moment like this? She opened her eyes. Drake's lips were enticingly close.

"Don't I deserve a kiss?" she asked after Drake had missed his cue.

"You certainly do; but not here. Not in a parking lot with a hundred guys watching."

"Oh?"

"Patience," he said. "It's our first kiss. You don't want a cheap memory, do you?"

"I don't?"

"No, you don't. If you can wait, I'll make it worth your while."

Isabel pouted. She frowned and narrowed her eyes. Then she noticed a man off to the side, staring. She had never seen him before, but he looked vaguely familiar. At six-foot-four, he stood taller than Drake. He had wavy brown hair and blue eyes a shade darker than Drake's. But those biceps and quads; no doubt, they shared the same personal trainer. His face was distinctive and bold; a mixture of California surfer and Spanish royalty.

"This must be Berringer," she said.

"And you must be psychic," Barry said, obviously pleased that Drake had talked about him.

"No," Isabel said. "I'm just a careful listener. Drake must've warned me, I mean, *told* me about you a hundred times. Is that your Corvette?" She pointed across the parking lot to the new white convertible that gathered dust from the passing cars.

"Ah, yes, the love of my life." Barry smiled at the machine and then extended his arms to the graduate. "May I?"

That uncertain look on his face; was he asking Isabel or was he asking Drake? Isabel answered by reaching out for a courtesy hug. She knew little about Berringer Dees except that he and Drake had been roommates since enrolling at Stanford and close friends for years before that. He was in his third year of medical school, but unlike Drake, Barry had been committed to a token amount of studying to maintain his "A" average.

Isabel and Barry embraced, and a heartbeat later, Drake yanked at her sleeve. "Enough of that. We've got places to go and things to do."

"Like what kind of places?" she asked.

"Like the Bold Knight to start. We have reservations and a half-hour to get there."

Barry laughed. "The Bold Knight, huh? Well, you do have shoes and shirts. They are required, you know."

Drake scowled. "You'll have to excuse Barry. It's way past his curfew. He's not accustomed to being in public."

"Listen to me, Isabel," Barry said. "Don't let the old man get away cheap. Ask him why you're not going to the Rainbow Room. It's your graduation for God's sake. You should be doing it proper."

What was Barry talking about? The Rainbow Room was one of the fanciest restaurants in the city of New York. Drake wasn't that impulsive. He was certainly well-to-do but not obscenely rich. Why would Barry tease her like that?

Drake poked his buddy in the ribs. "Hey, who's that sitting on the hood of the 'Vette?"

Isabel glanced at the car. No one actually sat on the hood, but a couple kids were standing way too close. Barry furrowed his brow then disappeared to chase them off. Meanwhile, Isabel slipped off her graduation gown and fluffed the folds of her dress.

"Stunning, to say the least," Drake stammered, exactly as she had predicted.

"You like?" Isabel twirled.

"Hey, remember, Drake," Barry said as he returned. "You just got your learner's permit. If you ask me, she's too hot to handle."

"Rest assured, Barry, she's in good hands. Don't bother to wait up."

The Bold Knight, when they finally arrived, proved to be a definite step above a barbecue at Almaden Lake. White linens, candlelight, friendly staff, and a fancy menu of seafood and steaks; how could Isabel complain?

Nonetheless, she had one nagging question as they sat down and ordered their meal; why was Drake waiting for the first kiss? She had given him permission to go to the next step, so *let's get on with it.*

But then came the hors d'oeuvres, the lobster, the strawberry parfait, and a long stroll back to the parking lot and Drake's Camaro. Still no kiss. No declaration of love. No hint of undying passion. What was Drake waiting for?

He helped her into the Camaro and pushed her dress away from the door. "We have one more stop."

Isabel's confusion grew. She had no idea what Drake had planned. Where was he taking her? Not to some sleazy motel; that was for sure. She knew him better than that—or certainly hoped she did. As they raced through San Jose, Drake never said a word. That seemed frightening enough. Then he detoured through Alum Rock, passing the porn theaters and the X-rated bookstores. Isabel felt her heart sink. She had never imagined a graduation like this. She had never been so wrong with her assumptions.

Another detour and they climbed a steep mountain road. The housing projects fell behind, but up ahead—more hills and darkness. Isabel had a feeling. Her first trip in Drake's car might be her last.

"Keep your eyes closed," he said without elaboration.

Isabel did, concerned that she might need to add a prayer. Drake slowed the car, eased onto a gravel embankment, and stopped the engine. Absolute silence. What was his next move and how could she possibly resist? Before the start of her prayer, she peeked out of the front window and gasped. She had never seen this before.

The view was tremendous. No dark, isolated forest; the entire city of San Jose was laid out in front of her in a dazzling display of orange and white lights below, stars above. She was five thousand feet above it all—at lovers' point, Mount Hamilton. Now she felt embarrassed. How could she ever suspect the face of an angel? That would never happen again, she vowed.

They stepped outside and held hands by the railing. The air was cold. A slight breeze rustled Isabel's skirt. Far below, the city traffic whispered like a rolling surf. From behind, a transformer hummed in the dark. She turned around and recognized the open dome of the observatory. Incredible as it seemed, some people drove up the hill to study the stars.

"Beautiful, isn't it?" Drake wrapped his arms around her waist and kissed her once. Isabel shuddered, blaming a chilling wind. He kissed her again, and now she felt the warmth of his lips.

"A kiss for every star," she begged.

"There must be a thousand stars out tonight."

"Okay," Isabel sighed, melting into his arms.

On that night, they kissed, and talked, and admired the stunning view. Isabel could not have planned a more perfect graduation. Drake stood by her side, sharing his heart and promising her the stars and the sky.

"I don't always believe in destiny," Drake softly said as they strolled along the embankment, "but from the first moment I saw you, I knew that we were meant to be as one. Isabel, you have a certain style. I can't explain it, but there's something about you that makes me come alive. If I didn't know better, I'd say I was in love."

"If you are in love, Drake, then come out and say it."

"Then more to the point. Yes, Isabel Espinosa, I love you more than heaven and earth combined."

She smiled and told him, "Drake Phillips, if I didn't know better, I'd say that I'm in love."

He kissed her again and held her tight. He gently rested his chin on her flowing black hair. This memory would stay.

For once, the world was back in step and going Isabel's way. She had begun to believe that the evil Ross Hutten was no more than a temporary, albeit painful, setback in her romantic life. From the start, her real destiny lay with Drake. *He* was the man who truly understood the meaning of love, respect, and commitment. He was the man who would prove Charlene wrong.

Contrary to Charlene's steadfast belief, there were men in the Bay Area who did not automatically add the price of a motel to the cost of a date. There were men who knew the proper way to treat a woman. Drake was, in every sense of the word, a true romantic. Now, if he could only comprehend the realities of life with a woman like Isabel.

***

At a sidewalk café in downtown Palo Alto, she explained her precarious situation. "The choices are pretty clear; we have three ways, and *only* three ways, of getting together. I can take the bus to the mall, and you can meet me there. Or, if I'm lucky, and my mom lets me have the car, I can meet you at your house."

"Third option?"

"Same as today; I drive and meet you somewhere."

"Technically," Drake said, "that's only two ways of meeting. And each involves that beast of a car. How many more miles are left on it?" He glanced sideways at the big, green Chevy that was parked up the street.

"Don't complain. It got me here, didn't it? Honestly, I never thought the day would come. I can stay out until midnight; I can date any man I want; *and* I have a car—well, sort of."

"Wonderful," Drake grumbled.

"But whatever happens; we have to be careful. Unfortunately, you can't come to my house. I mean never, never come to my house. Not if you want to see me alive when you turn twenty-six."

"I don't understand," Drake said. "Your mother knows you're dating. Doesn't she want to see *who* you're dating?"

"Desperately. But she'll never ask to meet them, especially if I tell her it's a white boy."

"Why is that?"

"Are you kidding? She's deathly afraid of you guys; rich, white guys, that is. Understand, Drake, she grew up on a farm with migrants. That's enough to kill her confidence. But she also speaks with a lisp—a very pronounced lisp. I'm used to it, but most people aren't. So she's self-conscience; both about her upbringing and the way she talks.

"I'll give her credit though; her English is good. Very good, actually. But regarding you, she wouldn't have a clue what to say. I mean, it's incredible. She'll yell at me and accuse me of sleeping with a hundred men, but she refuses to meet a single one. And that's fine by me."

"That's a shame. Things being as they are; I'd like to meet her."

"Trust me," Isabel said, "you wouldn't."

"Someday perhaps. Of course, someday you'll have to meet *my* parents."

"Yes, we'll get around to it."

Drake took an uneasy deep breath and forced out the next words. "Someday like, oh, this Friday night, huh? How does that sound? They're dying to meet you, and I said we'd stop by."

"What?"

"I'll tell you what. Cocktails and gossip start around eight. We'll drop in, you'll smile, say a few words, and then we vanish. Fair enough?"

"What are you talking about?" she said, sternly.

"Friday night party; you, me, Mother, Father."

Isabel groaned. Did he just say, "Meet the parents?" Her stomach convulsed into a hundred knots.

In a flash, her worst nightmare played in front of her eyes. There she was; standing in a grand, ostentatious courtroom; Drake's father and mother sitting on a throne, casting judgment, watching every move, and keeping score with a vengeance.

"Did you see that?" the father bellows. "She ate the crepes with her fingers."

"I have never seen such manners," the mother shrieks and points an accusing finger. "Mexican, you said? No wonder."

Drake rises to his feet. "She's only eighteen. How could she possibly know?" He pleads, but it's no use; Isabel is too young and too minority to have any sense.

Isabel shivered and looked away. Drake knew everything about everything. How could his parents be any different? Party with the parents? This was much too soon.

She gazed at him with sad eyes. "Listen, Drake, I'm not ready for a big step like that."

"What do you mean 'big step?' We're not running a marathon. It's no more than crab cakes and artichoke hearts. Easy. You'll go there, laugh at my jokes, and we leave. A half-hour at the max."

"I don't have a single decent dress."

"We'll buy you one."

"My hair's a mess."

"We'll have it done," Drake said.

"I'm—"

"No more excuses. It'll be fun. I promise."

Isabel folded her hands on her lap and nodded. The bright side, if anyone dared call it that, was that she would finally get to see his house and the house of his parents; yet another insight to Drake himself.

He had said that he lived in a modest bungalow on a quiet Palo Alto street; his only company being a roommate—Barry—and a stack of law books. Isabel wanted to believe that, but somehow the image of nightly beer busts popped into her head. She gave Drake credit, up to this point, for being exceptionally neat and well mannered. That was good. But most men wouldn't know a dust mop if they were handed one. Most men had more clutter and trash than a neighborhood dumpster. Could Drake be any different?

He never talked about where his parents lived in San Francisco. Isabel pictured a quaint two-story Victorian on California Street with a small bush as a front yard and a bay window overlooking the cable car tracks. Sure, his father was a San Francisco lawyer, but Drake's tuition must have been cleaning the old man's pockets. Luxury seemed unlikely. If Isabel settled on modest expectations, like a comfortable house and amiable parents, she might be able to survive the coming days.

It took a while for the concept to settle in. But after the misgivings faded, she began to look forward to a day of shopping, hair styling, and witty conversation with a group of strangers who were at least a generation older than she. That was Drake's world, and sooner or later, she would need to enter it, hopefully in style.

Friday quickly arrived, and before she knew it, Isabel was scouring the racks of Bullock's. Drake stood by her side, charge card at the ready. Armani, Dior, Yves Saint Laurent; it was such an odd feeling for someone on a ten-dollar-a-week allowance to sift through the fine designer gowns of Paris and New York.

Isabel pointed, and the sales manager jumped. What a difference from her last visit when she could only touch the fabric and flip the price tags. After finding the perfect low-heel pumps and basic pearl earrings, she picked out a black chiffon dress. It had a modest neckline, pleats for an elegant flow, and a hemline that tickled her knees. Good enough for now.

"On schedule and on budget." Isabel gave a confident smile as Drake checked his watch and offered to carry her bag.

Drake nodded. "We'll stop by the house, get changed, and then head up 101. How's that?"

"What's the rush, Drake? *Your* house is also on the tour. I expect the full treatment."

"That's what I'm afraid of," Drake said. "Don't expect a mansion."

"Don't worry," she said. "I am not one to judge."

Drake grimaced. "We'll see."

After a short drive, Drake pulled into the driveway of his Palo Alto home. Isabel smiled. She had read him like the proverbial book. His rented, three-bedroom ranch house seemed respectable enough; a plush green front lawn, birch trees for shade, ceramic geese, and full bloom gardenias and heather. That was nice, but when she stepped inside the house, it became clear that a couple of Stanford men shared the same place.

She roamed the hallways and back rooms, searching for clues to the real Drake Phillips, but what she found was an eclectic mix of books, furniture, and bland everyday curtains. Most of it was Drake's, and most of it screamed for a woman's touch.

"I don't spend a lot of time here," Drake said.

"I see," Isabel muttered and moved to the kitchen. "However, now we're getting somewhere." She gawked at a hanging set of copper pots and pans, a dazzling array of Sheffield knives, and a floor to ceiling spice rack. She rapped on a full keg of beer. "Apparently you guys like to eat and drink."

"Survival rations," Drake said.

"If you say so," Isabel said, shaking her head. "And where is the roommate tonight?"

"Barry had a last-minute errand."

"Where do I change?"

"My room. Down the hall; to the left."

"Here you go. Keep yourself busy." Isabel pulled out an old recipe magazine. "Find us a tuna casserole. We'll have it tomorrow."

She had made it clear from the moment she stepped into the hallway; no following to the other room, don't bother to try. Drake didn't. But that never stopped Isabel from considering the obvious.

She got to his room and shut the door. Drake's scent permeated everywhere; that same exotic, impossible to place fragrance. She sat on the edge of the brass bed and wondered how many other women had done the same. Did they all make love to him here? Was she the first to shy away from a first-night roll in the sack? Isabel shuddered. That bed sizzled with too many questions and not a single comforting answer. She got dressed and out of that room as fast as she could.

"Take a good look, Barry," she called out when Barry walked into the house with a six pack of beer. "I'll be the envy of the party, and you'll miss it all. What a pity."

"Not quite, hon." Barry set down the beer and stared at her dress. "I'm on assignment to chaperone you two."

"Come again?"

"Hey, be nice to the boy," Drake said. "This is the third week in a row that his date's canceled. What was it tonight? Her father died again?"

"So it seems," Barry said.

"Well, let's get moving," Drake said. "The 101's backed up, and we're already late."

Isabel helped Drake straighten his collar and tie, and then she stood back to admire her escort. God, he was gorgeous, again. That dark blue Armani suit was no chain store rag. Perfectly tailored, exquisite material, elegant style; his entire wardrobe proved to be impeccable. Isabel glanced in the hallway mirror. No question about it; she and Drake made one beautiful couple.

Drake ushered her and Barry into his van and immediately headed for San Francisco. On the way up, Isabel took a careful look at the van's custom features; tinted windows, swivel seats, fully equipped stereo system, and a fully stocked, refrigerated wet bar. The wet bar was a problem. She felt nervous enough that night without seeing that booze in the back. What if the cops pulled them over and searched inside? What if the cops arrested them all—for whatever reason—and threw them in jail? How would she explain that to her mother? How could she possibly make bail?

Isabel shrugged. Not to spoil the mood, she kept quiet. She didn't say a word. Her more immediate issues; how to keep wrinkles from her dress and how to keep dirt off her Ferragamo shoes. She had no clue that, before the night was over, a crease or two would be totally forgotten.

They arrived in the city and parked the van. Almost immediately, Isabel knew that something was wrong.

"Your parents live here?" she said with a gasp.

"For the past fifteen years," Drake said.

Isabel felt a twinge crawl up the length of her spine. This was not the house she had imagined. She hesitated to call it a house. She gazed at the three-story, Nob Hill, grand mansion. It had about ten thousand square feet of opulence; elegant white columns, beautiful brick façade, massive double-door front, and about a hundred French windows to peek through. It was almost like stepping into the royal palace of Monaco—if she could imagine what a palace would be.

Immediately, the butler approached, greeted Isabel, and took her sweater. He led her through the foyer to the central hall. Again, she felt overwhelmed by the grandeur; a four-foot crystal chandelier overhead, a stone fireplace off to the side, Persian rugs on each wall, an elegant oak staircase leading to the second and third floors. Somewhere in the background, a violinist played the best hits of Strauss and Stravinsky.

"Tell me I'm dreaming. I've never seen anything like it." She ran a quick tally of the party; ten couples, mingling and drinking, laughing, and snacking on smoked salmon and wild mushroom fricassee. The women hinted of the diamond and pearl crowd, weighing heavily with designer labels and business cards of the best plastic surgeons in the Bay Area. Thankfully, Isabel had youth and beauty on her side. The men there could see that. Now if they would only quit staring.

As Isabel took in the surroundings, the housemaid approached Drake and passed him a note.

"Thanks, Teresa," Drake said. He turned to Isabel and said, "Hang tight for a sec. I've got to step away."

Before Isabel could catch her breath, he excused himself and disappeared down a corridor.

"Good Lord, Barry," she said. "His father owns all of this? He never hinted."

"I'm not surprised," Barry said. "Yeah, they've got this place and a house in Hawaii, Paris, Switzerland, Monte Carlo, you name it."

"Wow."

"But I'll give you a clue; it's his mother's house, not the father's."

"His mother's?" Isabel said.

"A few years back, she plunked down some small change and got herself a bargain."

"Small change?"

"Helen's the one with the old money," Barry said. "Generations of greenbacks, handed down like a priceless heirloom. This here's just a token. When *her* mother dies, they'll split up the crown jewels, and Helen can buy fifty of these shacks."

Isabel sighed. "All this and her husband still has to work for a living."

Barry chuckled. "Make no mistake; no one here *has* to work for a living. And a bit of free advice; if you want to stay alive tonight, there are two words you keep to yourself—idle rich. This is one family that still has a modicum of pride."

"Trust me, Barry; my one goal tonight is to stay in the background."

"That's smart."

She stood close to Barry and whispered, "Any more secrets?"

"What? About Drake's family?"

"Yes," she said.

"Did he mention his brothers?"

"Vaguely."

"I can tell you this," Barry said. "Drake has an older brother, Jackson; PhD in philosophy. This guy can be a real charmer. You might be lucky and see him tonight." Barry winked.

"You're holding back," Isabel said. "I can tell."

"Then there's Raymond. Most down-to-earth fellow I've ever met. He'll be on your side."

"What do you mean 'side?' What am I getting myself into?" Isabel frowned. Suddenly the room seemed a bit cooler.

"Heads up," Barry whispered. "Drake's on the move."

"Come on, Isabel," Drake said. "There's someone I want you to meet." He beckoned her to follow.

Isabel obliged while Barry searched for a glass of Chardonnay.

Drake opened the library door and there he was—the father, William Phillips. He stepped from his desk and immediately extended his hand. God, he was big. Not in the corporeal sense as much as the way he carried himself. Authority. No nonsense. Speak your mind and get to the point.

Isabel sensed an ambitious and confident attorney who had honed his image to the point of perfection. She noted his consummate attention to detail; from the fit of his Armani suit on his six-foot frame to each carefully placed artifact on his desk. She glanced at his perfectly styled hair and the hint of gray by his temples. Was this going to be Drake in the next twenty years?

"He's talked a lot about you." William gave a courtesy smile. "You seem to have made my son happy, and that, my dear, is no small achievement. Keep working your charms. We'll be seeing you around."

Talk about pressure. Lucky, Isabel didn't have to charm the old man every day. How did Drake ever live up to the expectations? *That* was no small achievement. But she had a gut feeling; there was a lot of mutual respect and admiration between father and son. *Interesting* was one word that came to her mind. *Curious* was another. She had to find out more.

"Will you be joining us at the party?" she asked William.

"Right. Right. I have a few papers to sign then I'll be out." William gave a slight, almost military nod to his son.

Moments later, Isabel and Drake were back in the ballroom.

"You see," he murmured. "Thirty minutes and we're out of here. And my father is the toughest. You breezed through like a champ."

"But I didn't say a word. *He* didn't say a word."

"It's all body language," Drake said.

"Oh, yeah? Then read this body language." She pinched his elbow until he yelped.

"Hey! What's that for?"

"That's for not telling me your parents lived in a palace."

"You never asked."

"I shouldn't have to." Isabel poked at his rib then noticed a tall, thin man gliding their way. "Who's that?"

"Trouble," Drake said.

"How do you mean?"

Drake grabbed a shot glass from the passing butler, downed half of it, and faced his older brother. "Jackson. Yes, a rare pleasure, isn't it? Will this be a cameo appearance, or are you here for the duration?"

The gaunt man in a tweed suit smiled but ignored the question. "So, whom do we have here?" Jackson looked straight at Drake but obviously referred to Isabel.

"We have Isabel," Drake said.

"Isabel ... Isabel ...?" Jackson fished for a last name.

"Espinosa," Drake said. "Oh, and by the way, Isabel, this is Jackson—the first born."

"Espinosa," Jackson said, barely moving his eyes from Drake. "What an unusual and musical name. You know, I believe Teresa's maiden name was Espinosa." Jackson's hand floated to his chin, and he stroked the few wisps of a beard. He glanced at Isabel. "Your first visit to the house?"

"Yes, it is," she said. "Drake was eager to show it off, although I never—"

"Oh, really. That is so atypical of the boy. He has always struggled to cultivate that charming, down-home image of his. A home like this does tend to color a woman's opinion."

"I've formed my own opinion of the boy long before we arrived here." Isabel wrapped her arms around Drake's elbow.

"Yeah, you tell him, honey," Drake said. "You might as well get used to her, Jackson. Because when you see me, you'll be seeing her." He gave her a pat on the arm. He gave a smile to his brother.

Isabel let loose a heavy sigh. Barely into the *hors d'oeuvres* and her nausea had already taken hold. Why were the brother and father so abrupt, so cold and aloof? It couldn't have been anything that Isabel had said. So far, she had barely said a word. She folded her arms and moaned. She desperately wanted to fade into the background.

What kind of party was this? Where was the small talk about weather, dogs, and shopping for college clothes? These guys were much too serious and much too wrapped up in their personal affairs. Drake was wrong; this didn't look or sound anything like a party.

Then the noise and confusion took a turn for the worse. Drake waved at his mother, Helen, as she walked into the room.

"Oh no," Isabel groaned. How much worse could Mrs. Moneybags be? Could the years of affluence, pampering, and shoe licking sons have created anything but a fifty-year-old spoiled child? *Let's get this over with*, she wished.

"Isabel, there you are!" Helen sang with a huge grin as she approached. "I'm so glad you could make it tonight. Drake's already told us that you might be a little shy. But you know, my dear, he never mentioned how pretty you are. Oh my goodness, yes. And I simply love that color on you. Basic black—you can't go wrong."

Helen beamed like a Christmas star. Isabel could see it in a glance. Helen Phillips was a hundred percent cheerleader. She had blond hair—short and styled. She was slender but shapely. Energetic, enthusiastic, forever smiling. What a beautiful woman. And those baby blue eyes; those were the same gentle eyes that she had given her son. No need to look it up; this was God's definition of a giving mother.

Isabel gave Drake an icy glare then smiled at Helen. "I wish that Drake had told me more about you. Your son can be a little shy with the details; if you know what I mean."

"Oh, I do. I do. His father's the same way in that one respect." Helen flagged a server who passed by with a silver platter of appetizers. "Isabel, you have to try the smoked salmon mousse. Here, tell me what you think. Fabulous, would you say?"

Drake offered the first review. "Too much olive oil; not enough lemon."

Isabel smirked. "Perhaps you have a better recipe?"

Helen laughed. "He didn't tell you, did he?"

"Tell me what?"

"I wouldn't be surprised if Drake *does* have a better recipe. I would expect that; after spending four summers at the Cordon Bleu in Paris. Omitted another fine point, did he?" Helen nodded. "You should know that our master chef here is fluent in hors d'oeuvres, entrees, pastries, and French—Parisian French, that is. And also Italian, Spanish, and German."

"Tell me the truth." Isabel narrowed her eyes at Drake.

"Ah, *oui. C'est vrai*," Drake squeaked. "*J'avais presque oublié.*"

"A shame," Isabel said, "that I don't know a word of French or Spanish. I might be tempted to say a few words of my own." She smiled at Helen. "I suppose you have a bundle of stories about your little boy."

"Oh, you bet I do. I'll tell you what; Drake, sweetie, why don't you take Barry to Maureen and introduce them? Yes, and take your time while you're at it." Helen waved Drake off with a wag of the hand and a smile. She waited until Barry and Drake had sulked away to the far side of the hall.

Helen, to Isabel's delight, became a wealth of trivia and vital statistics. Off and on during the course of the soirée, she exposed the true Drake Phillips and Berringer Dees. It was such a pleasure to hear the unabridged version.

Isabel saw Drake and Barry squirm in the corner. Obviously, they didn't appreciate Helen revealing the intimate details of their intensely private lives. Vulnerability seemed to be one trait that never suited Drake. But Helen was relentless. She simply loved to brag about the kids.

Isabel heard that Drake and Barry had been friends since the early days of military school outside of Los Angeles. *Toddlers in dress blues* is what Helen called them. From the way they acted, they could have been twins separated at birth. For years, it was almost impossible to tell them apart. Eventually, they both enrolled at Stanford, they both earned a private pilot's license, and both achieved black belts in karate. Both men, it seemed, were destined to follow the personal and professional footsteps of their fathers.

Barry's father lived in Brentwood with his Hispanic wife. He had a thriving practice as a neurosurgeon and couldn't wait for his son to work at his side. Barry had a forty-foot sailboat. His father owned a seventy-foot yacht. Barry had a new girlfriend every week. His father had been married for thirty years.

Drake's father managed a large law firm in San Francisco. He was counting the days until his son joined as a partner. Drake flew his own Cessna; four seats but plenty of power. His father owned a Learjet, executive style, ten seats, and the pilot always on call.

"Anything else I should be aware of?" Isabel asked, trying to keep mental notes.

"Yes," Helen said. "Drake's last girlfriend was named Lisa. He remembers her well."

Chapter 7

SATURDAY MORNING cartoons blaring from the TV. Some old man screaming that his truck won't start. Doors slamming. Toilet flushing.

I must be home. This sounds so much like San Jose. Isabel woke to the reality of life in the South Bay. Last night must have been a dream. That was Cinderella up at that Nob Hill castle, not some poor girl who raced to get an old Chevy home by midnight. There was barely enough time for a goodnight kiss and certainly no time to leave a glass slipper.

Would Drake ever call again? After last night, Isabel wasn't so sure. She thought that she knew him, but now it was clear that he stubbornly held many more secrets. Drake Phillips lived in a different world, where money and women kept passing his way. What did he ever see in a woman like Isabel? What on earth could *she* offer him?

To be with a man like Drake seemed a beautiful dream, but Isabel told herself to prepare for the worst. She could try her best the please him, but at any moment, he could grow tired and move on to more exciting, more sophisticated prospects. His first love, Lisa, could simply snap her fingers, and Drake would irresistibly dance back to her embrace. With so many beautiful women around, why would he ever settle down? Why would he settle for anything less than perfection?

Isabel worried about that. She loved Drake dearly and wanted to spend the rest of her life with him, but if he were ever to let go, it sure would be nice to feel solid ground beneath. She hated the feeling of being cynical, but the memories of Ross Hutten remained fresh. The lesson learned was not to get burned.

She leafed through the pages of her college catalogs. In the long term, a good education seemed the best solution. Even if she never married Drake—or anyone—she would have a chance for a good job and a decent life. Then she wouldn't be stuck at home, fighting with her mother over the last can of deodorant. A college degree meant a responsible job, and a responsible job meant more money, independence, and much higher respect. True romance was tough, but a good education was practical and much safer than waiting for a handsome prince to swing by with a royal carriage.

Isabel dug out the bulging white envelope that held the registration forms to San Jose State. Carefully, she filled in each blank exactly as they required. This was her first university test. The answers came easily until she reached the bottom line. PLEASE SUBMIT REMITTANCE stood out in bold, undeniable print. How far could she get with a hundred dollars in the bank? Not one step farther than the student union cafeteria.

She had one chance, a long shot at that. Charlene kept a bank account, and between those funds and a summer job, Isabel might be able to squeak by with her first year's tuition. With nothing to lose, she went to step one of her master plan; catch Charlene in a good mood.

"Mom, can we talk?"

Charlene sat at the dining room table, clipping coupons and stacking them according to food products, kitchen cleansers, and cold remedies. That did not bode well. She was fretting about money and waving a mean pair of scissors.

"You haven't seen the paper, have you?" Charlene said.

"No, mom." Isabel sat opposite Charlene and kept her college brochures on her lap.

"I left it on the counter. Someone's got it."

"Mom, do you remember when I graduated? I told you about San Jose State and their accounting program. It's supposed to be one of the best you can find. Well, I'm thinking if I sign up now and work extra hard, I can graduate in four years. You know, get my degree and work for IBM or something like that."

Charlene finally looked up. "Haven't you figured it out yet? It's not going to happen, *Mija*. Your father and me can barely keep food on the table as it is."

"I know I can do it if you give me a chance."

"You don't understand. We don't have any money. Not a single dime."

"You don't have to pay a hundred percent," Isabel said. "I can help. I can help a lot."

"Truth is," Charlene said, "most people don't need college. Look at your sister. She never went, and she's got a good job."

"Good job? Mom, she's a telephone operator. She gives out phone numbers eight hours a day."

"She makes good money. Besides, you don't need to hang around those college men."

"What?" Isabel said.

"That's what you want, isn't it? An older man who knows what he's doing."

"Oh God. You're not back on that, are you?" Isabel slumped in her chair.

"Fernando—now there's a boy you should be seeing."

"Fernando from the convenience store? His only ambition is to work the day shift. And that's only because he wants to get his GED at night."

"Well, that is ambition," Charlene said. "A GED—that's the same as your diploma, isn't it?"

Isabel shuddered.

"I'm just saying you should talk to him. Get to know him before you run off on a wild chase."

"I'll keep it in mind." Isabel trudged to her room and tossed the registration forms into the trash. What was the point? No money, no school. She didn't need an MBA to see that. She didn't need a college diploma to recognize a dead end.

She curled up in bed and stared at the ceiling. Opportunity seemed to be slipping away, and the chance of a university degree seemed more elusive than ever. She sighed. What good was a new boyfriend if she didn't have the education to keep up?

She turned on her Pioneer turntable but kept the volume low. After listening to both sides of her Carole King album, she still felt worried but less on-edge. Good music always helped to lift her spirits. Then the phone rang, and suddenly, the topic of college and good music seemed a moot point. Helen Phillips was on the line.

"Drake gave me your number," Helen said. "I hope you don't mind that I called."

Isabel frowned. She had a sinking feeling that bad news was coming. She guessed that Drake had taken the easy way out and put an end to an obviously futile romance. If only he had had the guts to end it himself.

"No," she sighed. "I suppose it's all right."

"Isabel, this might sound a little forward, but I asked Drake not to see you today. I thought that you and I could meet for a while."

"Well ... okay." Isabel nearly cried. She shivered at losing college and a boyfriend in the same morning.

"Great," Helen said. "Then how's this for a plan? We could meet up here and have tea at the Saint Francis. And afterward; Eduardo for a treatment. You know, like a manicure and facial."

"I'm listening," Isabel stammered, trying to shift gears to a happy mood.

"Then there's a boutique I found on Maiden Lane. Everything there is cashmere or silk. I'm sure we'll find something you like."

"That could be fun," Isabel said, trying to hold back a squeal. "What time?"

"Drake said to meet him at two. He'll take you here then we're on our own. How's that?"

"I'll be there."

Isabel felt a warm glow and goose bumps. But two o'clock? That gave her less than four hours to eat, dress, and study. So she put together a plan. After breakfast and a quick shower, she slipped into her blue cotton jumpsuit and headed for the local library.

She browsed the aisles and stacks until she stumbled onto the one book that might help in a crisis like this; *The Complete Guide to Manners and Etiquette, Volume 1*. This was serious. Isabel had been invited to have tea at the Saint Francis with one of the richest women in San Francisco. This was not burger and fries at the high school cafeteria. Helen was the mother of the man she loved. There was no margin for error and no room for disappointment.

She scanned the brittle pages of the dusty old book. She hoped that the rules hadn't changed in the past forty years. She memorized the last chapter on thank you note writing, set the book on the shelf then rushed to Drake's house. So many details, so little time.

In Drake's living room, she nervously put on the last touches of makeup.

"Look at me, Drake. What do you think? Too much eyeliner or not enough blush?"

"Everything's perfect." Drake didn't bother to look.

"You're not just saying that, are you?"

"Stop worrying. I've known my mother most of my life, and she has never been one to criticize. Go out and splurge. Make the dear old lady happy."

"Not perfect," Isabel said, staring at the mirror and fixing her mascara, "but the best I can do. Let's do it."

Drake set down his paper and stood behind her. He looked in the mirror. "As I said; totally perfect."

After a quick ride up Highway 101, he dropped her off at the Nob Hill mansion and then headed for Sausalito and drinks at the marina yacht club. Now, Isabel was on her own. She rang the doorbell and gave her name to the butler. Then she waited in the foyer for Helen to appear. A last check a mirror showed that Isabel still looked good. Nervous perhaps—butterflies and apprehension— but the mirror didn't show that.

In the reflection, she saw Helen gliding her way. She was elegant to say the least. With her white pantsuit and navy blazer, Helen looked plenty happy just the way she was.

"Excellent timing." Helen grinned and led Isabel outside to a late model, white Jaguar XL. "You're going to love Eduardo."

"Eduardo?" Isabel asked.

"A specialist in cuticles, French tips, and rejuvenation. It's hard to find a man like that. Your nails look in good shape, Isabel, but he's going to hate to see these." Helen merged her Jaguar into traffic and tapped her fingernails on the steering wheel. "He'll say, 'Helen, didn't I tell you to stay out of the garden?' I'll apologize profusely and promise that it won't happen again. He'll laugh, hold my hand, and we'll do it again next week. We have a routine."

"You know I have to ask," Isabel said, reluctantly. "About Drake's fingernails. Are they—"

"Manicured?" Helen said. "Of course. Every week, like his father's. It's one thing to be born with a pretty face and hands. It's another thing to take care of them. Drake does a good job, I'd say."

"You taught him?"

"There was me, his father, and his nanny."

"Drake had a nanny? That's precious. I'll remember that."

Isabel laughed. She relaxed in her seat, stretched her legs, and set her purse on the floor. Suddenly, the trip to the city had become fun and productive. Every corner brought a new revelation. Not only did Isabel learn more about Drake—his childhood and teen years—she soon discovered the importance of a manicure, pedicure, facial, body wrap, and leg waxing. Eduardo—as Helen had said—had proven to be a true master at his job. It was a pleasure to watch him work.

At the tea room on Powell Street, Isabel finally understood the difference between crumpets and scones. She drank tea from Ceylon and sampled her first cucumber sandwich in an elegant surrounding of crystal chandeliers and gold-leaf sconces.

"I've learned," Helen said, "that you can place anything between two slices of bread, chop off the crust, and call it a tea sandwich. Now this dessert, on the other hand, is a tea room specialty. Here, try some."

"Scrumptious," Isabel said, tasting the impossibly sweet cake. "What is it?"

"Tiramisu is what they call it. I call it heavenly."

Isabel couldn't help but smile. There was such a joy about Helen. She never hid behind the rules of etiquette. No one needed a book to understand her motives. She was simply a best friend to her son's best friend, and Isabel had no problem with that.

Later that afternoon, at Drake's house in Palo Alto, Drake kicked off his shoes while Isabel went on about her date.

"See what your mother got me?" She pulled a pair of tan gloves from a shopping bag.

"Cashmere?"

"I never felt anything so soft," Isabel said.

"What are mothers for?" Drake said.

"Your mother perhaps. *Mine* is a special case."

"How's that?"

Isabel plopped onto the sofa and poured herself a pomegranate iced tea. "Do you have any more sugar?"

Drake passed the bowl of sugar cubes. "Trouble in paradise? Or business as usual?"

"How about a trade; your mother for mine. If you want, I'll throw in the old man and his dirty old truck … and his tennis shoes with the holes in them."

"That's tempting," Drake said.

Isabel pouted. "You know it still ticks me off when I think about it."

"About what?"

"My tuition. I told Mom that I couldn't go to school without it. I told her I have the grades, but I don't have the money. You think she cared? You think she would loan me two cents to get started? Think otherwise. I'm sorry, Drake, this would be a perfect day if I didn't have to think about Mom."

Isabel frowned. The sweet iced tea failed to coax a smile.

"How can I help?" Drake asked, sitting next to her.

"Understanding and patience, because I've decided to go back to school—with or without Mom's wallet."

"Great, tell me how."

Isabel crossed her arms. "I'll get a job, maybe two, during the summer and work nights during the school year. If that's what it takes, then that's what I'll do. It's as simple as that."

Drake leaned back on the sofa. "That's a bit harsh."

"How do you mean?"

"Look, it's not going to do me any good if you're dead tired when you get home or here. The classes are good, but this job thing, I don't know. How about a compromise?"

"My mother does not compromise," Isabel said. "Unless you count the time she said I was dumber than *half* of California."

"I'm thinking about us," Drake said, grinning. "Long term, that is. I'm thinking that I can pay for your tuition year by year if ... if and when you get some free time, you spend it with me. Fair enough?"

"I'm sorry?"

"I'm serious," he said. "I'll put you through school. It's as simple as that."

Isabel sat up straight and listened carefully. "Say that again."

"I can help you with most of your homework, but you're on your own when it comes to math problems. We have a deal?"

Isabel drew in a deep breath. The only image that popped into her mind was of her holding a diploma at a San Jose State graduation. What a sweet image it was. She looked at Drake's eyes. "It's expensive," she said. "Extremely expensive."

"Don't you think that you're worth it?"

"Certainly, I do. But in case you're wondering; sex is not part of the deal."

"Never crossed my mind. But how about a kiss between partners?"

Isabel smiled and found it hard to keep from smiling. She gave Drake a kiss and a bit more. But her deal was firm. After a grateful romp on the living room sofa, she excused herself and hustled home to sign up for classes. It turned out to be a pleasant day. She had made a new friend, secured her tuition, and tossed away those disgusting want ads from the newspaper. What a perfect way to start the summer.

***

And what a summer it was. From that point on, Drake kicked her life into high gear and never stopped to let her breathe. Her romance books sat in the closet and gathered dust. Why bother to read a single paragraph; Isabel Espinosa was living the fantasy.

Twice a week, they flew to Lake Tahoe in Drake's plane to have breakfast and visit with friends. Every Sunday, they circled the San Francisco Bay on Barry's sailboat and headed for the open sea whenever the mood struck. Neiman-Marcus and Nordstrom; Isabel knew every rack by heart. Although she never asked for a single dress, ruby, or dollar bill, she was never surprised if suddenly they appeared. A token here, a favor there; soon it became too much to hide in her drawers at home.

"No problem," Drake said, offering her a spare closet in the guest room of his Palo Alto house.

Plenty of stylish clothes, but Drake made sure that they never hung in one spot for long. Every other night became a four-star event; the Mark Hopkins, the Carnelian Room, the Fairmont. Certainly, those were among the best San Francisco restaurants, but how could Isabel ever forget that one August night and the lobster and artichoke dinner at the Rainbow Room, courtesy of the father's jet and a New York City limousine.

Then there was Helen and her box seats at the Opera House; Swan Lake, Otello, Il Trovatore, Madame Butterfly. Isabel gushed nonstop with her appreciation and couldn't hold back her admiration. A Saturday night ballet or opera in San Francisco seemed much more satisfying than sitting at home and fighting over the TV remote.

Isabel had no complaints. She experienced luxury at its best. Throughout the summer, she applied the same rules to Drake; go anywhere, do anything, see anyone—as long as she got home by midnight on a weekday. Why risk another round of embarrassing questions from Charlene? Why give up the few privileges she had? As far as Charlene knew, her daughter was simply cross-town, visiting cousin Cathie or shopping at the mall. The summer was way too short.

Chapter 8

"THERE ARE TWO things you protect," Helen said. "Your money and your image. Today, we work on your image. Now think about entering a room filled with strangers. Think about that one second you have to make a first impression. Whatever you do, whatever you say, do not squander that second."

Helen drilled her ingénue with a vocabulary of Mikimoto, Cartier, Gucci, and Luis Vuitton. Helen nurtured her. Drake did the shopping. Before long, Isabel had the look, walk, and feel of old money on her back. It was such a delicious, satisfying feeling. The only distasteful part came at Drake's house when she had to change back to her tattered jeans and climb into the old Chevy for the trip home. Someday, when she was married to Drake and living at his house, she wouldn't have to make the midnight run, but today, it was simply a matter of adjusting to the circumstances.

It began as a typical Friday evening; theater in the city, followed by a four-course Moroccan banquet, followed by indigestion and insomnia for the rest of the night. As the Saturday morning sun rose over San Jose, Isabel's head remained firmly planted in her pillow. She felt totally exhausted. But Drake Phillips—consummate planner and schedule maker—was already worried about slipping his weekend plan.

"Hey, I got tickets to the Giants' game. First pitch, two o'clock."

"Drake, darling, I just woke up. Give me a chance to think straight." The fog in her head took forever to clear, and when it did, she pictured herself spending another cold, windy afternoon in Candlestick Park. How could she ever sit still on some rock-hard excuse for a cushion and watch a bunch of overpaid juveniles spit tobacco and grab their crotches? And don't talk about extra innings. A pain in the neck. A pain in the butt.

"Didn't we see them last week?" she asked. "How about I skip the game and meet you for dinner?"

"Tell you what; you come with us, and afterward, I'll make you duck à l'orange. I'll make it the way you like it. You know you could never resist."

"I'll think about it," Isabel said.

"Try to be here before one."

Drake hung up, and less than a minute later, the phone rang again.

"Yes, Drake, what is it?"

"Isabel? It's me—Colette."

"Sorry, Colette. I thought you were someone else."

"Drake, huh. Is he the one?"

"Yeah, and only."

"You don't sound too thrilled about that."

"Not at this hour," Isabel said.

"So where have you been? Off on a different planet?" Colette didn't realize how close to the truth she was.

"I've been busy."

"Sounds like it. I mean, you get a couple dates with some guy in a hot Camaro, and we never see you again. Don't you know; you can't get rid of me that easy. Us alumni have got to stick together, thick and thin. Don't you agree?"

"Sure, why not," Isabel said.

"How about a little fun for a change?"

"I'm listening."

"Come to the mall and I'll tell you." Colette seemed purposely vague. Apparently, she was up to her old mischief.

"This better be good," Isabel said, suspiciously.

"He is. Trust me."

Isabel wasn't sure if the 'he' was for herself or Colette. Either way, she had found a good excuse to avoid that god-awful Candlestick Park. She agreed to Colette's offer and told her goodbye. She tossed back the covers of her bed and swung her feet to the floor. She gave a good yawn, a relaxing stretch, and a peek through the window outside.

Nice day, Isabel guessed, unaware that her day was about to change for the worse. She stood and found her slippers. Once again, the phone rang. Once again, it was Drake.

"What's going on," Drake said. "Did you leave the phone off the hook?"

"I was talking to Colette."

"What did she have to say?"

"Oh, not much. You know; girl talk. You wouldn't be interested."

"On the contrary," Drake said. "I certainly would like to catch up. You can fill me in when you get here."

"If I remember," Isabel said, curtly.

"Fine. I'll be waiting."

Drake didn't have to wait long for another excuse and one more disappointment. Isabel drove up Highway 101 to his house in Palo Alto, parked in the driveway, and stepped out. As Drake washed off the back of his van, she offered a half-hearted apology and her own agenda.

"I wanted to tell you on the phone," she said, "but you didn't give me a chance. Colette wants to go shopping, so I'm going to meet her at the mall. We'll catch up on old times—like you said. That means you and Barry have the afternoon to yourselves. I'll see you both later."

"What?" Drake's hose dribbled to a halt.

"You get nine innings of belching and swearing. That's gotta be your dream."

"What are you getting at? You haven't seen her in months. You said she moved out of town."

"I said she was *thinking* about it."

"You know, I thought we had a date," Drake said. "That's why I made the plans."

"One day without me; you'll get over it."

"I can't force you to go." Drake took off his sunglasses and looked at her with fatherly eyes. "But you can write off duck à l'orange tonight."

Sent to bed without dinner. Isabel sneered. Last time that had happened, she was ten years old, and she had spilled hot cocoa on the sofa. "Fine, I'll have a hot dog with Colette. Oh, and by the way, I have to change here. Be out shortly."

She rushed to the guest room and slipped into her shopping clothes; white cotton slacks, burgundy blouse, diamond earrings, and a gold bracelet. Drake loved that outfit, but on this occasion, when Isabel passed by, he gave her an icy glare. No kiss today, Cheri.

Colette, on the other hand, became a welcome sight as she stood in the parking lot of Macy's. Finally; someone with a smiling face and friendly hug. But that man by her side; if that was her boyfriend, then Colette had certainly upped her game. The man stood much taller than Colette and appeared a bit older. His thick, wavy black hair must have been robbed from a poor, innocent, young boy.

"Julian's on summer break from City College," Colette said. "He's going to have lunch with us, okay?"

"Sure." Isabel smiled and Julian blushed.

"Technically, he's a sophomore," Colette said.

"That's true," Julian said. "I've got one more year at City then it's down to San Luis Obispo."

Isabel gave him a three-second assessment. Thick glasses and pensive eyes. A wisp of a mustache, close to the skin beard. She picked up the hint of old books; either from his mannerisms or the scent on his sweater.

"Majoring in philosophy," she guessed.

"Poly Sci," Julian said. "I'm more of a doer than a thinker."

"Great," Isabel said. "Let's do something about lunch. I'm starved."

Despite her skepticism about Colette's plans at the mall, lunch was fun. Julian loved to talk, and strangely, he talked mostly to Isabel. Monterey jazz festival, politics in South Africa, women in the workplace, and dogs; Julian had opinions and spoke his mind. *Nice guy*, she surmised. He would certainly make Colette a fine boyfriend—or husband—as the opportunity presented.

Isabel set aside the last of her relish dog and glanced at a dessert menu. "Let's see what else looks good."

"Good idea," Colette said, facing Julian. "Okay, girl time now. Julian; go look at the bell bottoms, huh? Isabel and me; we got some catching up to do." She dismissed him with a wag of her hand.

"What do you think?" Colette asked when her friend was out of sight.

"About what?"

"Julian. Do you like him?"

"Sure," Isabel said. "What's not to like? He's cute, smart, and polite. You two are going to hit it off fine."

"No, no, no," Colette said. "I asked if *you* like him. Would *you* go out with him on a date?"

"What are you getting at?"

Colette nervously laughed. "Here's the situation. I like Julian, but he's a little too cerebral for my tastes, if you know what I mean. So, he's a libertarian. Big deal. Like I'm supposed to be impressed. Like I'm supposed to know what it means."

"Will you get to the point?"

Colette squirmed. "Bottom line, Isabel; I want to go out with Julian's brother—his younger brother. He's a roadie for Pink Floyd. And I would simply die to see Roger Waters backstage."

Isabel sipped her iced tea. "Great. You have my blessing; if that counts for anything."

"Then you wouldn't mind a double-date with Julian?"

"Pardon?"

"That's the one condition for a hookup. I fix Julian up with somebody suitable. Like you, Isabel. Then I get a backstage pass. Long term; it could work out for the both of us. We have nothing to lose and only our future to gain."

Isabel raised an eyebrow. Julian was cute, granted. But his shirt was a polyester blend from Taiwan, his shoes were scuffed at the heels, and he drove a Japanese truck. Worst of all, his fingernails cried out for a long-overdue manicure.

"Sorry, Colette, you know that I'm seeing someone."

"Come one. I don't see no ring on your finger. You can cut loose for one night. I know you two would hit it off."

"You're serious. Aren't you?"

"Listen," Colette said, "I know Julian. I know what he likes. You've got the long dark hair, the pretty face, the big, uh, smile. Yeah, that's it; you've got the big, happy smile."

"He likes Mexican women with big boobs. Is that it?"

"I didn't say that."

"Incredible," Isabel said. "Tell Julian; if he wants Mexican, he can sample Juanita. She's got Cinco de Mayo on the brain."

"It's a concert, Isabel. And jazz at that. I thought of good music, fun, Julian, and you. Pink Floyd and Roger Waters—that was more or less an afterthought."

"Two things. First off, like I said; I'm seeing someone. That's important. Second; I'm trying to get out of San Jose—for good. And these guys you meet, well, how can I put it? They're just spinning a hamster wheel and getting nowhere fast. Ten years from now, they'll be in the same house with the same job. That's not what I want."

"That's what you think of Julian, huh? He's some kind of rodent?"

"I didn't say that."

Colette scowled. "And you probably think *I'm* getting nowhere fast."

"You know that's not true."

"You've changed, Isabel. That's for sure. Now, you've got your Gucci purse and those diamonds. And you think you need a Mercedes to show them off. I don't know what's gotten into you. You used to save your pennies. You used to pray for any kind of sale at Macy's. *That's* the Isabel I used to know."

"I'm the same person, Colette, except I have new clothes and a few expectations. There's nothing wrong with that. I've grown up a little."

"Where's Julian," Colette grumbled. "I can still find someone who appreciates an honest man."

She stormed off, leaving Isabel with an order of apple pie and the bitter taste of a friendship gone bad. Four years of close ties, good talks, and good parties—gone for the sake of someone's taste in clothes. Isabel felt a wave of sadness.

She stepped into the dressing room of Macy's and slipped into her standby sweatshirt and pants. No doubt, the frumpy clothes would've pleased Colette. Diamonds, it seemed, made her mad. It was a rare day that Isabel looked forward to going home, but she grew tired of fighting with everyone who purported to be on her side. Why did so many people remain so stubborn?

She drove home, eager to find a friendly face or someone without ulterior motives. But as she pulled into the driveway, she was once again disappointed. Charlene scowled as she clutched her handbag and paced the front porch.

"You didn't tell me you were taking the car," Charlene snarled as Isabel dangled the Chevy keys.

"You said you were doing the wash all morning."

"Not without Tide. I got you running around with your boyfriend, and I'm sitting here while the laundry piles up."

"That's not true."

"Like yesterday," Charlene said. "You come traipsing in at twelve-thirty. What's the matter? Couldn't say 'no' again?"

"Mom," she whined.

"Whatever the excuse; it's not going to work no more. From now on, if you want to go somewhere, you take the bus. This car is off-limits."

"Why? Because I came home late? That's not a crime."

"It was a mistake from the start," Charlene said. "You get freedom with no responsibility. I knew this would happen."

"There was an accident on the road last night. I was lucky to get home when I did."

"Now you don't have to worry about traffic. You'll be riding the bus or sitting at home." Charlene snatched the keys, hopped into her car, and rumbled down the road.

Isabel argued in vain with the blue smoke of the Chevy exhaust. "Why won't you listen to me? We had an agreement, and it was working; if you didn't need the car, I could have it. Truth be told, Mom; you hardly go anywhere. This has nothing to do with Tide, or laundry, or leaving you stranded. If you want control, you certainly have it now."

She sat on the front step and wondered how everything went wrong. In one day, she had had a fight with Drake, lost her best friend, and lost the car. She had plenty to complain about, but there was not a soul around who would listen. Instead, she grabbed a fistful of brownies and retreated to her room.

Isabel plopped onto her bed and cranked up the volume to the Chicago VI album. She was home alone, and no one cared about how loud the music was. No one cared if she was a victim of circumstance or merely a woman with a mind of her own. After playing *Feelin' Stronger Every Day*, she came to the only conclusion that made sense; she did nothing wrong and the brownies were fantastic.

Later on, Charlene returned, but it didn't matter. Isabel remained holed up in her room, content to hide away from everyone gone mad. She pulled out her Seels and Crofts album and doubted that she would ever be a *Diamond Girl*. Regardless, she played the song until she wore out the track. As she stuffed the album into its cover, the doorbell rang. *Now what?* she asked herself. *Bad news or really bad news?*

She dragged her feet through the hallway and scooted by Charlene without saying a word. But she finally saw a smiling face.

"Special delivery," the man at the door said. "Sign for the box and have a nice day."

Isabel did and then hurried back to her room. She opened the box to find a dozen red roses and an apology which read; *Regrets are cheap, and I have a million. Won't you please help me to work them out? Meet me at the park a half-hour from now.*

That was easy for Drake to say. *He* still had a car. He didn't have a mother who was arbitrary and cheap. Even so, Isabel perked up with a plan. She felt determined to avoid her mother at any cost and eager to make up with Drake at any cost.

She slipped into her denim jeans and floral blouse and dashed out the front door. Thankfully, she didn't need a car or permission to go to the park, which was a half-hour away by the safe route or twenty minutes via the shortcut. The direct route seemed better, until it became the longest twenty minutes of her life.

She walked the neighborhood streets, fixed in her own world, content to keep to herself. But halfway to the park, the distractions became too much to ignore. Rock music blared from one house. Eyes peeked out from another. Old trucks rolled down the road. Old cars blocked the sidewalks.

Suddenly, Isabel became aware, and the crime stats began to make sense. Slowly, she picked up her pace. Quietly, she cursed; why did she wear those shoes with the one-inch heels? Why did she slip on her favorite gold bangle? Then again, this was *her* neighborhood. There was no reason to feel scared.

Off to the left, a man walked out of a stucco house and slammed the screen door closed. Isabel took one glance and kept moving. The image stayed with her; Hispanic with a goatee and ponytail, tattoos, plenty of fat. Plenty of sweat, no doubt. He walked to his truck, pitched a beer can to the back, and drove down the road. Isabel breathed in a sigh. *Never walk this way again*, she promised herself.

She crossed another block and felt a shiver run up her spine. The same truck slowly rolled up from behind. It passed by Isabel and stopped ahead in a driveway, in the middle of the sidewalk. Trouble had to follow. She saw two men inside; the same fat guy, now with a skinny white passenger. She gave it no more than a glimpse. If she had stared, they might get the wrong idea. More likely, they came with the wrong idea.

She crossed the street and kept a steady pace. Her heart pounded. From the heavy footsteps behind, she knew that the fat man followed.

"What's the rush, *chica?*" he slurred. "Too nice to walk alone."

Isabel ignored him and kept her eyes forward.

"Come on, talk to me," the man said. "I'm trying to be nice."

"I'm already late," she snapped.

"I got a ride. I'll take you anywhere. Where you headed?"

Isabel could almost feel his hot breath on her neck. She whiffed the pungent odor of cerveza and tried not to be sick. She aimed for the middle of the street and glanced behind. The guy's friend cruised by in the old truck. As he passed her, he rolled down the window and smirked. Then he tapped the brakes and blocked the easy path ahead.

Isabel raised her voice. "I told you to leave me alone!"

The fat man laughed. "Come on, I just want to be friends. No harm, huh?"

Isabel thought about her open-toe shoes. She thought she could outrun the big man, but the truck itself—or the man inside—definitely not. She flashed on her mother's car. Why had Charlene been so cruel to hoard it? And Drake's car; why had he parked so far away?

"Come on, *chula,*" the big guy slurred, "talk to me. Be nice. *Simpática,* huh?"

Isabel felt a tug on her elbow. Instinctively, she turned and slapped the man's face. Hard. The man scowled but hung on tight. Isabel felt stuck in place. She couldn't run and couldn't fight. She could probably scream. She took in a deep breath, ready to yell at the man or anyone near. Then she heard a familiar sound from behind. She held her breath, not sure if it was real or wishful thinking.

She let out a breath as fear flipped to relief. A black Camaro rolled closer. White stripe, dual exhaust—without a doubt that had to be Drake. But Lord, he drove slowly. No squealing tires, no gunning of the engine, no rush to save the woman he loved. Isabel jerked her elbow free as Drake came to a stop in front of the truck. He casually stepped out of the Camaro and looked at the fat man.

"Having a little trouble, are we?" Drake's voice held steady as if he was gazing at a flat tire or a stalled truck.

"No trouble here," the fat man snarled.

"I was talking to the lady," Drake said.

The man latched onto Isabel's sleeve and sneered. "This is *my* lady. And like I said, we got no trouble."

Drake shook his head then tugged at the same sleeve. Suddenly, the bad situation turned frantic. The slow-motion drama switched to a blur of bone-jarring moves. Isabel cringed as the fat guy wound up and swung at Drake's head. Luckily, the sucker punch never got close. Drake easily blocked it and countered with a jab to the gut. The man doubled over and groaned, spewing beer to the pavement.

Before Isabel could say a word, she felt a solid push on her hips as Drake coaxed her into the Camaro. He closed the door behind.

"Sit tight," he told her.

From where Isabel sat now, she couldn't see much. But she did glimpse a blur as the skinny guy burst out of the truck. She saw a baseball bat swing at Drake's head, and she saw a miss. A moment later, she saw two men laid out on the ground. Drake, thankfully, remained standing.

Isabel blinked, and the scuffle ended that fast; but not before Drake got in the final touch. He grabbed the baseball bat and pitched it onto a neighbor's lawn.

"This belongs at the ball park," he said to the downed man, "not on the streets!"

With her pulse racing to the verge of a bursting heart, Isabel couldn't stop shaking. She closed her eyes as Drake drove off. She kept them closed until they arrived at the lake. Some visions were best wiped from her mind, she figured. Some memories never belonged.

Finally, when they parked by the beachside, Isabel regained a hint of composure. Cautiously, she opened her eyes. She knew what she had to do next. She hopped from the car and raced to the driver's side. There was only one vision she wanted to hold forever. There was only one memory worth keeping.

She watched Drake as he stepped out. He was confident, calm, and self-assured. Not one hair was out of place. Despite the horrendous encounter, Drake kept his poise, kept his style, and kept his priorities clear.

"We're a bit late for our walk," he said. "But I brought a bottle of iced tea. I thought you might like it."

Isabel ignored his offer and instead gazed into his steel-blue eyes. Then she moved in and hugged him as tightly as she could. She breathed in his mysterious cologne as she felt her heart rate drop from frantic to walk in the park peaceful. A feeling she never wanted to lose.

"Thank you," she whispered.

Drake led her by the hand to their favorite bench. They sat and took in the shade of a cottonwood tree. Isabel ignored the family picnics and the kids. She ignored the dogs and the barbecues. Instead, she kept her eyes and her attention on Drake.

"Before we start our walk," Drake said, caressing her cheek, "I have a couple questions if you're up to it."

"I'll try," she said.

"First, do you still love me?"

"Now that's an easy question," Isabel said. "Of course, I do."

"Then I apologize for this morning—for making assumptions about us that were totally out of line." He brushed back a strand of Isabel's hair that had fallen across her eyes. He went on, "I assumed that just because I wanted to go somewhere, you would come along. Obviously, that's not always the case. I can see why you felt pressure, and I can see why you backed away. That's only natural. But what I'm trying to say is; if you need your own space, let me know. No more pressure, no more assumptions—from me or anyone else. I assure you, Isabel; my one goal in life is to make you happy and safe. You have to believe me."

Isabel felt a warm glow as if a light bulb in Drake's head had suddenly switched on. After all this time, Drake finally realized that she was not simply his better half or his personal shadow. Isabel was an independent woman with her own family, her own friends, and her own desire for privacy.

"I appreciate that, Drake. I know that we both can be strong-willed ... occasionally. If we have to make a few minor adjustments here and there; well, that's only natural."

"I was hoping that you would say that."

"And your other question?" she asked, growing a grin.

"Other question?"

"You said you had a couple."

"Oh, yeah," Drake said. "And how can I phrase it; why on earth were you walking down that block? I know guys like that, and they prey on women like you. Lord, what were you thinking? What were you doing?"

Heavy sigh. "Okay, I don't know what 'women like me' is supposed to mean, but the truth is, it comes down to this; I don't have a car anymore."

"No car?" he said.

"Yep, and that means I'll be walking down a lot of blocks, except a few by my house. My mom pulled my license, so to speak; at least temporarily."

Drake shrugged. "Honestly, no car is no problem. I'll swing by your house and pick you up. I'll be a chauffeur, so to speak."

"Come on, Drake, I told you about that. If my mother got one look at you, she'd blow up like the Hindenburg."

"There is one other option," he said.

"That would be what?"

"Your own car. That's the safest and the *only* way to go."

"I thought about it," she said. "However, with seventeen dollars in my bank account, that'll buy me cab fare to the Ford dealer. Question is; how would I get home?"

"That's where we can deal."

"Deal?" Isabel asked. "Like you and me. Or me and Ford?"

"I'll tell you what we can do." Drake paused as though shifting through a dozen gears. "How's this; I'll make the payments on, let's say, a reasonable car. And you, in exchange, you'll stop by and visit whenever you can."

"Are you serious?"

"Try me," he said without blinking.

Isabel leaned back on the bench and considered Drake's deal. She recalled the argument with her mother, and she relived the nasty stroll through the neighborhood. She considered her limited choices and asked Drake the most important question, "Can you make it blue?"

"I can make it any color you want."

Isabel squealed like a little girl with a new Barbie … or a new car. Too excited to walk around the lake, she hustled Drake to his feet and led him down the path to the Camaro. She couldn't wait to get to the dealer. She almost got too excited to ask him another question that had crossed her mind. She gently poked his elbow.

"Tell me this." She looked to his eyes. "How did you ever wind up on that block? I know you weren't driving to the house."

"That's true," he said, keeping his gaze forward. "You didn't show up at the park, so I gave up waiting and took the long way home. Turned out to be a good idea, you think?"

"I suppose," Isabel said, trying to understand his logic but failing to do so. Of course, it didn't matter at this point, because she desperately wanted to put the drama of the afternoon behind her. "I suppose we can move on like it never happened."

"I agree," Drake said. "So what do you say; find us the shortest route to Ford."

"Trust me; I know exactly how to get there."

By the end of the following week, Isabel got her wish. She drove home with a sparkling new 1973 Mercury Capri, complete with stick shift, AM-FM radio, eight-track player, and a beautiful blue metallic finish. It was impressive, practical, and so much classier than walking the streets or sliding into a big green Impala.

As Isabel explained to Charlene, "I got a job in Silicon Valley, and I'm paying for the car on credit."

"Smart move," Charlene said. "Now take care of the car."

Charlene smiled. Getting a job; that was her idea from the start. It had taken a while, but her daughter had finally made the connection; real life, real job, steady income. It was a lesson learned the hard way.

Isabel beamed. She now had the freedom to go anywhere she pleased, anytime she pleased. She floated on a cloud and felt like a million dollars. It was an incredible feeling, and she owed it all to the man she loved.

Chapter *9*

"YOU BLEW OUT the engine to the 'Vette?" Isabel lifted her palms. "What does that mean? I don't understand. How do you blow out the engine? Dynamite? Come on, Barry, talk to me."

She pleaded in vain as Barry stormed his way through the Palo Alto house. He griped about the Mustang loaner car in the driveway. He cursed about waiting two weeks for a new engine. He walked out and slammed the door behind.

"Leave the poor guy alone," Drake said, feigning symphony. "It'll take him a while to live this one down."

"Live what down?" she asked.

"Crossing the red line when he shouldn't have."

Isabel narrowed her eyes and glared at Drake. "Is that so? And where were you when that happened?"

"Not behind him," he said. "Not even close."

"One of these days that boy is going to kill himself."

"I wouldn't be surprised, but hopefully it's not today."

"Why?" Isabel asked. "What's happening today?"

"Don't you remember? Ten thousand feet. Star formation. Relative work."

"Skydiving again." Isabel groaned.

Of course, she forgot. How could she possibly remember every detail of their jam-packed schedules? Every day, since the start of July, Drake had dragged her to yet another of his parties, or friends, or sport of the week. Whether it was scuba diving off Costa Rica, karate matches, or rafting down the American River in Colorado, Isabel had tagged along, content to sit by and watch as Drake and the others kept themselves amused. But today, she had a feeling; her patience and tolerance had reached a new limit.

It began as a typical afternoon in Yolo County. Isabel gulped her strawberry lemonade at a picnic table that had not seen rain for an entire season. It was hot, dry, boring, and exactly the same as the last trip to the airport. She stared through the shimmering heat to a distant almond orchard. She pitied the migrant workers. But at least *they* had someone to talk to, someone to help share the tedium. Isabel's only company became a bag of chips and a hungry squirrel. And the squirrel didn't care to listen.

Overhead, a DC-3 droned. When it was barely a dot in the sky, the engine slowed, and ten more dots emerged from its side. Drake and Barry were jumping again; circle formation, ten jumpers linking arms for eight thousand feet. Isabel had seen it plenty of times, and the novelty had long expired.

"Last jump of the season," an old man said. "Twenty-man star then it's back to the dorms for the youngsters."

"You'll be one of the twenty?" Isabel glanced at the man's harness and chute.

"And my granddaughter," he said. "She'll be thirteen come October."

"Granddaughter?"

"Yep. Gave up her dolls for a beautiful Para-Commander."

"Wow!" Isabel said. "I'll bet that she's never bored."

"And you can bet I'm proud," the old man said, grinning. He said, "Take care and enjoy," and walked off to a waiting plane.

Isabel returned to watching the persimmon trees dehydrate in the sun. Her boredom lasted until she got to the bottom of her lemonade and until Drake got his feet on the ground. He abruptly threw down his harness and helmet and marched to Isabel's table. From that look in his eyes, he wasn't coming to review the crosswinds.

"Who was that guy you were with?" Drake got to his point.

"Who?" Isabel asked.

"That guy—the one with the white hair. What did he want?"

"Him? We were talking about next week. You know, his last and final jump of the summer."

"Ten minutes for that?" Drake said.

"How do you know how long it took? You were a thousand feet in the air. You couldn't have seen a truck from where you drifted."

"Seriously, what were you doing? Getting phone numbers or giving them?"

"Seriously, what's the matter with you, Drake? This hot air going to your head? Or did you go up to fifteen thousand again?"

"Jesus, don't start with that."

"What do you expect?" she said. "Every place we go, you go off and dump me like a dog on a leash. Don't you get it? I'm bored. I'm tired of sitting here. I'm tired of talking to myself and the same old squirrels."

Drake let his shoulders slump. He sat across from Isabel and calmed his tone. "Why didn't you tell me in the first place? You want someone to talk to; that's not a problem. How about Ginger? She's done her last jump, and she may be sidelined for a while. Bad ankle, I think."

"You don't need to hire a babysitter." Isabel folded her arms.

"No, I mean it. You probably have a lot in common."

"Like what? Skydiving?"

"Well, maybe not that," Drake said. "But you'll find plenty else, I'm sure."

Isabel flashed on a dozen conversation topics from dogs to recipes to scuba diving and jealous boyfriends. Then she flashed on the most obvious topic. "Why not skydiving? If Ginger can do it, then why can't I?"

For a moment, Isabel couldn't believe that she had said it. Then Drake's eyes opened wide, and his jaw dropped. His scowl grew to a grin. Isabel knew that she had struck a chord.

"Are you sure?" Drake asked.

"Totally," she said, gulping. Suddenly, she felt torn between the fear of leaping from a plane and the fear of summer-long boredom. Her silence, by default, confirmed her decision to start a new adventure.

"Then I will make it happen." Drake nodded. He patted Isabel's hand then hurried to make a plan. He disappeared but quickly found the best woman instructor on staff. He immediately arranged and paid for a short private session. When he returned, he seemed more excited than a young girl with a Para-Commander.

"Anything more than the basics," he said, handing Isabel a release form, "and you might change your mind."

"Anything *less* than the basics," Isabel said, "I might wind up dead."

"Not a chance," Drake said. "Let's do it."

Isabel signed her name then signed up for the thrill of her life. She borrowed Ginger's bright yellow jumpsuit then rented boots and goggles. She met the instructor for one hour of training. During the session, she learned the elements of skydiving; leap from the plane, arch your back, count to three-Mississippi, pull the cord, and look for the nearest cow pasture. Easy enough for a young girl or an ambitious woman.

On the way to the pickup point, Drake threw in his own tips. "Forget about 'streamers' or a 'Maye West.' Personally, I've never seen one. But just in case, this is your emergency pack."

"I know," Isabel said. "And if anything *does* happen, you'll be right above me."

"Think of me as a guardian angel."

"Last chance," Barry said as the DC-3 landed for a pickup.

Isabel shook her head. "Next stop, two thousand feet." She stuffed her hair into the helmet. She adjusted the straps on the goggles. Her heart was racing, but she smiled the best she could.

As the DC-3 climbed, she took her place beside Drake, Barry, the instructor, and a dozen others—mostly beginners like herself. There were no smiles except on those two guys sitting next to her. Sure, Drake and Barry could laugh on the way up; they weren't sitting next to the open door with nothing but rocks and pavement below.

"If I die," Isabel said to Barry, "you tell my mother I was hit by a bus."

"Whatever you say." Barry gave her a wink and a nasty laugh.

Minutes later, the pilot slowed the engine.

"What's happening?" Isabel asked.

"He wants us to leave." Drake tapped her hand. "Don't worry. Whatever happens, I'll be behind you every step of the way. Relax and enjoy the scenery."

What step was Drake talking about? Isabel stood with her face in the door. She tightly held the metal frame. The next step was a half-mile below. The butterflies in her stomach were enough to make her float.

"See you at the target!" Drake yelled.

"What?"

"Jump!" Drake screamed, and Isabel let loose. The instructor and Drake followed.

For a heartbeat, everything seemed still. The roar of the plane, the stinging wind—gone with the adrenaline rush. Only one thought remained in her throbbing head; *Pull the cord and open your eyes.*

She did, and a breath later, the soft tug of a canopy cradled her with a gentle rocking. She looked to her feet. The farms below spread out in a patchwork of green and brown. Beautiful. Absolutely beautiful. Total, undeniable freedom.

So this is how a bird feels. Isabel floated with the wind and left her troubles behind. She felt a thousand miles from San Jose and a thousand miles from any hint of a problem. For a short while on a hot Saturday afternoon, she felt a power inside of her that let her fly anywhere and do anything. This was a joy worth living for.

When Isabel hit the dirt a hundred yards from the target, she had one thought on her mind; fly up and jump again. She stood, yanked off her helmet, and let her black hair tumble to her waist. A glance to the sky and she saw Drake and Barry floating down to greet her.

"My God, Drake, why didn't you tell me it was like that?"

"I thought I had."

Isabel squealed and moved closer to Drake. She grabbed him and kissed him hard until a gust of wind ballooned the canopy and knocked them both to the ground. Barry stomped on the fabric. With a sly grin, he shook his head until they came up to breathe.

"Falling out of a plane," she said, "now that's an aphrodisiac."

Isabel went home and wrote in her journal. She wrote about her excitement today and her plans for tomorrow. She wrote about her dreams, her goals, and how no one could stop her now. Like an opening door, she saw a new world; beckoning her and tempting her with new possibilities and promises.

Her next step to following those dreams came on a Tuesday morning flight to Lake Tahoe, California.

"Teach me to fly this thing," she casually said to Drake and Barry as they passed over Pine Grove.

"No joking?" Drake gave her a skeptical look from the pilot's seat.

"Of course not. I'm tired of sitting in the back. I want to work the steering wheel myself."

"It's called the yoke."

"Whatever. I want to learn to fly this machine. Takeoffs, landings, radio; how hard can it be? I mean, it's a safety thing too. What if both you guys got food poisoning or heart attacks? Then what? For sure, we crash into the mountain."

Barry laughed. "She's got a point. Dual heart attacks are way up this year. It's not safe to keep her in the back, untrained."

"Well then, Captain Espinosa," Drake said, flashing a mock salute, "welcome aboard."

The contortions came next as Barry climbed to the left rear seat and Drake slid to the right front. Isabel took control in the pilot's position. Suddenly, the plane didn't feel like an egg crate anymore. She peered over the cowling and felt like an old lady driving a monstrous Cadillac. Countless instruments and dials. Knobs and levers in the oddest places. And where was the speedometer? Her mouth went dry as she gingerly gripped the yoke.

"Now what?" She faked a smile. She had no intention of backing out.

"We start easy," Drake said, glancing between her and the sky. "Left. Right. Up. Down. Using only the yoke. Gradual turns, no hurry."

"Like this?" Isabel twisted the yoke, and the Cessna banked like an obedient falcon.

"Keep the nose on the horizon and don't let the airspeed drop below seventy."

"Why?" she asked.

"Remember that crashing into the mountain thing—that's why."

Isabel eagerly followed each of Drake's commands as they circled above the San Joaquin Valley and cruised along the Sierra foothills. Up a thousand feet and down five hundred.

"Turn left," Drake said. "Shallow bank to a heading of three-two-zero."

Isabel watched the horizon; she watched the gauges; and she felt her heart pound.

"She's a natural." Barry laughed.

Drake yelled over his shoulder, "You know if this works out, we'll get Isabel in front and a poker game in back."

"Why wait?" Barry reached into his pack for a deck of cards. "I can deal you in now."

Isabel had her own plans. The flying seemed fun and challenging, but the freedom it represented felt immense. If she had her pilot's license, she could take off whenever she wanted and go wherever she pleased. She could spend the day in Sonoma, or Big Sur, or the Hearst Castle in San Simeon. Even better, she wouldn't have to beg the guys to take her there. She wouldn't need to drag them from their precious football games.

"When we get back to San Jose, Drake, you'll sign me up for lessons. Won't you, please?"

"I've never seen you like this. It's very becoming; I'll tell you that." He grinned at his new co-pilot.

Isabel nodded, and she remained adamant. When they returned to the Bay Area, she talked nonstop about runways and airports and what to wear to Santa Catalina. Drake shook his head but faithfully kept his word. He signed her up with one of the best woman flight instructors he knew.

Isabel felt on the cusp of an unstoppable roll. She had her own skydiving instructor, her own flight instructor, her own style instructor—Helen—and now that the fall semester had started, she had university instructors to keep her schedule booked solid from now until graduation.

Home, lately, had become simply a place where her pillow sat. According to Isabel, the less she spent there, the better. Why bother with people who believed that putting a woman through college was like sending a dog to Yale; just didn't make sense.

"Education begins at home," Charlene insisted. "Forget about school. Go back to your job. Save money. Learn to raise a family."

Isabel dismissed much of her mother's advice but had to agree on the first point. Education, at least for Drake Phillips, truly did begin at home. As Isabel worked her way through Accounting 101, Drake had graduated from Stanford. He became a partner in his father's firm. Quickly, he learned the finer aspects of law; mergers, acquisitions, IPOs, and the fundamental first principle—look prosperous, be prosperous.

With that lesson in mind, William bought Drake a top of the line Mercedes-Benz coupe. It came with a car phone, black leather seats, and a flawless, pearl white finish. It epitomized a beautiful machine— the perfect image for any ambitious man. But this one, according to Drake, lacked the perfect color.

Isabel was stunned when Drake described what he did on that last night in November. "What do you mean, you hit a pole?"

"Don't worry about it," Drake said. "I'll have another one tomorrow."

"That's not what I meant."

"This one's going to be silver," he said, "with a black interior and high-speed radial tires."

Isabel had a sinking feeling; between school, flying, and every-other-day parties, both she and Drake were on the same road to emotional and physical burnout. They both pushed themselves to the limit, running a marathon at a sprinter's pace. Sooner or later, something had to give, something was bound to explode.

"Drake, honey, I'm telling you; you gotta slow down. And I'm not referring to your car. You've got every second of your life planned in that book of yours. You're always doing some job or running somewhere. For once, why don't you sit back, relax, and do nothing?"

"December seventh," Drake said, chuckling like a mischievous child.

"What's that?" she cynically asked.

"That's the one afternoon you have to keep free."

"I'm afraid to ask why," Isabel said.

"Just tell me you'll take the day off."

"Let me think about it, Drake. I've got finals and about a million presents to buy. If the seventh is a Saturday—"

"Now, who's busy?" Drake frowned then checked his schedule book. "Okay, we'll make it the ninth; two weeks before Christmas."

"Fine. I'll pencil you in."

Drake grinned like a Cheshire cat. Unlike his usual mile-a-minute conversations, he seemed unusually tight-lipped about his plans for that particular event. "I promise you a relaxing getaway. One memory to last forever."

Isabel never believed him for a moment. Relaxing to Drake was like the pope and a bottle of Jack Daniels; just never happened. She waited patiently for the afternoon of the ninth, and when it finally arrived, Drake said one word—Tahoe—and Isabel knew exactly what was coming next.

She envisioned their typical Tahoe schedule; fly up to the lake, meet friends, drive to some restaurant, meet more friends at the lodge, celebrate until ten, fly home, and get Isabel home by midnight. What getaway? Drake had put together a recipe for a nervous breakdown.

Nevertheless, she went along and hoped that the high country air would calm Drake and get him to listen to the voice of reason. She hoped to see a hint of sanity. But when they got to the lake, the rush continued. Drake scrambled in the airport parking lot to find a Jeep that his friend had supposedly left.

"I've got the key." Drake showed it to Isabel. "But a car would help."

"We really have to talk," she said. "This is supposed to be a mini vacation. So far, we've been racing from one point to another."

"In due course, I'll be yours. Patience, my love." Drake found the car, helped her in, and kissed her on the cheek. He started the engine, but before it had a chance to warm up; they raced again to the south shore of the lake.

"New French place," he said. "We have to check it out."

Isabel was wrong. The fresh, cold mountain air didn't slow him a bit. When they arrived at the restaurant, he still seemed a raw bundle of nerves.

"Drake, we have to talk about slowing down. I think that when the New Year comes, we'll make a few changes. Resolutions, as it were."

Isabel peeled off her coat and scarf and sat down at the table. In other circumstances, she would have drowned herself in the ambience. In front of her was a panoramic view of Lake Tahoe and the surrounding mountains. To the left, a violinist played. To the right, the warm flames of an open-hearth fireplace crackled.

The soft light cast a ruddy glow to Drake's face. This should've been a perfect night for romance, but for some reason, Drake seemed incredibly tense and distracted. His eyes darted. He squirmed in his seat and toyed with his menu.

"Where is the waiter?" He glanced at his watch.

"Drake, sweetheart, we came up to relax. Please, sit back and take a deep breath."

"Oh, now he comes."

"You're not listening, are you?"

"*Bonsoir, monsieur-madame,*" the waiter said. "Would you like a drink to start off? Or some hors d'oeuvres?"

"*Ah, bonsoir, monsieur,*" Drake said, taking every opportunity to speak French. "*Nous voudrions un soir parfait. C'est facile, n'est pas? Et pour commencer, on va prendre le foie gras frais en gelee, s'il vous plait.*"

"Oh, sorry," the waiter said, faltering, "I don't speak French. Actually, I suppose, none of us do."

Drake grimaced and let the menu drop to his lap. "*Quelle honte.*" He sighed. "Then bring us your house pâté and some iced tea."

The waiter disappeared. For a moment, Drake sat quietly and stared across the table. His look of disappointment slowly dissolved into a quiet smile. Then he sat back and snickered and finally let loose with a tremendous laugh.

"Once again, Isabel, you are spot-on. This is no way to unwind. Do me a favor; ignore the false start. Let's reset and try again."

Isabel smiled, which she did whenever Drake said that she was right.

"Excuse me." Drake slid his chair and stood. "I need to use the phone."

Before she could scold him on table etiquette, Drake disappeared to the phone in the hallway. And before Isabel had scanned to the bottom half of the English-translated menu, Drake returned with a slight change of plans.

"Finish your drink and let's go," he said.

"Where to?" she asked.

"A small step back in time."

Isabel shrugged. "I have no idea what you mean."

Soon enough, she found out. After a short ride to the lakeshore, they swapped their four-wheel drive for something a bit more nostalgic. Isabel couldn't believe her eyes, but there it was; their transportation for the rest of the evening. A one-horse sleigh, complete with sleigh bells, chauffeur, thick woolen blankets, and a thermos of hot chocolate.

"Drake, you are a hopeless romantic." She stood on her toes to kiss him. She wrapped her arms around his waist and pulled him tight. Even with her mittens on, Isabel could feel the muscles in his back begin to relax. The tension drained from his body as any thoughts of deadlines and schedules melted in the arms of a beautiful woman. Nothing else seemed to matter except sharing an undying love and holding hands in the wide-open, star filled skies.

Another kiss then they climbed to the leather seat. They huddled close with the blankets drawn tight. The crisp mountain air tingled Isabel's face and cleared her mind. It felt invigorating. She couldn't have planned a better way to end a nonstop, yearlong race.

The driver snapped the reins, and the horse took off with a shudder. Isabel sighed. She could not recall a more soothing sound than the crunch of snow beneath an open sleigh and the jingling of harness bells on a cold December night. The view of the lake seemed heavenly under a full moon. Forget the rest of the world. Isabel sat by the man she loved, and nothing else mattered.

Drake kissed her when they stopped by a knoll to listen to the night sounds. His warm breath went straight to her heart.

"Don't ever leave me," Isabel sighed and held him close.

Perhaps it was the child in him that she loved; an unspoiled innocence, mischievous but kind, eager to please, and always willing to do the right thing. Here was Drake at his simplest; no fancy car, no plane, no super-rich, super-enmeshed family. There was nothing but the man himself. He looked at her and offered his love and a few generous words.

"Isabel," he softly said, "I know that once in a while, it can seem a little chaotic."

"I have no complaints."

"Tonight, if I look distracted, there's a very good reason."

"Why is that?" she asked.

"Something's been on my mind for a while. Something I've been meaning to tell you. But I've never found the best moment or the best words. Hopefully, when I say it tonight, I won't scare you away."

He shifted in his seat and took a deep breath. "There's this woman, you see. I've known her for quite a while, and well, I have to be honest. She has this power, this energy that, how can I say this? Whenever she's around, I can't help but feel alive. It's no wonder I fell in love with her on that first date. No wonder I love her to this day. She has the face of an angel and the smile of a child. She's the most beautiful woman I know. And ... and *if* my luck holds out, that same woman will take this ring and agree to be my wife."

Drake fumbled through his pocket and came up with a small box, definitely a ring box. Isabel's eyes widened when he flipped open the lid and flashed a huge diamond.

"Marry me, Isabel," he said. "Give this old man a reason to live."

Isabel threw off her mittens, slipped on the ring, and let the tears stream from her eyes. "You don't have to say another word, my love. The answer is 'yes.' "

Chapter *10*

DRAKE OUTLINED a one-year engagement.

"Fine," Isabel said. "I understand that you're busy at work. You've got new clients, and you're trying to open a branch office in the South Bay. A wedding *could* be a major distraction."

"That's not quite the reason," Drake said. "As it turns out, nineteen is about a year too young."

"You're kidding," Isabel said abruptly. "What difference can a year make?"

"Professionally, a huge difference. A year from now, I'll be marrying a woman in the twenty-to-twenty-nine age bracket. I would *not* be marrying a teenager."

"Your *image* is what's driving you?" She widened her eyes.

"No, Isabel. What's driving me is *our* future; not only a year from now but thirty years ahead. In the long run, twelve months will seem like the blink of an eye. When we get married, 'forever more' will mean exactly that."

Isabel took in a deep breath. "When you phrase it that way ..."

"Meanwhile, I promise; between now and next December, if you have one moment of boredom, you let me know, and I will fix it."

Fun and excitement. Once again, Drake knew exactly what to say. He eagerly worked a deal that Isabel could live with. She put away the *Bride* magazine and agreed to ease off the pressure of a wedding date ... for now.

A full year of diversions was what Drake had promised, and that was precisely what he delivered. Once again, Isabel was catapulted into a whirlwind of dinner parties, theater parties, business parties, parties at thirty thousand feet, and parties in international waters beyond the Golden Gate Bridge. She barely had a moment to breathe. The months sped by like blurred signposts on a wide-open freeway.

She woke up one morning and flipped the calendar to September. She glanced at the calendar pages and wondered where the summer had gone. The months had passed so quickly, something had to be wrong. How could she have possibly run through a season like that without writing a single word in her journal? Despite the nonstop activities, Isabel had a feeling that something fundamental was horribly missing.

"Missing?" Drake asked as he stretched his feet on his living room sofa.

"I mean, from my life," Isabel said. "I don't feel, oh, what's the word? Fulfilled. Yeah, that could be it. I am not fulfilled."

He scowled. "You want to explain that?"

Isabel squirmed. "How can I describe it? I know I've done a lot of stuff, but sometimes it feels more style than substance. Whatever that means."

Luckily, Drake had a perfect memory, and he gladly helped her to recall their recent highlights. "How about Vancouver last week? What would you call that?"

"Yeah," she said, "that was a nice trip."

"And your flying lessons. You wouldn't call that nothing, would you?"

"But I've never gone anywhere by myself. More often than not, I sit in the back seat. You and Barry sit in front; in control."

"Then go someplace."

"Good point," she said. "I think I will go somewhere; like maybe Santa Barbara tomorrow. I'll fly down, catch a cab to the city, have lunch, and do a little shopping. Then I'll come home."

"Sorry, Isabel, tomorrow we jump in Antioch. Skydive before the winds pick up then dinner in Berkeley. Remember?"

"Somehow, I thought you would say that."

"Twenty more jumps to a thousand. For you, that is. You don't want to stop now, do you?"

"I don't?" Isabel asked.

"Of course not. It's a big milestone, and you are this close. If you want to go flying, go ahead. But save it for Monday."

"Classes, Drake. You know that. I've got accounting or economics every day of the week. No way can I take a morning off. To be honest, I should be studying instead of tagging along with you to your karate match."

"See," Drake said, "another example."

"Of what?"

"Something you've done during the past year. You're a college woman now; sophomore at State. That's one year down and three to go."

"Wonderful. An entire year at that place and I never made a single friend."

Drake sat up straight and coaxed Isabel to sit beside him. He gently caressed her hair and gazed at her with his dazzling blue eyes. "In a few months, we'll be married. You'll have a new house and plenty of friends. No need to worry about that."

"Yes, I know." Isabel groaned as an epiphany took hold. She had finally discovered the missing elements. She finally understood what she needed more than anything else; privacy and a life to call her own. A day never went by without Drake talking about *his* schedule, *his* family, *his* friends. He spoke nonstop about *his* plans, *his* money, and *his* valuable time away from work. Well, no more of that. Isabel felt due for a change. And that change, she realized, had to start with herself.

Next Saturday morning, she drove to Drake's house with a detailed account of *her* schedule and *her* plans for the day. "I'm flying to Monterey," she said.

"We can't," Drake said. "I've got a karate match at ten, and I told the old man that we would see him at two."

"No, I said that *I'm* flying. By myself. In the plane."

"Not in this overcast." Drake scowled. "You're essentially grounded."

"Grounded?" she said sharply. "What are you, my mother?"

"It's an aviation term," he said. "It means that you're not safe unless I'm with you."

"That's not it. You're afraid, aren't you? Maybe someday I won't need a chauffeur. That's what it is. Go on, you can admit it, Drake; you need me a lot more than I need you."

Drake laughed. "If you want to believe it; go ahead. Oh, and while you're at it, why don't you forget who's paying your tuition. And who owns the plane. And who paid for that Chanel purse."

Isabel turned a beet red and yelled to Drake's face, "And while *you're* at it, why don't you forget about the whole weekend? Give my regards to the old man. *I'm* staying home." She dumped out her purse. She scooped up her wallet, cosmetics, tampons, and hairbrush. Then she threw the purse to the floor and disappeared out the door with scarcely a "goodbye and leave me alone."

She drove home and locked herself in her room. She yanked off her necklace and stared at the engagement ring that dangled at the end. The two-carat, flawless diamond no longer sparkled. The luster of the princess cut suddenly faded. Isabel's heart—definitely jaded. She plopped onto her bed and folded her arms. A pounding headache took over. It didn't have to be like this, she told herself. The pain, the frustration, the complications; none of it had to be if Drake had listened more than he talked.

She longed for the simple excursions; walks in Hellyer Park or kissing on the boardwalk in Santa Cruz. Love was never a problem when all she had to worry about was cotton candy on her shirt or sand in her shoes. Simple and easy made for the best romance.

Apparently, Drake concurred. After a week on his own, he proposed a start-over plan. He offered an apology of sorts; beginning with dinner at the Bold Knight, followed by a nighttime stroll on Mount Hamilton. As he reminded her, that was the place of their first official date and one of their best.

Isabel wasn't too keen on the start over concept, but a casual walk in the autumn breeze seemed like a good effort to move forward, a good way to clear the air. On Saturday night, she met Drake at the Eastridge Shopping Center, and from there they caught the expressway. On the drive to the restaurant, Drake didn't seem too keen on the small talk. It seemed as if he was saving his speech for a public spot.

Fine, Isabel thought. She turned up the volume to a Joni Mitchell song and tried to relax. It was good music, but the stress in her back and head returned when the song ended. Drake flipped the station to his favorite. *Taking Care of Business* came on. Immediately, Isabel clenched her teeth and searched her purse for an aspirin. Nevertheless, she kept quiet and kept her fingers off the radio button.

At the restaurant, she tried her best to maintain a civil tone. They sat down at the candlelit table, but she soon realized that Drake was trying too hard to reset the clock.

His Armani blazer was the same that he had worn on her graduation night—a dark blue that favored the azure in his eyes. His burgundy silk tie was the same as before. Only difference; Isabel now knew that he had bought it at the Galeries Lafayette in Paris. Then there was Drake's cologne; splashed on more than usual. It took her back to their first meeting at the park in San Jose. She had some good memories from the park; it was a shame that things had to change. It was a shame that recent bad memories had to intrude.

Isabel thought about tonight and wondered if things would ever change for the better. She wondered if Drake's start over plan would somehow switch to a 'definitely over' catastrophe. She felt guilty for thinking the worst of an innocent meal. For a while, she enjoyed the strawberry lemonade.

"You might try the swordfish." Drake began with a safe topic. "I understand that the chef has a good marinade."

"I'll keep it in mind," Isabel said.

"Did I tell you about Barry?"

"What about him?"

"He blew out another engine to the 'Vette."

Isabel chuckled. "Not again. What does he do? Recycle or toss them away?"

"Yeah, I've to ask him if he gets a volume discount."

"Did I tell you that my sister got promoted?" Isabel said.

"Supervisor, if I recall," Drake said.

"As of last week."

"Pretty good job, I bet."

Isabel nodded. She studied her menu and tried to decide; when was the best time for a serious talk—before the appetizers or after dessert? She saw prime rib and Idaho baked potato on the menu, so naturally, the meal came first.

The waiter came and left, and Drake settled back to give his updates. He took a sip of wine. "Did I tell you about Mother?"

"What about her?"

"She's off to Monaco for three weeks."

"Monte Carlo, you mean," Isabel said.

"Starting tomorrow. She wants to get away for a while. She says that it's beautiful in autumn."

"So I've heard." Isabel slipped off to a daydream. Running away to a foreign country; why couldn't she do that herself? A few weeks alone would do it; long enough to catch her breath, long enough to retrieve a hint of her sanity.

The waiter dropped off the meals, and Isabel drifted in and out of Drake's well-rehearsed monologue. She kept her mind on her meal and kept her opinions to herself. She savored the Yorkshire pudding and stayed with a positive outlook. So far, there was no drama.

For the second half of his perfect date, Drake coaxed her for a nostalgic ride up to Mount Hamilton. He had planned to show another stunning view of the stars and the city. Isabel agreed to the ride, hoping for a not-so-stunning conversation on boundaries and personal freedom.

She kept quiet until they were halfway up the hill to Lovers' Point. Then she turned down the radio and casually asked, "Did I tell you about Colette?"

"What about her?"

"She invited me," Isabel said.

"Where to?" Drake asked, keeping his eyes on the road.

"Just a party."

"A party?" he said. "Is that so?"

"Yeah," she said. "Didn't I tell you?"

"No, you didn't. I would've remembered."

Even in the dark, Isabel could see him scowl. "Could've sworn I did."

"So, what, uh, what kind of party was it?"

"A welcome back for the students," Isabel said. "Off-campus, but nearby."

"*When* was it?" Drake asked.

"Next weekend. Saturday."

"Saturday?" Drake grimaced. "We're having dinner with the Biancas, remember?"

"Can't be, Drake. You told me that they were going to L.A. that weekend."

"We'll fly down to meet them."

Isabel sighed. "Admit it, Drake. The bottom line is you don't want me out of your sight."

"Now, you know that's not the point."

"Then you tell me; what is the point?"

Drake gave his own sigh and spoke a bit louder. "I don't understand why you feel this need to go places where men can check you out. You're my fiancée. We have obligations to family and friends."

"They have a jazz band there," she said, raising her voice. "I haven't seen Colette in over a year. And give me a break. I am not going there to meet men. It's a stupid party, for God's sake. If you can't handle that, you definitely have a problem!"

"I have a problem? I can't turn my back on you because the minute I do, you're out there making the rounds. What kind of engagement is this? What kind of fiancée are you trying to be?"

Isabel narrowed her eyes. "I'm a fiancée that you should be able to trust. If you can't even do that, you tell me; what do we have?"

"Show me you deserve to be trusted. Tell me that you're not going, and *then* I'll think about trust."

"What kind of lawyer double talk is that? Come on, Drake, we both know what's going on here; you're jealous, plain and simple."

"You want plain and simple talk?" he said, nearly shouting. "Let me put it this way. Maybe you can understand it in these terms. If you go to that party, then the engagement is off. If you don't act like a fiancée, you certainly cannot be one."

"Fine!" she screamed. "Then it's over. I'm going to the party, and no one tells me otherwise."

"I don't believe this. What do I do; I pluck you out of the slums, treat you like some all-mighty virgin princess, and this is how you repay me? My God, Isabel, give me some respect and act like an adult."

"I don't need to hear this." She crossed her arms. She screamed at Drake. She begged him to slow down the car and stop.

"That's what you want?" He threw up his hands and slammed on the brakes. "Then that's what you get."

Isabel bounced off the dashboard as the Mercedes screeched to a halt. Before Drake could utter another word, she jumped out the door and vanished down the dark mountain road.

Drake rolled down the window and shouted, "Isabel, get back here! You're acting like a child."

Isabel ran down the centerline until it faded to black. She kept running until she slipped and fell on the gravel by the ditch. She cursed at her scraped knee. Outraged by his antics, she stood and cursed at Drake. Up the road, he spun around. His headlights lit up the sky like a beacon. Isabel found a bush and hid behind it.

So this is what we've come to. I'm standing here in the dark, and you're out there, thinking that you're my salvation. Sorry, Drake, I don't need you to tell me who I am or what I want. I was doing fine by myself two years ago. I can do fine by myself now.

"Isabel, come on! We can talk about this!" Drake shouted, but no reply. Up and down the hill he drove, shouting and cursing and pleading in vain. He drove by Isabel a dozen times, passing her, and missing her, and getting more frustrated with each tap of the brake.

Isabel knew, of course, that the walk down the mountain was much too long and dangerous. But she also knew that Drake would never give up. After a half-hour of shivering in the cold air, she grudgingly stepped back onto the road and into Drake's waiting Mercedes.

"I'm still going to the party," she muttered.

"Then it's over," Drake said his final words for the night.

Isabel twisted off her diamond ring and shoved it into the ashtray. That was *her* final word.

Chapter *11*

ISABEL SURRENDERED the chateaubriand. She gave up on the day trips to the spa and weekend trips to New York and Vancouver. She turned away from rides in a Mercedes-Benz and flights in a Learjet. She banished the dream of a palace on Nob Hill in San Francisco. She chased away the most eligible bachelor from Stanford University. She felt sick to her stomach from her loss. Her head hurt from anger. Her heart filled with loneliness.

But when she woke up on Saturday morning and stared at the sunrise painting in her bedroom, she gave a short prayer, grateful for what remained. She still had a home; her parents' bungalow as it were. She still had transportation. Her Mercury Capri payments had been cleared eight months in advance, and the family Impala ran like a champ. She still had two semesters of prepaid college tuition. Best—she now had freedom and a life of her own.

Although it seemed impossible to ignore the past, Isabel sensed that a new, bold adventure lay ahead. She looked forward to seeing Colette again and eagerly planned for a girls' night out. It seemed a good start to a new direction.

She switched on her turntable and turned up the volume to *Goodbye Yellow Brick Road*. Isabel easily switched to an upbeat mood. Finally, she got invited to a party where she could pick out her own clothes and her own makeup. Finally, she found a party where Drake couldn't complain that her skirt was too short or her heels too high.

She could open her blouse down to the third button if she wanted or wear that forbidden cherry lipstick. For this party, there would be no chaperon hanging off her neck or jabbing at her ribs. There would be no icy glares or tapping of a watch. Strange feeling for sure; Isabel had just split up with the man of her dreams, but she never felt so confident.

When eight o'clock came, she put her plan into motion. She slid into her black slacks, slipped on her lavender top, and draped on her eighteen-inch Mikimoto pearls. She eased into her Ferragamo heels. A touch of Dior perfume from Paris, and she was good to go; except for one last chore. She opened her wallet, took out Drake's photo, and banished it to the bottom of her sock drawer.

"He was a good man," Isabel said, "but unfortunately, not the one for me."

When she arrived at the off-campus fraternity, she couldn't help reminiscing about Drake and his old habits. A pity he had not been invited, because he would've loved a party like this; old Victorian house, free-flowing draft beer, loud rock and roll, beautiful women, and just enough men to be rowdy.

She found Colette and confessed to being nervous. "It feels funny. It's been so long since I've gone solo."

"You do remember how to flirt, don't you?" Colette said.

"According to Drake, I never forgot."

"You've got your accountants on the left and your premeds on the right. If I were you, I'd go easy for a while. Start with the spreadsheet boys. You just have to wink, and they'll follow you home."

"Thanks," Isabel said. "But honestly, I'm not looking for a man at the moment. I like the music, and I came to catch up—with you, that is. It's been a year, Colette, I'm sure you've got a story or two to tell."

"I've got a hundred," she said. "And I'll start 'em off, once I get my tequila sunrise."

"Sounds like a plan."

"How about you, Isabel? Something to drink? How about a Rum and Coke or a Long Island iced tea?"

"Not for another year or two," Isabel said. "Maybe some punch, *un-spiked*, if you please."

"That's funny." Colette laughed. "I'll get you a Tom Collins." She wandered off in search of the bar, leaving Isabel alone and undefended.

She waited for Colette as long as she could. But when it seemed as though Colette had forgotten her or had gotten distracted by liquor or men, Isabel wandered from room to room in search of her own diversion. It didn't take long before she found her first challenge. She stumbled into the billiard room and found a trio of men who seemed desperate for attention. The tall man with the wavy blond hair set his beer mug on the windowsill and went on with his story.

"... and then he came running through the camp, yelling something about Australopithecus and a million-dollar grant. 'Nice concept,' we said, 'but hey, show us the proof.' So he grabbed a couple picks and brooms and drove us out to the site. 'New Mexico nomad,' he kept calling him as if a moniker made it valid. 'Ten thousand years old.' I mean, I didn't want to laugh at the guy, but what can I say; you just don't get your Pleistocene hunters wandering through the desert. Needless to say, the early Navajos didn't have horns, and his wandering nomad was an ox. Civil War vintage, I believe. After that, yeah, he switched majors to philosophy. We never saw him again." The blond haired man laughed well after the punch line. He kept laughing as long as he could.

Isabel smiled even though she had missed half the story. She smiled because the man was cute—with or without those little-boy dimples in his cheeks. There was a quiet pause, so she thought fast and improvised. "Archaeology, huh? What do you think; would a woman like me have any future in studying the past?"

"That depends," he said, showing his incredibly white teeth.

"On what?" Isabel said.

"That depends on what you're studying now."

"Let's say accounting."

"Accounting? That means going from a ten-key to an Acheulean hand axe."

"A what?" she said.

"An Acheulean hand axe. That's what they used before chain saws were invented."

"I know what an axe is. But why on earth would I want one?"

"Extra credit," he said. "If you can make one, then you get an automatic 'A' in Wilson's class."

"I don't know. It sounds like a lot of work." Isabel desperately wanted to turn the conversation away from the Stone Age.

"Can't be that hard," the man said. "I mean, it's not like you're carving Mount Rushmore. It's a piece of flint with a point at the end. Oh, and by the way, I'm Brad. Brad Thompson." He extended his hand.

"I'm Isabel," she said, stopping at the first name.

"Well, Isabel, if you're going to swap majors, I can help you get that 'A' in archeology."

Instantly, a hundred images flashed through her head. It seemed as though an archeologist had asked her out on a date. That meant more stories about the Stone Age, travels to boneyards in the Mojave Desert, prospecting for artifacts, and guiding a mule. Not too appealing. But it also meant that Brad—if he stayed with archeology—would soon be a university professor at San Jose State or Stanford, no less. Brad had possibilities. Isabel was about to offer her last name and a phone number when Brad got a tap on the shoulder.

"It's my sister," said the man doing the tapping. "She's on the phone, and she won't talk to anyone but you."

Brad shook his head and apologized. "Sorry, Isabel, this sounds like another crisis. Third one today, I suppose." He excused himself and disappeared to the back room.

Just as well, she surmised. *No sense competing with another woman. She can have the man with the rocks.* Isabel crossed the hallway and found Colette by the bar.

"Any luck?" Colette asked.

"Not looking for luck. Remember, I came to see you and swap a few stories."

"Forget about me," Colette said, nodding at a football player. "Go out and make your own story."

"Too soon for that. I hate when things happen too fast." She smiled then grimaced. "Maybe you can help me to take it slow. Here comes that bone collector again. He's a maybe yes, maybe no. Help me to sort it out."

"Oh God, he's a definite 'yes.' Cute and stylish; I'd take him home in a heartbeat."

"You think so, huh?" Isabel took a second look at Brad Thompson, a different light so to speak. His camel-hair sport coat and burgundy sweater gave him a strong masculine presence. But still, that clean-shaven face belonged to a grade-school boy. His bright blue eyes lit up like a sunrise when Isabel glanced his way.

Brad quickly approached and flashed a killer smile. "So are we on for Saturday night?"

"Saturday night?" Isabel said, taken aback by his assumption.

"Sure. I'm thinking dinner in the city. Good food. Great conversation. A couple hours to remember the rest of the week."

Not a bad offer, Isabel mused, considering that she had only planned on great conversation with Colette. Even though Brad was not a high-power attorney, he seemed to have potential. And he had eyes that were bluer and more honest than Drake's.

"I'll tell you what," she said. "Let's make it lunch. No farther than Palo Alto. We'll discuss anything but accounting and fossils."

"Not a problem," Brad said, grinning. "We can talk about anything you like."

"Then for starters; how about your friend's sister?"

"Who?"

"The one who can't get along without you."

"Oh, her." Brad shivered.

"Are you and she, you know, good friends or *really* good friends?"

"Susan? Oh God, no. Not Susan. She's a patient of mine, kind of."

"A patient?"

"She's seven months pregnant. I'm in the last year of premed. She's looking for second opinions, and I'm too nice to send her away. Which, I suppose, is my biggest fault; I'm way too nice." Brad laughed.

"You're going to be a doctor, are you?" Isabel's voice suddenly carried a melody.

"Hopefully, in a dozen years we'll have one more cardiologist roaming the hospital halls."

"Did you say cardiologist? As in Stanford?"

"Or radiologist or gynecologist. Anything but an archeologist."

"Oh, come on," she said, "there's nothing wrong with collecting fossils."

"If you say so." Brad smiled again. From the way he looked at her, he would've believed any story she had to offer.

Isabel walked away from that party and finally saw the light; she didn't need Drake anymore. She could have any man she wanted. With an easy wink and smile and a "you're terribly cute," any man would drop at her knees.

Sure, Isabel was depressed for a couple minutes when she broke up with Drake. She fretted a couple minutes more about getting her affairs in order. But those worries belonged to the past. Now, she had a doctor standing in line; and that was merely the beginning.

The stars aligned perfectly for Isabel that night. School was good. Home life was tolerable. Brad Thompson could make her dream of tomorrow. What else could she ask for? All things good seemed to fall into place; except a small loose end by the name of Drake Phillips. In a grand display of horrible timing, he called her the night after the party and begged to meet her at the Great Wall Chinese restaurant. He said he had an important message to relate, some atonements to make.

Isabel was dubious. What could Drake possibly offer except a hundred apologies and a guarantee for a hundred more? *A horrible mistake*, she warned herself. The more she listened to Drake, the more trouble she would find. Still, the memories—both good and bad—ran deep. She took a deep breath, forced out the words, and pinched herself for being weak.

"I'll meet you," she said. "Let's hear what you need to say."

She waited patiently until Thursday night. Then she drove to the Great Wall, expecting her patience to be tested. Once again, her intuition proved to be true.

Drake sat down at the table, ordered his meal, and jumped immediately into his speech. He couldn't wait to tell his side of the story.

"Babe, I've been kicking myself for days. I mean, I screwed up big time. This party of yours, what can I say? I was wrong, a hundred percent wrong. What I said was totally out of line. If I could take it back, I'd do it in a flash. And, uh, and you know, Isabel, you can stop me whenever you want."

"I'm listening."

"Sorry," Drake said, "I'm the one who should be listening. It's that you tell me things, and for some reason, I don't hear. Okay, maybe I don't want to hear. But I'm telling you; from this point on, things are going to change. Darling, you gotta believe me."

"Drake, I want to believe, but—"

"Understand where I'm coming from. I mean, you can't blame me if I get all wrapped up. I love you—you know that. I can't stand to be away for a heartbeat. I know it's not healthy, but that's the way I am. You know it hurts; it hurts me, and it hurts you."

Drake paused when the waiter dropped off the Cokes and food, although it seemed more like he paused to get Isabel to respond.

Isabel dropped a straw into her Coke and sipped. She gazed down at her chopsticks and across the restaurant to a young couple holding hands. She slowly swung her gaze to Drake. "Tell me again, Drake. These changes, what's going to be so different?"

"We are. You and me; a brand new start. I'll trust you. You trust me."

"I've heard that before," she said.

"I'm serious," he said. "From now on, if you want time alone, just say the word. A day, a week, three weeks in Monte Carlo. Whatever you want."

"Why should I believe you?"

"I've never lied to you, have I?"

"You've never been *caught* is what you mean." Isabel aimed her chopsticks and uncovered the essence of their relationship; Drake was living his life from the dark side of a one-way mirror. He knew all about Isabel. He knew when she got home and when she woke up in the morning. He knew when her classes began and how many miles she had put on her car. He knew every little secret and every little shame. Isabel was living her entire life under his microscope, and somehow that didn't seem fair.

Drake's eyes began to glisten, and he raised his voice as if he and Isabel were the only customers in the restaurant. "You want me to beg. Is that what you want?"

"Please don't do this, Drake."

"Okay, I'm begging." He split apart the dishes of egg rolls and mu shu pork. He tightly held her hands. He bowed his head and stared up at her with pleading blue eyes. "I love you, Isabel. As God is my witness, I would do anything, anything to get you back. I'm asking you; I'm begging you. Take my life in your hands and show me some mercy."

By now, people were staring, and Isabel was thinking; thinking about that night on Mt. Hamilton. She wondered if a short 'I'm sorry' would change a long pattern of jealousy and control. She wondered if the name Mr. Start-Again would be his ultimate moniker.

She released his hands. She bit into the egg roll and burned her tongue. The sharp pain cleared her head and took her attention away from Drake's seductive eyes. The more she thought about the problem, the clearer the solution. A trial separation—as painful as it seemed—seemed the only road out of a very difficult situation.

"Drake, I wish I could believe you. I so desperately want to believe you. But you know it, and I know it; there's no way we can get it to work. I've tried to understand. I really have. And I've realized that some destinies were never meant to be. Sorry, my love, we have no choice; we have to say goodbye."

Isabel slid her chair and stood for a last look at a desperate man. Then she grabbed her purse and a fortune cookie. She dashed for the door. Poor Drake never knew what hit him. In a second, she was gone; gone from the restaurant and gone from his life.

She got to her car and cranked on the engine. Then she cracked open the fortune cookie. The cookie was empty, but her fortune was clear; "You will have a full life ahead with no one but rich, interesting men to cater to your every need." That was a fortune she could live with.

Luckily, Isabel had a new man to kick start her new adventure. She had a good feeling about Brad; intuition perhaps or a growing self-confidence. One way or another, Brad was going to be with her for a real long time. She had no complaints about that. Brad seemed to be the kind of guy who could put the fun back into romance and the romance back into dating.

Sure, he had the looks, dollars, and smarts to fit in with the rich boys, but to Isabel, Brad was little more than a playful puppy, a stray dog who wanted nothing else than love and a little attention. How could she go wrong with someone like that?

On a warm Saturday afternoon, they agreed to meet at a Palo Alto bistro and have some coffee and conversation. Isabel drove up at noon, parked her car in front, and looked out to see Brad running to her door. It sure seemed as though he was wagging his tail and eager to plant a wet kiss on her face.

"Whoa, what was that for?" She was caught by surprise when Brad gave her a peck on the cheek.

"Sorry, I thought that it would ease some of the tension. You know, first date jitters and all that."

"Who said this is a date?"

"Sorry," Brad said. "I guess I got a little anxious."

"I have a cure for that." Isabel urged him close for a whisper. Then she reached up and surprised him with a passionate kiss on the lips. "Now, *that* is the start of a date."

Too bad her old fiancée wasn't around to see it. It was certainly a legitimate reason for Drake to get jealous.

Isabel sat down with Brad and ordered a cappuccino and cake. For himself, Brad got a café au lait and a few chunks of biscotti. Not much to eat, but then, as Brad insisted, he was there for the company and not the food. Isabel agreed. She decided that it was more than enough to sit there and talk and get lost in Brad's piercing blue eyes. She hated comparisons, but Brad was about the cutest guy she had ever seen. Those dimpled cheeks, those broad, muscular shoulders, and that never ending smile. No doubt about it; this was a man worth keeping.

"Did you ever make one?" Isabel asked.

"One what?"

"A hand axe. You know, for the extra credit."

"Nope. Never did," Brad said. "Made an ashtray once, but that's not quite the same."

They both laughed. And Isabel knew deep inside to trust her hunch. Brad could certainly make her forget any trauma of the past. She sensed a romance born again; a romance conceived through the notion of innocent fun and starry-eyed dreams. There was something about Brad that made him so full of joy and spirit. He was like a grade school boy discovering a new world; wanting to touch everything, meet everyone, see every place.

"Next summer," Brad said, "I want to spend a week at the Louvre in Paris. Can you imagine; seven days, studying the masters. Monet, Rembrandt, Renoir. Can't wait to see 'em in person."

"That's so romantic," Isabel said, recalling her own Paris, where she had seen the true masters like Gucci and Louis Vuitton on the Champs-Elysees.

"And then," Brad said, "a week in London; jogging in Hyde Park, or—"

"Shopping at Harrods or high tea at the Savoy?"

"Could be fun," Brad said.

"Sounds like you have your entire life planned to the minute." She recalled another man who had the same habit.

"Only to the nearest year. I have one more year of premed, four years of medical school, a few years as a resident, and so forth and so forth."

"That's a lot of work, Brad. How could you possibly squeeze a moment for us commoners?"

"Commoners, no. But for you, Isabel, I have as much time as you can imagine."

***

Brad—as Isabel soon discovered—certainly meant what he said. From that lunch date on, every spare second became devoted to the woman of his dreams. Almost every day for the next two weeks, they met at his place in Mountain View. From there, it was dinner, books, theater, or their favorite; passionate romance on a cool leather sofa.

Isabel—as Brad soon discovered—certainly meant what she said. No sex without marriage. No marriage without everlasting love. Until that happened, she compensated by spending every spare second being provocative, witty, entertaining, and stunningly beautiful. She played with Brad and teased him; but just enough so he would beg for more. French perfume and a sheer cotton blouse; whatever it took to drive him mad.

Once in a while, she would hint of her past, revealing only enough to keep Brad intrigued. For the most part, her escapades with Drake had to remain a secret. She talked about sailing off the Monterey Coast with her ex-fiancée. She shared the intensity of a ninety-second skydive. But to give Brad every detail of her life would no doubt overwhelm him and strip away the remaining mystery.

As Isabel had learned, it was best to keep romance clean and neat. Complications—as in surgery, flying a plane, or romance—rarely resulted in a good ending. And she hated stories without the fairytale ending.

By the third week in October, she was back on track to her original dream. In three years—she predicted—she would get her college degree and be happily married to a rich, handsome doctor who believed that the universe revolved around her. Undoubtedly, she pushed for lofty goals, but she never did plan on a fragile heart.

On a Friday afternoon, the phone rang in her room.

"Isabel, we need to talk," Brad said, breathless.

"What's the matter, Brad? You sound upset."

"Something's come up."

"Something bad?" she said. "I'm afraid to ask."

"Can't tell you now," Brad stammered. "Meet me at Chez Antoine in a half-hour. Please be there."

Isabel unsteadily hung up the phone. She had never heard Brad this agitated. Bad news always came abruptly. Isabel felt confused until she pieced together the scenario. Fancy restaurant, public place, and three weeks of ideal romance added up to only one possible outcome.

For some insane, incomprehensible reason, the man of her dreams was setting her up for the big dump. That had to be it. At the restaurant, there would be too many witnesses and no chance to make a horrible scene. She ran through the gamut of possible outs for Brad; old girlfriend, overwhelming schoolwork, too expensive to date, too many expectations, the ghost of her ex-fiancée.

She knew that the thing with Brad was too good to be true, but she didn't know if she should feel angry, sad, disappointed, or apathetic. Isabel leaned toward anger. She was angry that Brad didn't know a good woman when he saw one.

As quickly as she could, she dressed in her fighting black Chanel pantsuit. She grabbed her handbag and headed up Highway 101 to Chez Antoine in San Mateo. As soon as she pulled into the parking lot of the restaurant, she saw Brad. He got out of his van, waved excitedly, and rushed over.

"It's about time you got here," he whined.

"I got something to say about that." Isabel stepped from her car and squared her shoulders with him.

"Me first," Brad said. "I was going to say it during dinner, but this, this can't possibly wait. I've known you for three weeks, yes? Now, granted that's not very long, but it's long enough for me to realize what's going on. I've seen what you've done to me, and I'm sorry, Isabel, I have to say it fast; there's no other way. Darling, I love you more than anything in the world. I can't imagine living without you, and I can't wait to get married. So, would you ... will you, please marry me?"

"What?"

"Marry me. Wear my ring and be my wife." Brad pulled out a beautiful, one-carat sparkler to light up her eyes.

Isabel's mouth sank to the pavement. "My God, what can I say," she barely squeaked.

"Say 'yes.' "

"Yes ... yes," she said.

Chapter *12*

"YOU JUST KILLED Drake. You know that, don't you? You aimed the gun and yanked on the trigger." Barry became enraged when Isabel popped in to give him the good news. It seemed her recent engagement had caused more of a fuss than she expected. Thank goodness, Drake had already left for work.

"He'll get over it," Isabel said, feeling no need to apologize or explain the situation.

"My God, Isabel, I've never seen anyone so cold-hearted."

"Hey, I don't deserve that. You want a shark, talk to your roommate. I don't have time to stick around." She jabbed at Barry's chest, and the ring flashed like a one-carat dagger.

"Oh no, you don't. There's no way you're going to skip out and leave me hanging."

"Barry, please. Please, please. You're his best friend. You can break it to him. You don't need me."

"You coward. That man's given you everything. He busted his butt to satisfy you. Now you've got the gall to turn your back and pull this stunt."

Isabel narrowed her eyes. "You know, what they said was true; you guys are twins."

"Come on, this is a joke," Barry said. "You're not getting married."

"Of course, I am." She held up her ring to prove it.

"That doesn't mean anything! Tell me the guy's name."

"Yeah, right," Isabel said. "How stupid do you think I am?"

"When did you meet this guy? Last month? Last summer?"

"If you're implying that I cheated on Drake, you're dead wrong."

"That's not what I meant. I'm just trying to figure out how you can love this guy after, what, three weeks?"

"Let me put it this way; *this guy* and I already set a wedding date. We're getting married in two months. What do you think of that?"

"You could've married Drake. You never gave him half a chance."

"Stop defending him, Barry. I'm supposed to be your friend too. Think about *my* feelings."

"Look, Isabel, I know you better than you think. And I know Drake. It's obvious by now. You kids love each other, but you; you're too stubborn to admit it."

"Don't you get it, Barry? I do love him. But I can't live with someone who treats me like a child. My entire life; it's been the same. I've always had someone standing over me, following me every step. First, it was my mom then it was Drake. So help me, I am not going to sign up for a lifetime of that. Now, you tell His Royal Highness that I never want to see him or his money again."

Isabel slammed the door on Barry's face and hopped into her car. She sped out of Drake's life and slipped over to Brad's. A graceful exit if ever there was one. In reality, she did have a mountain of remorse. The next day, she sat in class and worried about next semester's tuition, and next year's car payment, and her token room and board fees at her mother's house. Drake, despite his faults, had proven himself to be a generous man. He had given her whatever she wanted. Except for that little matter of trust, he would've been perfect. But as Drake used to say, *"C'est la vie."*

Isabel's newest question became; how perfect was Brad? So far, he seemed to be a dream come true. At first, it felt strange to be with a man who was willing to sit down and listen to each of her problems. He never said a disparaging word. For once, she could hear her own thoughts and speak her own mind. There were no phone calls in the middle of the night and no after-class lectures. All that Brad expected was a chance for lifelong commitment. Eternal love and mutual respect; now that was a dream to believe in.

Once again, the simple things made Isabel smile. The best part of her day was to watch Brad as he reveled in the basic chores at his apartment; building a new bookcase, roasting a French Cornish hen, or sketching his dream home in the country.

"I don't know where it's going to be," he told her, "but I know we'll get there; redwood trees, five acres of land, wide-open skies. That's what a man needs. Plus a woman to love."

Isabel gave a long, deep sigh. All *she* needed was passion and romance in one beautiful package. Luckily, she seemed to have it in front of her. She counted her blessings as she gazed at Brad. Here, she had a man who was in great physical shape; handsome, strong, and healthy. Despite his good looks, Brad had a heart like no other man she had known.

She remembered the day, not long ago, when he picked up an injured cat. He took it home and sutured its leg. With compassion and a good hand, he got it back on the path to well-being—a happy ending for both owner and cat. Isabel remembered that day and the visions she had of marrying a doctor. She remembered feeling happy again. Hopefully, her blessings would grow.

She wondered about Brad's parents; they must have done something halfway smart. Surely, his father was not a gambling truck driver who ran off every weekend to play cards. His mother probably never laughed at *his* friends or told *him* to get a real job.

She asked Brad, "Talk to me about your folks. It's my guess that they love you *and* support you."

"How could it be otherwise?" He chuckled.

"I mean it. I want to hear all the good stuff. I want to hear how they spoiled you from the day you were born."

"That covers a lot of territory."

"I figured as much," Isabel said. "And if you can spare a minute and a half, I'll tell you the good my parents have done."

"With time left over—from what you implied."

"Listen, Brad, I don't want to criticize my parents. But things being equal, I'd rather not talk about 'em."

"Suit yourself. But there's only one way to get to know my folks; you have to meet them." He lit up with a broad grin. "And now that you've brought up the subject, how about Friday night? Dinner at their place. If I call now, I can get us in around seven."

"Good idea, Brad, but it's a little too soon."

"Fine, I'll make it seven-thirty."

"I was thinking more like the middle of December."

"Come, on, Isabel, they're not going to bite. They're not criminals. They're just plain everyday attorneys."

Isabel moaned. She thought she had seen the last of her lawyers. "Both of them?"

"How about that? Honestly, they're about as down-home as you could ask for. My father, for instance, well, he does just about everything."

"You mean like cooking and cleaning and shopping? Because that would be a real down-home father."

"More like divorces, wills, lawsuits, you name it."

"I see." Isabel sighed, returning to her image of the typical lawyer. "How about your mom?"

"Works for a company; nine to five routine. And *she* helps with the cooking."

Isabel cringed. She imagined a couple of rich, white, nose to the grindstone attorneys who had dedicated their lives to work and raising a decent son. What would they say when that same son brought home a plain, everyday, Hispanic woman from the middle-class side of San Jose?

"Then tell me this, Brad; what exactly have you told them about me?"

"They are expecting some beautiful grandkids."

"Dear Lord."

"I'm kidding." Brad chuckled while he gave her a hug.

Isabel was not amused.

When Friday arrived, she climbed into Brad's van and rode to his parents' home in well-to-do Atherton. Despite her initial reluctance, she soon discovered a pleasant surprise. She met the parents, and it quickly became clear; Brad had spoken the truth. He folks weren't like other attorneys. Isabel didn't have to close her eyes to pretend that they were real people. After a while, she didn't want to close her eyes at all.

The father, Ed Thompson, was the image of his son. He looked the same, spoke the same, and wore the same style of clothes. Seeing that, Isabel began to believe; *Brad Thompson, you're going to stay young forever. And that's what I like in a man; a great body and a timeless face. Don't you dare think of growing old.*

She also began to wonder why she wore her most expensive Dior suit and Mikimoto pearls. The Thompsons were not pretentious snobs. They weren't snobs in the least. Everything about them said "down to earth" or "middle of the road."

Their house was a modest ranch style; set on a quaint, half-acre, wooded lot. They had a flower garden of asters and mums in the backyard and a well-manicured lawn in front. A classic picket fence bordered the street.

They had furnished their home with a mix of antiques and Early American pieces, mostly purchased by Marie, Brad's affable mother. They had a large dog, a small cat, and long ago they had a goldfish or two. Ed and Marie also had a charming daughter, Amy, slightly younger than Brad. Amy favored the mother in both style and appearance; brunette, tall, thin, and pretty. She seemed nice. In total, Ed and Marie had two kids, two American cars, two incomes, a small mortgage, and a huge Stanford tuition.

Moderation seemed to be the Thompson theme. Keep an even keel and sail in a straight line. Don't make waves and live a long, healthy life. Debauchery, to them, meant two martinis and a round of bridge or canasta with the neighborhood friends. They seemed to thrive in a white bread niche. They took everything in stride; including the prospect of having grandkids that would be half-Hispanic and half-white. Isabel called that a welcome relief.

On the way back to Brad's apartment, Isabel begged for a personal review. "Come on, Brad, you can tell me. What'd they say?"

"You passed," Brad said. "Charm, etiquette—very high marks."

"I've been practicing."

"So you have." Brad chuckled and shot back his own request, "Now, you can tell me."

"What's that?"

"When do I meet *your* parents?"

Isabel choked. *Why is it they always ask?* "Please, Brad, we already discussed that."

"That was before we got engaged."

"The situation's the same," she said.

"Sooner or later, your mom's going to find out. You can't hide me forever."

"Oh, I wish." Isabel considered her options and came up with her best and only compromise. "Okay, we'll give her one week."

"From today?" Brad asked.

"No, one week before the wedding. I'll tell her then and not a moment sooner."

"That's two months away. It sure doesn't sound fair."

Fair, did he say? What did that have to do with a mother like Charlene? Charlene had so many flash-paper rules, it was impossible to figure out what she wanted or how to please her. An engagement ring? Most mothers would be thrilled. But for Charlene, it was like a diamond handcuff, being shackled to a man for the rest of her disgruntled life.

Brad said that no family could be that cynical. "What's the worse that could happen if you told her now?"

Isabel mumbled something about whacking a hornets' nest and running to save her skin. She drew a picture of the end of the planet. "Wouldn't work in a million years."

"Please," Brad said. "She does have a right to know."

"Nope. No way."

"I can't let you go home until you say 'yes,' "

"I might be here for the next twenty years," Isabel said.

"If that's what it takes."

Isabel saw nothing less than a parade of red flags as far as her mother was concerned. But as they pulled into the driveway of Brad's apartment, she slightly softened her mood.

She felt the regrets coming on fast, but she cautiously said, "Very well, I'll mention your name and take it from there. No guarantees. I may not even talk about the wedding or the ring."

"It's a beginning."

The next morning, she caught her mother raking leaves in the backyard. The sun was out, and the autumn air felt crisp and clear. It was a perfect day for a heart to heart talk; a perfect opportunity to tell Charlene about the man who had made her daughter so happy. Isabel took a deep breath.

"Mom, what would you say if I had a boyfriend?" She began with an easy question.

"I'd say I wouldn't be surprised."

"And what would you say if someday he proposed?"

"You're not pregnant, are you?" Charlene steadied her rake and glared at Isabel.

"No, Mom. I told you I don't sleep around."

"Yeah, well, you're only nineteen. Come back in five years when you're serious."

"Yeah, but Mom. What if I don't want to wait? What if he proposes next year or next week? I'm just trying to think ahead."

"Then I'll tell you what's going to happen." Charlene wiped her brow and frowned. "He's going to leave you next year or next week. It don't matter if you're married or not. If he gets the urge, he'll be gone in a flash. I'm telling you, Isabel, do yourself a favor. Don't fall for any man who talks about love. It's a game; nothing more, nothing less. The longer you stay out of the game, the better off you are."

That short and to-the-point opinion came straight from the mother of the bride. Regrettably, Isabel went back to her original plan; not one more word about weddings or men. The longer she held off the news, the better off she was. She did herself a favor with Charlene and fell back to her usual topics; dogs, weather, and Carlos at the *carniceria*.

When she next caught up with Brad at a small Italian restaurant, she once again apologized. She tried to explain the family situation.

"I don't think they're intentionally mean," she said, "but my parents do have a way with words. Especially my mom. Her words make me feel incredibly small."

"Your folks can't be that bad," Brad said, holding her hand. "I mean, you seem to be fine. They must've have done something halfway smart."

Isabel laughed. "You want a family to be proud of? Let's start with you and me and plan it from there."

"Someday, I'll meet your mom; you know that. But tonight, over dinner, I want to talk about you."

"What about me?" She grabbed her plate of spinach-and-mushroom raviolis and sprinkled on the parmesan.

"As you said, we should have a plan."

"About what?"

"You and school," he said. "Somehow I get the feeling that you don't want to be an accountant when you get out of State."

"Maybe so. It's the middle of November and I'm already bored. The classes are dragging, and my grades are slipping. But the tuition is cheap and the commute's easy. Besides that, what else can I do? My high school counselor said I was good for banking or the highway patrol. And I sure don't like guns."

"Come on, Isabel, you must have some kind of dream."

"I've got plenty of dreams," she bashfully said. "But they're more back of the mind fantasies for now."

"Give me an example."

"You'll laugh."

"Tell me," Brad said.

Isabel smiled. She sipped her passion fruit tea and reached back to those nearly forgotten dreams. "I want to paint," she said, feeling suddenly proud. "Oil pictures on canvas. Seascapes, landscapes, portraits. I want to paint every style. I want my own gallery and I want customers to stand in line. That's it; I want to be an artist. I can't believe I finally said it out loud."

"Surprising," Brad said. "But then, maybe not. You do have a flair for style and fashion."

"Definitely not inherited," she said.

"And definitely, we'll need to do something about it."

"Like what?" Isabel asked, feeling somewhere between curious and skeptical.

"Like next week," Brad said. "I'll call the San Francisco Institute of Art. We'll see what it takes to get you in."

"Are you serious?"

"Of course, I am."

Isabel squealed until customers stared. Then she realized, "It's expensive, you know."

"If I have to work nights to get you in, I'll do whatever it takes to make you happy."

Isabel found it hard to catch her breath. She heard the word 'happy.' She saw a gorgeous and obliging man in front of her. She felt terrific. There had to be a link. Suddenly, she felt unstoppable. "Oh, and by the way," she smiled, "my other fantasy."

"Name it."

"I want a Mercedes-Benz. A fast, black one. Any model as long it matches the color of my hair."

"That's great," he said. "How many pictures would you have to sell to afford that?"

Isabel laughed and laughed again. Never before had she felt so much alive. She finally had the man and the life that she had always imagined. Obviously, from the start, her real destiny lay with Brad. He was the one person who would turn her luck around. He was the man with the happily ever after. She stared at his face and that beautiful smile. Dear God, here was a kindhearted man. Isabel felt so lucky to have known Brad, if only for a moment. Then, without realizing, she blinked, and the moment was gone. The lights flickered, and everything went black.

Chapter *13*

ISABEL HAD ALREADY busted curfew, and Charlene wondered if she would follow up with an outright lie or a simple half-truth. Charlene wondered why bother to ask. Isabel had been home on-time or early for the past several weeks, so why not let this one tardiness slide? She drifted into a light sleep on the sofa, only to be woken abruptly by a loud ringing.

She grumbled as she reached for the phone. Nobody called that late except drunks or relatives with bad news. Either way, she hesitated to answer. On the fourth ring, she fumbled the receiver then held it to her ear. The woman on the line did not seem drunk.

"Ma'am, this is the Palo Alto Police Department." The voice was soft and professional, but the words were stabbing.

Charlene gulped, hoping for a wrong number. The caller didn't oblige.

"Do you know an Isabel Espinosa?" the woman asked.

"She's my daughter. Why, what'd she do?"

"Ma'am, there's been a car accident. Your daughter's been involved."

"What?"

"Your daughter, Isabel. She's at Stanford Hospital."

"No, she's on the way here," Charlene said.

"Ma'am, I have a report that her condition is critical. I would urge you to get yourself to the hospital as soon as you can."

Charlene set down the receiver and stared at the phone. It sure seemed like a scary dream. Did she hear the phone ring, or was it part of the dream?

"Ma'am, listen to me." The voice seemed faint, almost like static. A truck rumbled in the street, and Charlene wondered if that noise was the one that had jarred her awake. She glanced to the side as Leo stumbled into the room and grabbed the phone.

He held the receiver to his ear and listened until his hand began to shake. "Get your coat; we have to go."

"Go where? What are you talking about?"

"The hospital." Leo hung up the phone and coaxed Charlene to her feet. "They said she's at Stanford."

"What's she doing there?"

Leo shook his head but sprung into action. He snatched Charlene's coat and passed it to her. He told Randy to stay cool until Ruby showed up. Then he rushed to the bedroom and changed into his work clothes. He grabbed a jacket and hat. His shoes were half-tied, and his shirt draped over his pants. His socks didn't match, but he stood halfway out the front door as Charlene struggled to zip up her coat. Getting her to move was like prodding a glacier.

"She can't be in the hospital," Charlene muttered. "She's supposed to be here, and she's already late."

"Doesn't matter now," Leo said, sternly. "We have to move!"

"I don't understand."

"What's to understand?" he said. "We get in the car and get on the road."

He hustled her to the driveway and helped her into the old Chevy. Then he cranked on the engine and cursed until it sputtered to life. The hospital was thirty miles and forty minutes away on an empty road. Leo figured on a half-hour for driving plus ten seconds for parking.

"They do that," he said, giving Charlene's hand a squeeze. "They tell you that it's serious to make you rush. But it can't be that bad. Remember her neck? They said *that* was serious. She missed school for a couple months then she was better."

"Why does she do this to me?" Charlene raised her voice and stared through the windshield. "I told her to get home before twelve. So help me, I'm going to ground her for a month."

She tightly gripped her handbag and stiffened her spine. She shuddered when she saw the approaching sign; Emergency Entrance—Stanford Medical Center.

"It's got to be a mistake," she said. "Are you sure they said 'Stanford?' "

"I know what I heard," Leo said, snagging the closest parking spot. "And I know that we have to keep moving."

Like a bad dream that refused to fade, Charlene could not shake the feeling of dread. She could not wait for the words, "Go on home. It's nothing more than a misunderstanding."

She dragged herself through the automatic doors and headed for the admissions counter. She scanned the faces in the waiting room, hoping to find someone familiar. Ten patients in the lobby and not one of them was Isabel. Was that a good clue or bad?

Leo stood at the sign-in counter and confronted the woman sitting behind it. "My daughter's supposed to be here," he said calmly.

"Her name?" The woman with the nametag 'Alicia' kept her eyes on a chart and picked up a pen.

"Espinosa. Isabel Espinosa."

Alicia set down her pen. She placed her hands on her lap, looked up at Leo, and dolefully rose to her feet. "Could you come with me, please?"

Alicia beckoned Leo and Charlene to a small consultation room down the hall and away from the noise of the visitor lobby. "I'll let them know that you're here."

Charlene tugged at Alicia's sleeve. "What about my daughter? You can't leave without telling us what's wrong."

"I'm sorry," Alicia said. "Dr. Linoff can explain."

The door clicked as Alicia left. Leo and Charlene were once again alone in a room that seemed barely bigger than a closet. A beige wall, three small plastic chairs, a colorful print of gardenias on the wall. None of it was welcoming. Most of it compounded Charlene's frustration.

The worst part was the hospital smell; that disinfectant, sterile scent that took her back to childhood and reminded her that hospitals meant only one thing—people, especially loved ones, go in sick and come out dead. History didn't lie, and so far, this trip fit the pattern.

She paced the tiles until the hallway door swung open. She stepped aside when a man walked in. Charlene looked at his green smock and matching surgical cap. She guessed that he was Dr. Linoff. Hopefully, he was the man with the answers. When Linoff slipped off his cap, Charlene got the full view of his worried face. He looked tired or stressed. He looked pale and gaunt, but the hint of gray sideburns told her that Linoff had plenty of experience. But experience at what, she wondered.

A police officer stood at Linoff's side. He had the same thin face and worried expression. He was young, athletic, and too good-looking to wear a face like that. Charlene tried to guess; which man had the worse news?

"You're Mr. and Mrs. Espinosa?" the doctor spoke first.

"Where's Isabel?" Charlene said. "Is she okay?"

"I'm Dr. Linoff, and I'm sorry to say your daughter's been in a car accident."

"I know," she said. "But is she okay?"

"Please, sit down." Linoff pulled out a chair for Charlene and made sure that she took it. "First, let me tell you that Isabel is alive. Now beyond that, it's going to be a tough call. With the trauma she's had, I have to be honest; I've seen it go either way. We're doing as much as we can, but frankly, the next couple hours, that's going to be up to her."

"I don't understand. Does she have whiplash or what?" Charlene lifted her palms, looking for an easy answer.

"Truthfully, we have several problems. I'll try to be straightforward." Linoff grabbed a chair, sat down, and placed his palms on his knees. He glanced at Leo but spoke directly to Charlene.

"Isabel has had severe head trauma, possibly a fracture. She's got compound fractures of her left leg—below the knee—and her left arm. She's got fractures of six ribs and a possible fracture of her clavicle—that's her collar bone. She has extensive internal injuries, including bleeding and possible liver, spleen, and pancreas damage. She has contusions over much of her body, but that's the least of our problems. Honestly, if she doesn't stabilize in the next couple hours, she may not make it through the night."

Charlene drew in a deep breath and felt her heart sink to her stomach. "Oh, my God. *Lo siento, Mija. Lo siento.*"

Leo held tightly to her hand and looked at Linoff. "When can we see her?"

"She'll be moving to ICU in a couple hours or so," Linoff said. "You can see her then. But I have to warn you; as of fifteen minutes ago, she was still in a coma. But talk to her anyway. Hold her hand if you like. Any kind of support could make a difference."

Although Linoff didn't exactly urge Charlene to pray, she knew that she had to. But before she could start the first word of her prayer, the cop stepped forward.

"Ma'am, I'm Officer Grissom. Understandably, it's been a rough night. I don't want to take up much more of your time. But if you could answer a couple questions, you could help me along."

"Okay," Charlene said, half listening, half distracted.

"Did you know the man she was with?"

"What man?" she said, glancing at Leo. "I have no idea where she went or who she saw. She never told me about a man."

Grissom put away his notebook and lowered his voice. "I'm sorry. The fellow that was in the van with her—Brad, Brad Thompson—he didn't make it."

Charlene took a shallow gasp and held her hand to her mouth. God rest his soul; Brad was dead. For the first time in her life, Charlene was saddened by a man she never knew. Whoever he was, Isabel had cared about him. That was reason enough to mourn for a stranger. Charlene felt a sadness as if she had known Brad herself. A moment, a year; how long did it take to know someone? She merely had a first and last name, but the pain she felt cut to the bone.

Brad Thompson; so fragile was his life, so unfair he should leave it now. A midnight crash, and a man was gone. How could anyone make sense of something like that? Charlene certainly couldn't. She reeled from a horrible heartache and a hundred questions. Who was the person? Where was he from? How did Isabel know him? Was he worth dying for?

She sank into a despondent heap. She wanted to pray for Brad— for Isabel—but the words wouldn't come. What difference would it make anyway? Does God show mercy for a mother's forgotten love?

"Is that why you're here?" Leo asked the cop. "To find out what he was doing with Isabel?"

"No, but we'd like to know what they were doing before the accident."

"You mean drinking, don't you?"

"It would help us a lot," Grissom said, "to know where they were."

Charlene scowled at the cop. "Isabel doesn't drink, and she would never date a man who does." Then she turned to Linoff and raised her brow. "You never told us; how's her face?"

"Her face?" Linoff said.

"Yes. Tell me she didn't hurt it."

Linoff gave a grateful sigh. "In a way, she was lucky. She has numerous contusions and a laceration about here." He touched his finger to his forehead above the left temple. "But don't worry; she still has a pretty face."

That small favor would carry Charlene for a while. There were way too many problems for a woman who hit the roof over sour milk. Isabel's brother and sister had to be told. School would have to be canceled. Friends and family would need to know.

"Later," Charlene said. "We'll sit down and come up with something to say." More likely she would never find a decent explanation.

The updates came slowly, and waiting was torture. Leo wandered the halls with a cup of coffee. Charlene sat on a hard, plastic chair in the corner of the waiting room. She would glance up as visitors or patients passed through, but mostly she kept her gaze down; hand on her lap, a silent prayer on her lips.

Once in a while, she would catch a glimpse of a blond haired, young man pacing in the next hallway. He had the same worried expression on his face, the same aimless wandering of his pace. She wondered who *his* friend or patient was. She wondered if his pain could come close to matching hers.

At three o'clock in the morning, Charlene and Leo got their first visit to Isabel's room.

"Fifteen minutes," Linoff said, "is the most we can allow."

Charlene stepped into the ICU and opened her eyes to a harsh new reality. She felt confused. The chart at the foot of the bed said 'Isabel,' but that woman sure didn't look like the daughter she had seen the night before. This patient was mummified in tape and bandages. There was a splint on her left leg and left arm. She had an IV in her right hand, an oxygen tube up her nose. She had a bandage on her forehead, and—as in the old days—a brace on her neck.

It was hard to tell, but a closer look said 'yes.' The patient in front of Charlene was Isabel. Her eyes were swollen and blue, but thank God, her face—that beautiful angelic face—had remained mercifully intact.

The monitors beeped out a steady rhythm. How else could anyone tell that she was still alive? She lay motionless and pale, barely a heartbeat away from death.

It was difficult to see her like that, and after a quick, "I'm sorry," Leo retreated to the hallway. He said he was a realist; he couldn't help, and it made no sense to worry. Charlene believed that he was more afraid that he would break down and cry.

She sat by her daughter. It had been so long since she had prayed; would God ever recognize her voice? The ICU was no substitute for a church, but it certainly seemed like the best opportunity to pray. The room seemed dark and uncomfortably cold. Charlene held her daughter's hand through the stainless rails of the hospital bed. She began to weep.

"*Mija*, why are you doing this to me? First it was your Grandma then your Uncle Joe. Don't you dare leave me like they did. Please don't leave me alone. I've got you and Ruby. That's it. No one else cares if I live or die. I'm sorry if you hate me. God knows I never meant no harm. I just wanted to protect you. You can't blame for that, can you?

"Dear God, please don't take away my daughter. Can't you see what she means to me? Don't do it. Don't punish her for my own mistakes."

Charlene prayed for God to listen, but how long would it take to receive an answer? A minute seemed like forever when her daughter's life hung in the balance.

"They said to give her three days," Leo said when he returned. "If she makes it that far, she has a good chance."

"What are they going to do in the meantime?" Charlene's blood-red eyes begged for a good night's sleep.

"You mean, what are *we* going to do?"

"I'm not going to leave the hospital."

"Yes, we are," Leo said firmly. "You have to go home. You stay here, and you'll make yourself sick."

"I'm already sick," she said. "What's a few hours more?"

Despite her steadfast devotion, Charlene had little choice in the matter. Visiting hours had been strictly posted no matter how much or how loudly she complained.

"Very well," she said. "I'll go home, but I'm not going to like it. As soon as we can, I'll be back at her door."

"Fine," Leo said. "We'll come together."

Charlene reluctantly shuffled out of the Stanford Medical Center, pausing only once at the reception counter to gather a phone number. She stepped aside as a tall, dark-haired man signed in as a visitor to the hospital. He mentioned his name, but Charlene barely made note.

"Berringer Dees," the man said. "Friend of the patient."

Chapter *14*

ISABEL SLOWLY stirred to strange voices and odd mechanical sounds. Immediately, she realized that this was not her home in San Jose. This was not even close to a familiar place.

"Come on," she heard. "Wake up now. Wake up."

Someone poked at her side.

"What's happening?" Isabel said. "What are you doing to me?"

"You've have an accident," someone said. "You're at the Med Center, and we're trying to help you."

"I don't believe you."

"Isabel, trust me; this *is* a hospital."

"Hospital nothing. You can turn on the lights and show me your face. I don't trust nobody!"

"Isabel, I'm Dr. Linoff. Dr. Trepp is here to assist. He's a neurologist." Linoff placed his finger on Isabel's face. "Normal contraction. Dilation. Same with the left."

"Tell me what you see, Isabel," Trepp said.

"What are you talking about? I don't see anything. Quit poking me and turn on the lights!"

"Isabel, the lights *are* on."

"Don't lie to me!" She screamed and sat up straight. At this point, there was only one thing she understood; strange men and a dark room meant a whole lot of trouble. She swung her arm to the side and felt a cold rail. Not enough to keep her confined, she figured. She lifted her leg and shifted her hips, intent on climbing over. But like a knife to her side, she felt a deep, stabbing pain.

"Oh God!" She winced and dropped her head to the pillow, unable to move without excruciating pain. Wherever she was; she knew she was stuck. She had no place to run and no way to hide.

"What happened to me?" She moaned. She accepted, for now, that the men around her were truly doctors.

"Okay," Linoff said. "Looks like we have another problem."

"What do you mean *another?*" Isabel said. "How many problems are you talking about?"

"Isabel, you got yourself banged up pretty bad. What you just felt is a small part of it. Please, whatever you do; do not move around. Don't make it worse than it already is."

"What else? What else is the matter with me?"

Linoff arranged her pillow and brushed the hair from her eyes. He patted her hand. "You're awake and that's encouraging. From what I've heard, you're also a fighter. That's going to help us through the next couple days."

"Days?" she asked.

"Months before we get done."

"God."

"But back to your first question," Linoff said. "Yes, we do have a long list of problems."

"Such as?"

"Let's start with your left leg; we have that in a cast up to your knee. And your left arm—likewise, up to your shoulder. Your ribs are taped, and your neck's in a brace. I understand that you've had one before. Go ahead, check it out."

Isabel lifted her good hand to her neck and traced the outline of a painfully familiar collar.

Linoff continued. "You've got internal injuries to your—"

"What about my eyes?"

"You'll get the best ophthalmologist we have," Linoff said. "Dr. Felder. I'll have him stop by as soon as he can. In the meantime, don't try to roll out of this bed. Promise me, you'll stay put and get some rest."

She scarcely nodded. She ran her fingers over her eyes. "Just let me see again."

Isabel had barely rested her head on the pillow when she felt a soft touch on her wrist.

"*Mija*, I'm here for you," Charlene softly said as the doctors left to consult.

"Mom?"

"I don't know what I can do, but I want you to know that I'm here."

Isabel took in slow, shallow breaths. She hesitantly turned and whispered, "I'm going to be all right, aren't I, Mom?"

"Of course, you are. I prayed for you last night. So far, it must be working."

"I'm scared, Mom. It's never been this dark. What am I going to do?"

"You do what the doctors tell you to do," Charlene said. "You'll get better. You always have."

"This is not like before. Not even close."

"Don't talk like that," Charlene said. "It'll take longer, but you can do it. I know you can."

Isabel uncomfortably followed the curve of her left arm and stopped at the top of the cast. With every move, she hurt. Every breath was a kick to the ribs. The plaster on her leg and arm, the brace on her neck; cause for anguish, to be sure. But the worst torture; she couldn't see her mother's face. Charlene sat two feet away in a room filled with nothing but darkness and desperation.

"Tell me what I look like," she said.

"Fine," Charlene said without hesitation. "You look fine."

"What do you mean, 'fine?' "

Charlene remained silent, as if carefully choosing her words. Isabel recalled their arguments about too much blush, the wrong color lipstick, and eyeliner that made her look like a tramp. None of that mattered anymore. Being alive was the greatest gift imaginable.

"They left your hair alone," Charlene said. "That's one less problem to worry about."

"One from a million, I suppose."

"I did bring your makeup," Charlene said. "For those dark circles under your eyes."

Isabel heard Charlene rummage through her handbag, followed by an awkward silence.

"I'll put it over here." Charlene placed a compact on the nightstand.

"That's not going to help me, Mom. I can't fix what I can't see."

"Sorry."

"You can do it for me," Isabel said. "You know what I like."

Charlene tried her best to cover up the black and blue but gave up when the tears washed away most of the makeup. Isabel's face streaked with sticky concealer.

"I'm no good at this," Charlene said.

"Then hold me, Mom. You were always good at that."

Charlene did, and for a while, Isabel felt better.

***

By Friday, despite Charlene's prayers and the best medical team in California, Isabel showed little evidence of improvement. Unstable and weak, she fought hard to keep her mind from drifting into the shadows. The medication, the injuries, and the pain kept her moving from one mental state to another.

Her most lucid time of the day was early morning; after she woke up and before the nurse hit her with another shot of morphine. And it was barely enough morphine to keep away the pain. From what she had heard, severe head trauma and pain killers did not go hand in hand. In total, Isabel had about two hours to carry on a day's conversation. Beyond that, she rarely made sense.

That morning, with Linoff at her bedside, Isabel quickly got to her point. "It's been three days, Dr. Linoff, and I still can't see. I'm tired of sitting here in the dark. I'm bored that I got nothing to do."

"I can believe it," Linoff said, scribbling notes on his chart. "But you know we're doing the best we can."

"That's what I've been told."

"Since we're on the subject, how about going for a ride?" He lowered the bed rails as the nurse came in with a wheelchair.

"Let me guess," she said. "Another X-ray."

"You should be so lucky. This morning, it's a CAT scan."

"Wonderful. Another morning with my head in a vise."

"After that test," Linoff said, "you can have the rest of the day off."

"A vacation, huh?" she said, sitting up straight. "That's what I need."

"Don't we all?"

Isabel felt envious. Linoff got to go home to his family and friends. Thirty minutes a day with Charlene and Leo was not quite the same. More often than not, it was a half-hour of work and stress; trying to stay awake, trying to be coherent, trying to keep from sobbing. No wonder she began to daydream about running away to fresh air and wide-open spaces.

"If my guess is correct, it's already the weekend." Isabel swung her legs over the side of the bed and struggled to stand.

"Close enough," Linoff said.

"If it's fine with you, I'd rather not stick around. You know, I do have places to go and people to see. Like tomorrow, I'm supposed to go up to Napa with, uh, with Brad, that is. He's got a friend up there and uh ..." For some reason, Isabel couldn't finish her last sentence. Something didn't feel right. She bit her lower lip and wondered what the problem was.

"You know, I totally forgot about Brad. I don't get it; he should've been here by now. Somebody must've told him about the accident."

Linoff drew in a deep breath. He carefully set his hand on her wrist. "Isabel, listen to me. Brad was ... Brad was in the accident. The same accident that put you here. They tried to help him. Believe me, they tried. But it was too late. His injuries were much too, uh ... I'm sorry, Brad died before he got to the hospital."

Isabel caught every other word, and the words that stuck didn't make sense. Why would Linoff suddenly become so evil?

"Did you understand me?" Linoff said, keeping his voice calm.

Isabel understood him, and she understood what she had to say. "Don't you dare tell me that!" she screamed. "Don't you *ever* tell me that! You know it's not true!"

"I'm sorry." Linoff snapped his hand back. "But Brad's dead. There was nothing we could do."

"Jesus Christ, I told you not to lie! Get away from me! Get out of my face! Take your lies and go somewhere else. Leave me alone!" Isabel threw her arms in front of her face and screamed. "Oh God, no. He can't be dead. He can't!"

She swung her arm to the side; half in anger, half to keep her balance. In frustration, she grabbed her pillow from behind and flung it across the room. She swung her cast like a baseball bat and fell halfway to the floor. Then, with the strength of a hundred angels or demons, she stood and flailed at the IV stand, sending it crashing into the monitors. She grabbed the water pitcher with her one good hand and hurled it over Linoff's head.

"God, no. Don't tell me he's dead." She collapsed to her knee and cried. Now the stabbing pain came straight from her heart. Brad Thompson, the man who had promised a lifetime of love and commitment, had come back into her life for barely a moment; only to be ripped away by some cruel parody of medical justice. For the next hour and the next day, Isabel cried, forsaking God and doctors alike.

Chapter *15*

DARKNESS; visually, emotionally, prospects for her future. Isabel sat in her private room at the Stanford Medical Clinic and tried her best to ignore the realities of a difficult—almost desperate—situation. Her one solace; a jazz or pop tape that she would slip into her cassette player every morning. Good music would set her mood and allow her to forget her pain—for a while.

Dr. Linoff tapped her shoulder. Suddenly, Andy Kim's *Rock Me Gently* and Isabel's compliant mood disappeared from the room.

"You have a visitor," Linoff said.

Isabel lowered her headphones to her lap. "Who?"

"This is Officer Grissom of the Palo Alto Police Department. He has a few—hopefully basic—questions that he'd like to ask. I've asked him to keep his visit to ten minutes or less. Definitely less, if you have any hint of stress. Is that okay with you?"

"Questions about the accident?" she asked.

"Yes," Grissom said. "This shouldn't take long. Think of it as a flu shot. It might hurt for a while, but then you won't see me for a year."

"Didn't this guy tell you," she grumbled, "I can't even see you now."

"Sorry," Grissom squeaked. "How about I start over? Miss Espinosa, please, what can you tell me about the accident?"

"I don't want to talk about it." She picked up her headphones and snapped them back to her head.

The clock was counting down, and Isabel didn't care. She couldn't see Grissom's badge. She couldn't see his gun or his pressed and starched black uniform. As far as she was concerned, Grissom's only measure of authority was his deep, professional voice. All things being equal, Andy Kim had a much better voice.

Linoff tapped her wrist and turned down the volume to the cassette player. "Give it a try," he said. "If you don't care for the direction that Officer Grissom is taking, then by all means, turn up the volume. We'll ask him to leave. I have no issue with that. But if you could assist him, then we could move on. Agreed?"

Isabel nodded and lowered her headphones.

"Okay, ma'am," Grissom said, "how about an easy question? Let's go back to one hour *before* the accident. Can you tell me where you were?"

Isabel moaned. "If I tell you that, *then* will you leave me alone?"

"Yes."

"Let's get this over with." She grimaced then took a deep breath to calm her mind. No flu shot was ever like this. Given the choice, she would take the flu itself over reliving the nightmare that put her in this place. She knew the pain that memories could bring, but if she kept her story short, hopefully, the pain would be fleeting.

"We went to a restaurant," she said, slowly gaining strength. "I think it was called the Olive Grove or something like that. On El Camino; that's where it was. And I know what you're getting at, but Brad only had one glass of wine. That's it; one glass. He finished it long before we left."

"You said the Olive Grove?"

"Yeah, that was the place."

"Very good," Grissom said. "Now can you tell me what happened after the restaurant?"

Another deep breath and she went on, "I remember climbing into the van and kissing him."

"That's all?"

"What do you mean, is that all?" Isabel scowled.

"I mean, that's all you remember?" Grissom said.

"Yeah. See, I told you I couldn't help."

"Okay," Grissom said, sliding his notebook into his shirt pocket. "One last question and I'll leave you alone."

"Ask away."

"What kind of day was it?"

"How do you mean?" Isabel creased her brow.

"What did you both do in the morning?" Grissom asked.

"What difference does it make?"

"Just go ahead and tell me."

"What can I say; it was the same Friday I always had. I went to school, went home, and ducked out to see Brad. What's wrong with that, and who cares what I did?" Isabel set her hand to her hip.

"Thank you, Miss Espinosa. That will do for now."

Isabel shrugged. She slipped the cassette tape into the player and calmly waited for her next shot of morphine. As Linoff said, it was time to move on.

And she did move on, until the next morning. Then she woke to a commotion that told her—once again—that Linoff was up to no good. A nurse went to her side. The nurse casually removed the IV and nonchalantly rolled away the stand and monitors. She slid the bedside table across the room.

"I'm thirsty," Isabel said. "If you're going to wheel me off to a CAT scan, at least give me a glass of water."

Before the nurse responded, Linoff popped into the room. "Morning, Isabel. How are you feeling today?"

"Be doing a lot better if you get this truck off my chest. It seems your darling nurse forgot my pain pills again."

"Today, you can blame me. I want you to have a clear head for a while." He moved in and adjusted the pillow.

"Clear head." Isabel faked a laugh. "I have no idea what that feels like."

"Do the best you can. Officer Grissom is back."

"I know. I can smell his Mennen aftershave. Tell me what he wants."

Grissom moved forward and took his place next to Linoff. "Isabel, I need your help."

"I already told you what I know."

"Yes, we had a good start," Grissom said. "And today will be short but unfortunately, not very sweet."

"It's your sweet time that you're wasting."

"Ma'am, I have one job today, and that's to convince you how important your statement is."

"Important or not, I can't remember." Isabel groped by her hips for a jazz tape. She realized that the nurse had removed each of the tapes and the cassette player. She sensed a cheap ploy to focus her attention.

"I understand," Grissom said, "but let me ask you this."

"What?"

"Do you have any idea why you're at Stanford?"

"Now *that* I can tell you. Seven broken ribs, a broken leg, a broken arm, and a busted shoulder. *That's* why I'm stuck in this god-awful place."

"That's not what I'm looking for," Grissom said.

"Then how about this dent in my head and the fact that I can't even see my face in the mirror?"

"That's not it," Grissom said.

"Do you want the entire list, or are you going to tell me?"

"You're here because of a drunk driver." Grissom finally got to his point, but Isabel failed to understand.

"I already told you," she said, "Brad only had one glass of wine. He couldn't have been drunk."

"No, not Brad. It was the other driver. The man who hit you was drunk."

Isabel began to shake. Hearing that update was like a blind-side hit. Until then, she knew only two facts; Brad was dead, and she was hurting. Who cared about anything else? But still it bothered her; what did it take to get the truth around here?

"What driver?" she said. "No one told me a thing."

"What are they going to say; you're lying here all busted up, and he's out buying a new car? You don't need to hear that."

"I just did."

"Ma'am, this guy's going to kill again if we don't stop him. This was not his first DUI. But I'll tell you, whatever we do; we have to make sure it's his *last*."

"Fine, you do that. But I already told you that I can't help."

Grissom moved closer and softened his voice. "That's correct. You said you can't remember."

"Well, I can't. Don't you think I've tried? I forgot about Brad for three days after I woke up. How do you think that makes me feel? I want to remember, but it's all blacked out. I can't give you something I don't have." Isabel felt her face flush. She sensed her blood pressure spike, and she didn't care if it was dangerous or not.

"I'll leave this up to you," Grissom said. "Say the word and I'll walk out. You won't have to deal with me again. Or I can stay and talk. I can tell you what happened. And if, by chance, you happen to remember anything else, you tell me. Between us, we can work it out. We'll keep that man from driving again."

Isabel said nothing while she felt the rage build within her. She curled her fingers into a fist, eager to strike or strangle the person who put her in that hospital bed. She narrowed her eyes, ready to scream at anyone who got in her way. She struggled to catch her breath.

Then she slowly exhaled and sank into her pillow. Like a cold slap on the face, she realized who she was and where she was. And she realized that she could do nothing by herself. For any retribution, for any justice, she realized that she would need the support of others. She heard Grissom retreat to the doorway, and she feared that her one chance for truth might be slipping away.

"Stay," she whispered. "Tell me what I need to know."

Grissom went to her side. He pulled out his notebook and flipped to the first page. "Very well," he said. "Now if you want me to stop, you let me know."

Isabel nodded.

"First off," Grissom said, "the accident happened Saturday night, not Friday. Nobody knows where you were before the accident. And as long as Brad was sober, it makes no difference to me. But this is what we have. It was late, close to midnight. You and Brad were in his van, headed south on Middlefield Road when you came to a red light. There was a little traffic, but the weather was clear. It should've been a perfect night for a drive. So, you sat there and waited for the light to change. So far, everything's fine.

"Meanwhile, we have this fellow named Huffnagle. He spent most of *his* night bent over a glass of rum. There was no doubt that he was legally drunk—well past the limit—before he hit the road. But he drives anyway and shoots down Colorado Avenue. Like a locomotive, he's not going to stop for anyone.

"The light turns red, but he doesn't see it or doesn't care. He's doing fifty in a twenty-five zone. He's got no intention of slowing down. A van—Brad's van—pulls out into a left turn. By then, there's no way Huffnagle could stop. He smashes into Brad's side of the van, killing him and throwing you into the windshield. That's when you busted up your head and chest. And when the door flew open, you were thrown flat to the street. That's where you broke your leg and fractured your arm. But you were lucky; *you* were still alive."

Isabel sank deeper into her pillow and struggled for air.

Grissom flipped to a new page. "Now it's your turn. Tell me what you saw that night. Give me your version of what happened."

"What for? You seem to have the full story. At this point, I don't think you need me."

"There's only one story the DA cares about, and that's yours. Without your testimony, ma'am, we don't prosecute. That's fundamentally what we have."

At this point for Isabel, nothing was fundamental. She would be willing to help; if she had something to offer. But asking her one question—or a hundred—about the accident didn't matter. Her answer would always be the same.

"It looks like you're out of luck," she said, "because I don't recall a single minute."

"You don't know if you don't try, Isabel. You can't quit on us now."

"Listen, nobody's quitting on you. But if you haven't learned it from Dr. Linoff, then learn it from me. I have one thing—and only one thing—on my mind; how do I check out of this blood sucking hotel? Beyond that, I couldn't care less."

"Message received," Grissom said. "But how about one last question?"

"That will do for today," Linoff said, sternly.

"What?" Isabel asked, as if she had the final word.

"Will you call me if you remember anything?"

"Sure, why not. Just leave your number with my secretary outside."

"Yes, ma'am." Grissom turned and began to walk off.

"One last question," Isabel said, raising her head from her pillow.

"What's that?" Grissom said.

"The other driver; whatever happened to him?"

"You mean, was he hurt? Well, you see, there's this one expression we have. They drink, you pay. His vehicle was wrecked, but he walked off with barely a scratch. It's more common than you think."

Isabel had a feeling that this cop was trying to get her mad. He was trying to get her so enraged that she would blurt out the truth of the accident. And she might have done that if she had remembered a single detail about any of the events. As it was, she drew a blank. She had no memories of that night and no idea on how to respond now.

And to the doctor's relief, she had no rage. Despite Linoff's discreet moving of his precious monitors and equipment, Isabel was in no mood to touch or toss anything. She was in no mood to do anything but sink into her pillow and let the pent-up air escape from her lungs.

Disappointment seemed to be a recurring theme that morning. She had disappointed the cop and left him empty-handed. She had disappointed Linoff for her slow recovery. She had disappointed Brad for failing to cherish their last moments together. With nothing left but frustration over a hopeless situation, Isabel chased everyone away and cried until the pain in her head and ribs took over the pain in her heart.

***

As winter approached, Isabel had one more voice, one more personality to reckon with.

"Isabel," Linoff said, "this is Dr. Wescott. To let you know up front, he's a psychiatrist here at Stanford. He's one of the best—if not *the best*—we have."

Isabel frowned as she sniffed the air. She heard the word 'psychiatrist' but remained far from surprised. Almost predictably, Wescott had arrived on cue, and also predictably, Isabel knew what to say.

She spoke calmly. "To let you know up front, Dr. Wescott, and for the record; yes, I do get depressed. I get angry. I get frustrated; mostly from being stuck in this place. But I am *not* suicidal. Surprised, Dr. Linoff? I know that you suspect as much. I know you check my pillow to see if I'm hoarding pills. I know that you told the nurse to keep away anything sharp.

"But to make it clear; suicide is *not* on my list. And you know what else is not on my list—psychiatrists. I know exactly how they work. I know how they can twist your head into believing anything. I know the games they play. So I'm sorry, Dr. Wescott, I am not impressed. Oh, yeah, another thing you need to know; I happen to be one of the better patients that Dr. Linoff has—if not his *best* patient."

"I'm not surprised," Wescott said; his voice deep, calm, and somewhat assuring. "Your body and your emotions have been through a lot. I won't patronize you by saying that what you're experiencing is normal, because it's not. Every patient—every individual—is different. People heal at different rates, and some, honestly, don't heal at all. Some plateau for months; some make steady progress. You, Isabel, will have your own pace. I don't expect miracles overnight, but between Dr. Linoff and me, we'll do whatever it takes to make you healthy again."

Wescott tapped her wrist then took her hand. "Pleased to meet you, Isabel."

Isabel shook Wescott's hand then released it. "Pleased to *officially* meet me? You also dropped by on Tuesday and Thursday; to observe, I presume. Yes, every doctor smells different. You, Dr. Wescott, what is that—Givenchy from Paris?"

"You may become accustomed to my cologne," Wescott said. "Because for the near term, unfortunately, your other visitors are on a restricted list."

"I know," Isabel said. "My mom can visit a half-hour a day. My brother and sister—even less."

"That will be it for a while," Wescott said. "No friends, no classmates, definitely no police. Our priority is to get you stable. Too many visitors—more often than not—leads to stress. We'll take it slow, and we'll get you better. I promise. We'll see you tomorrow."

Isabel groaned. Yet another promise that seemed impossible to deliver. Another man who wanted to control every minute of her day. The doctors left and sure enough; the monotony returned. Taking it slow seemed to be an understatement. 'Getting better' seemed a distant dream. Wescott may have curtailed Isabel's visitors, but no way did he cut back on her frustrations.

High above her bed, a color TV constantly reminded her of her condition; especially when it became obvious that television was meant for people who could see. The five o'clock news and daytime soap operas didn't bother her. It was easy enough to find someone worse off than she was. What troubled her was the constant parade of commercials that begged her to see the bright, new colors, or try out the new Lancôme eye shadow, or test drive the new Mustang. Who cared about that? From now on, her only color was black, and her only car was surely to be repossessed.

There was no way that Isabel could fake being a happy blind woman. Life was simply not the same anymore. A month ago, she sat in school; studying, laughing, and running to her next class. She looked forward to a happy marriage. It was the essence of her dreams.

Nowadays, she slept half the day and worried half the night. The sleeping itself seemed a practical way to pass the otherwise-boring hours. But the worst part came when she woke to the same old question; what time was it now—morning or night? Not that it mattered that much, but she always had to ask; was toast and cantaloupe on the menu or steamed carrots and turkey breast?

She dreaded the dead silence of the hospital room. Often, she would wake up with nothing but her own thoughts and a few pain killers to keep her company. She often called for someone to talk to. Any distraction was better than none. That was what she believed—until that one day in December.

Isabel had just finished her mid-morning nap; or it could have been her afternoon nap or her nighttime snooze. Either way, she was groggy, tired, and in no mood for cruel and unusual games. Someone stood beside her. The man remained quiet, but she recognized the scent. She nearly froze as the nightmare began.

"Who's there?" she said.

The voice was soft but unmistakably clear. "Isabel, it's Brad. Brad Thompson."

Dear God, what's happening now? She trembled and drew the bed sheet to her chin. In front of her, like an unholy apparition, she saw the ghost of a man who had no right to come back and haunt her.

"What do you want?" she stammered.

"We have to talk." The ghost floated to the foot of the bed and chilled the air with a shivering cold.

For sure, Isabel had lost her mind. She blamed the episode on a medical delusion and the lack of a good night's sleep. She didn't want to see Brad. He was gone forever, and she had finally accepted the fact. Coming back now could only aggravate a difficult situation. Bedside chat? No way could that help.

The apparition had to be the touch of death himself. She remained convinced; Brad was there for one reason only; to lead her back to a cold November night—to a crash that, by all accounts, should have claimed one more victim. Not tonight, she vowed. No delusion would take her down that dark road.

"Go away!" she screamed. "Leave me alone." She cursed at her pills. She cursed at the nurse for leaving her alone. She waved her arm in front of her face. It didn't help. Brad's voice hung in the air and begged her to listen. Isabel screamed again, but the nightmare only got worse.

Chapter *16*

ISABEL BEGGED for Brad to leave. She was sorry, but he was part of the past and part of a trauma that should never be relived. There was no point in discussing the good times or the bad. There was no point in talking about the future—especially if they had none. There was no need to break her heart again—especially when her heart had just begun to heal.

Good intentions or bad, this ghost had to go. Isabel screamed for the nurse to help. She screamed for anyone alive. She listened for anyone but Brad. Then to her surprise and immense relief, she recognized another voice.

"Listen to me, Isabel. It's me, Marie. Marie Thompson. Come on, wake up."

Isabel slumped against her pillow. "Marie, thank God. You wouldn't believe the dream I just had."

"After what you've been through, I can believe anything."

"It was so real. It was like he was standing next to my bed."

Marie gave her hand a pat. "Let me sit down, and you can tell me about it."

"Oh, never mind," Isabel said. "I'm awake now. I'll be fine."

"I brought someone else," Marie said.

"That's good. Who?"

The man stepped closer and spoke up. "Isabel, it's Ed Thompson. You know—Brad's father. Do you remember me now?"

There was that voice again; that deep, haunting, dreadfully painful voice from the past. Isabel sniffed the air. That had to be Brad. That was his cologne, his scent, his essence from a life that had been so painfully stripped away. Again, she trembled.

Marie kept talking as if she didn't hear the voice; as if she didn't see the same ghost.

"We wanted to stop by a week ago," Marie said, "but they said 'no visitors.' This was the first chance we had."

Isabel tried to make sense of it. Somehow, she understood that Brad's father stood in the room, but the old memories intruded like a smothering apparition.

"Sorry this took so long," Ed said, unaware that his voice came with a ghost.

"Please, leave me alone," Isabel said.

"We had to see you," Ed said. "You're alive, and that's the only good thing to come from the accident. Give us a chance. We want to help."

"Get out of here, Brad. I am not going to talk to you. You had your chance. You didn't have to die like that."

Suddenly, the Thompsons understood. Although Ed had the best of intentions, he was undeniably part of the problem.

Isabel raised her voice and pleaded for Brad to leave. She cried for anyone to help. Finally, the nurse ran in. She apologetically added one more name to the restricted list; Ed Thompson, former acquaintance and family friend.

"Sorry, Mr. Thompson," the nurse said, "you'll have to wait in the lobby."

It took a while for Isabel to settle down, but when she did, she began to confide in Marie. "Well, Marie, you might have noticed that I'm a little messed up."

"Tell me someone who isn't. But don't worry about Ed; he's used to hysterics by now. It's been what, over a month, and I still cry every night."

"You and me both. Except nowadays, someone has to tell me if it's night or day."

"So I've heard," Marie said.

"I don't think I'll ever get used to it. I mean, sitting here in the dark is bad enough, but I'm tired of them treating me like a child."

"How's that?"

"I haven't been spoon-fed in over eighteen years. But now, three meals a day, the nurse comes in, cuts up my food, and feeds me one piece at a time. Until I smell or taste it, I have no idea if it's pot roast or asparagus."

"One irresponsible driver," Marie said, "and your whole life is a mess."

"Tell me about it," Isabel moaned. "But whatever you do; do not break the rules."

"What rules?"

"Never, never talk about the accident."

"Wasn't planning to," Marie said.

"Why not? Everyone else wants to hear about it."

"Not me. I've already heard plenty."

"I'm sure you have," Isabel said.

"Then you tell me; what do *you* want to discuss?" Marie slid her chair closer. "The last time I saw you, we were splitting a bean salad at the Holiday Inn café. Remember that? Not much better than asparagus, if I recall."

Isabel nodded then mentioned the first topic that came to mind. "You know, it still burns me about that drunk."

"I thought we weren't going to mention the man."

"They said he's still driving around. Do you believe it? He kills Brad, puts me in the hospital, and then they give him back his keys. Is that stupid or what?"

"He still has to work," Marie said.

"Are you saying this guy has a job?"

"So to speak, he does," Marie said, hesitating.

"But let me guess; he has no insurance."

"He does have insurance. I'll give him credit for that."

Isabel hated to talk about any part of the accident; what happened before, what happened during, what happened afterward. She felt her blood boil with the very concept of the word 'accident.' She pictured the other driver as a typical drunk; some teenage kid with a fake ID and a six pack of Coors. His only ambition that night was to drive his pickup truck from one bar to another. His only goal; get loaded, drive home, and pass out.

She agreed with the cop on one critical point. "The guy's a total sleaze. Lock him up, and throw away the key. Then tell me when he dies."

"Amen," Marie said. "There's no reason for him to walk free."

"Or drive. Can't we just blow up his truck?"

"Yeah, with him in it. There's an idea." Marie paused then gently touched Isabel's wrist. "Are we talking about the same person?"

"I thought we were."

"You did talk to the police, didn't you?" Marie sounded more confused than Isabel.

"Sure. At least twice."

"What exactly did they tell you about the other driver?"

"Now that you mention it; not much. I got two things from the cops."

"What's that?" Marie asked.

"First, they want me to testify."

"And second?"

"If I do go to court, they can put him away for years. And that's fine by me."

"It figures they would tell you that." Marie hung her purse on the chair and moved the chair closer.

"What do you mean?"

"The police," Marie said, "and the DA have one goal; make it look easy. All you have to do is; give a deposition, show up in the courtroom, and let the jury do their work. Simple, huh? Do that, and it's goodbye, Mr. One-for-the-road."

"What's wrong with that?"

"Unfortunately, it's not going to be easy. And it's not going to be easy for me to tell you this."

"You know you have to, Marie. You know if I find out later, I'll be more enraged. And no one's ready for that."

"Okay, we'll talk," Marie said, leaning forward. "But tell me if I go too fast or say too much."

"I will."

"Then first off," Marie said, faltering, "you were hit by a Cadillac; a brand new, two-ton El Dorado."

"So the guy has a little money. It makes no difference to me."

"So they guy has a lot of money and a *lot* of influence. Essentially, here is what you're up against. The man that killed Brad and sent you to the hospital is a doctor; a rich orthopedics surgeon from Palo Alto. Ironic in a way. I mean, with one bottle of booze, he tossed out the Hippocratic Oath."

"No one told me that," Isabel said, feeling the shivers run up her spine.

"Regrettably, it's true. But listen, Isabel, I don't want to get you mad."

"Sorry, Marie, you're too late for that. I'm already mad."

"No, trust me. If we're going to get this guy—make him pay for what he did—we have to stay calm and keep two steps ahead."

"I don't understand."

"I apologize. They're giving me five minutes, and if I talk fast, it's only because we have to catch up."

"Then tell me what you came to say. I'll worry about understanding later."

Marie gave her another light tap on the hand. "Let me put it this way; Huffnagle's smart. He knows what *can* happen because of the accident. And he has two concerns. One of them is manslaughter. A conviction there might net him sixty days in jail. We'll call it a two-month vacation then he's back to work. It turns out to be a minor concern when you get down to it."

"Then tell me, what *does* he worry about?"

"He doesn't know it yet," Marie said, "but his number one problem is going to be me. Technically, Ed and me, but mostly me. We are going to sue his sorry butt for every cent he has. It doesn't matter that a day after the crash he went out shopping for the best lawyer he could find; as if that's going to help. That's his first mistake; a big one."

"How's that?" Isabel asked, trying to keep up.

"He's assuming that *his* attorney is smarter than we are. Not a chance."

"And the second mistake?"

"He's assuming that our son's death will slow us down. He thinks that we are so distracted, we can't do our job. Truth is, yeah, I cried nonstop for days. I still cry every night, and I'm trying hard not to cry now. I'm a mother, and that's what mothers do. But I'm also an attorney—a good one—and I'm going to make Huffnagle pay if it's the last job I ever do."

"I'm sure glad that you're on my side."

Marie laughed, probably for the first time since the accident. She seemed to relax, knowing that Isabel sat at her side. "My plan is simple; we're going to reach out and grab him by his financial balls. Precisely where it hurts."

"I hope you know what you're doing."

"I know exactly what I'm doing," Marie said. "And God help anyone who gets in my way."

Isabel nodded.

"Huffnagle's been a doctor for twenty-five years. His estate, I'm guessing, is worth millions. At this point, he'll do what he can to cover his assets. A real sweetheart, if you ask me. He's going to hold every dime he can. That means he's got one priority for the next six months; sell those properties and shuffle those accounts. Now, you know what that means. Next year, when we go to trial, he'll have nothing left to sue—on paper, that is. Now won't that be a shame? Of course, that's not quite how it's going to happen."

Isabel leaned closer, trying to catch each of Marie's words. She liked the idea of getting even, as long as she didn't have to get involved.

Marie went on, "For the past three weeks, we've had him followed. Believe me, he doesn't go to the can without my knowing it. If he goes to the marina, I want to know if he has a boat. If he flies to Tahoe, does he rent a room or stay in his cabin? I want to know where he banks, where he shops, and who he knows. When I get done, I'm going to own that SOB."

"I just wished him out of my head," Isabel said. "It seems you've got a lot more imagination."

"By the time we finish," Marie said, sternly, "he'll wish he were dead."

"What does Ed think about this? Sounds like it's getting personal. Very personal."

"Actually, a lot of this came from Ed. That's the advantage of doing divorces. He can dig up the dirt and sniff out the secret accounts. I'd be lost without him."

"From where I sit, you seem totally in charge."

"I wish." Marie sighed. "To be honest, we have a lot of work ahead. But there's no way we're going to slow down or stop. It's inevitable. Nobody kills our son and walks off. If we have to spend the rest of our lives doing it, Brad *will* be avenged."

That was certainly a good ambition for someone who could walk and see. Isabel, on the other hand, had her hands full simply waking up in the morning. "My only goal," she said, "is to put the whole mess behind me; even if I have to spend the rest of the year doing it. I don't want it to drag on."

"Don't worry. With your help and the Petersons', we can wrap it up in a few months."

"With whose help?"

"The Petersons'," Marie said, startled. "You mean, they didn't tell you about them either?"

Isabel shook her head.

"They're just the folks who saved your life." Marie stepped to the doorway and called for her husband. She spoke in a hushed tone then sent him on his way. She returned to the bedside.

"Isabel, I'm going to give you a small snippet of the crash. If you get upset, for *any* reason, let me know. Ed is looking for the doctor."

"I think I need to know," Isabel said with a gulp. "And don't wait for the doctor. He's the one who keeps me in the dark."

Marie lightly held her hand. She leaned closer and began with a hush, "The Petersons were in the car behind you. They're an older couple, incredibly nice. It turns out that they were coming home from a friend's house. Like you and Brad, they were minding their own business. Then it happened. Honestly, they were pretty much in shock; horrified, when you get down to it.

"Most of what they saw was a blur, but they did see you; lying there in the middle of the street. They told me this, and they swore you were dead. From what I heard, they were almost right. They weren't sure, but they helped you the best they could. The wife got her coat and covered you. The husband, well, he stood in the road and waved away cars. He risked his life to save you. Isabel, these are good people who helped you. They went out of their way to make sure you were safe. And no one told you about them, huh? Yeah, well, why should I be surprised?"

"But I don't understand," Isabel asked, trying to catch her breath. "What?"

"If they saw the accident, why do the police need me? They've got their witnesses."

"They can help," Marie said, "but it's *your* testimony we need. Unfortunately, without you, Huffnagle walks free. No question about it."

"Somehow, I thought you would say that." Isabel sank to her pillow. She felt pressure on her heart and her head. How could her already-messed-up situation get any worse?

Chapter *17*

CHRISTMAS WEEK at the Stanford Medical Center; there could have been worse places to be, but Isabel couldn't think of one. She was stuck in bed and blind to the Christmas cards that stacked up on her nightstand. She left most of them unopened. It didn't make sense to unfold a card and not read it. It didn't seem possible to have anything close to a 'Very Merry Christmas.'

However, one holiday greeting came sprinkled with a delicate—but exotic—cologne. She knew immediately that her ex-fiancée, Drake, was wishing her the best. Of course, in reality, she already knew. Drake had become the most persistent man that the hospital staff had ever seen.

The nurses told her stories about the man who came every day, any hour, and begged and pleaded to see the patient in room 127. They said his one request was to stop by the room and drop off flowers or simply say, "Hi, how are you doing? How can I help?" Nothing more than that; one minute from a good family friend.

Isabel wondered about that. Drake wasn't family. In some respects, he was barely a friend. What right did he have to intrude on her happy holidays? But she also understood the meaning of the word *inevitable*. It meant that Drake, through patience, timing, bribery, or attrition, would eventually work his way into her hospital sanctuary. It wasn't a question of *if* he would come. It was more a matter of *how* and *when*.

On a cold, lonely night in late December, Isabel chose to surrender to her inevitable fate. She passed along a message; *I miss you, Drake. Stop by and see me sometime.*

The nurse wrote up the note and said she would pass it along. Almost immediately, Isabel felt a knot in her stomach that she couldn't blame on yesterday's ration of meat loaf. She understood that she played with fire. She knew the danger of making her heart an open target. Visiting hours began in a half-hour, and without question, Drake would get the message. He would show up at her door with a dozen flowers and a Pandora's Box.

Even so, she couldn't resist the temptation of being at his side. During the holiday season, she had often thought of Drake and recalled the love of a man who had given her so much. She thought back to a time, long ago, when she was independent and self-assured.

She could walk down any street and have men turn their heads in unison. With Drake at her side, she could walk into the Top of the Mark restaurant and command the best table in the house. Lobster, caviar, chateaubriand, and cherries jubilee; anything she wanted, she got. All she had to do was smile and say, "Pretty please."

Nowadays, she had become confined to a stainless steel hospital bed. A carefree afternoon included a wheelchair excursion to the X-ray lab or a two-hour descent to the CAT scan chambers. Room service; that meant boiled potatoes, a green salad, and boneless chicken. For that special treat, there was always raspberry Jell-o night at the hospital café. Heads still turned when she passed by, but these days it was more of a sympathetic nod.

Isabel wondered; what would Drake think when he walked through the hospital door? What would he say when he came upon the woman wrapped in plaster and tape? Probably a token, "How do you do?" and "Call me when you get better."

Fair enough, but then why would she care what he was thinking? *This is not a date*, she told herself. It was nothing more than two friends getting together for coffee and conversation. No expectations and no obligations.

Still, for some reason, she felt compelled to look her best. This would be her big night out. It wouldn't be fitting to disappoint the man who had sacrificed many of his own nights on the off chance that he might catch a glimpse of the woman he had dearly loved.

In truth, Isabel did look perfectly stunning in her white hospital gown with a high neckline and draft up the back. It was simple and stylish, she believed. Hair and makeup; that was more of a problem. She had combed her long hair the best she could, and the nurse said it looked great. But there was no telling; she could have a hundred split ends and never know.

Question was; would Drake notice? Probably not. What with the leg cast, the arm cast, the neck brace, and the remnants of a big ugly bruise on her forehead, there was more than enough to keep him distracted.

No doubt about it; Isabel was a total mess. So why on earth would Drake want to see her like this? She had nothing left to offer. Suddenly, the regrets came. Maybe it was a mistake to invite him in. Maybe it was a mistake to expect anything more than a sympathy call and a courteous, "You're looking good."

She reached for the buzzer to call the nurse and retrieve her misguided invitation, but it was too late. Drake stood at the door.

"Isabel?" He called softly with a voice reminiscent of their first phone call.

"Drake," she said, doing her best to smile. "Welcome to my house. Now don't you be shy. Come in and set the roses on the table."

She waited for him to stutter something like, "You can see again? No one told me."

Instead, he said, "I have fresh water in the vase." It seemed that Drake realized his own predictability. Flowers, candy, or diamonds; he had always come prepared. He set the vase on the nightstand and let the sweet fragrance permeate the air.

"Vermillion red," he said. "Your favorite."

"You're lucky," she said. "Two days ago, I couldn't have flowers. Then I got this new room. Nice, would you agree?"

"Any room that you enter is automatically nicer."

Isabel flushed, feeling uncomfortably exposed. Now was the moment of truth. Drake would sit down and stare at what used to be a young and beautiful face. He would see the black and blue, and the scratches, and every small imperfection. He would stare at her leg in a cast and wonder if she would ever walk in a straight line. Poor Drake. How could anyone make small talk in a situation like this?

Isabel felt terrified. She couldn't see his face, and that meant that she couldn't read his thoughts. She had no idea if he was smiling, frowning, closing his eyes, or checking his watch.

"Starting to rain." He began with a weather report. "Looks like it's getting worse."

"If it's like yesterday's storm, I'll be awake half the night."

"Could be," Drake said. "I thought I heard thunder a while ago."

"Thunder?" Isabel shivered.

"Could've been a Harley. Yeah, that's what it was."

The allotted time was ticking away, and Drake wasted it on weather and motorcycles. Why did he bother to stop by? If he had nothing to say; *just come out and say it*. When it seemed that he had exhausted the topics of weather, décor, and hospital food, he stood and put on his coat. "Sorry," he grunted, "I'm being asked to leave."

Not surprising, Isabel supposed. Drake had seen enough. It seemed that the weak, vulnerable woman didn't suit his style anymore. The slow and blind patient seemed no match for a jet-set life. As he went for the door, Isabel felt the sharp sting of rejection. For the first time in a long time, a man had turned his back and walked away.

Might as well get used to it, she thought. *No man is going to want someone like this.*

Drake stood in the doorway. Isabel could feel his dispassionate stare. He muttered something and got no response. Then he spoke up, clearly.

"How about tomorrow?" he said. "Can I stop by?"

"I'll be here," she said, hesitantly.

"Likewise," Drake said. The smile in his voice became suddenly clear. "And for as long as it takes."

Isabel plopped her head on the pillow. *For as long as it takes?* What did that mean? Until tonight, she had only two concerns; what test was scheduled for tomorrow, and what was for dinner tonight?

Drake, it seemed, had longer-term plans.

Chapter *18*

THE NEW YEAR came, but Charlene stuck with the same old preaching. "It's not worth it," she said. "You don't need more aggravation. You've got enough problems without making it worse."

Isabel listened, but she wondered; what would it take to get her mother on the restricted list? Without a doubt, Charlene had become the main source of aggravation.

"Mom, don't you understand? I have to testify. That man has to pay for what he did. We can't let him walk like nothing ever happened."

"You're poor and Mexican. You get on the witness stand; they'll rip you apart. Is that what you want? Why can't *you* understand? It doesn't matter what you say; he's still going to walk."

"That's not true," Isabel said. "Someday, I'll remember the accident. And you know what; that's the same day he goes to jail."

"You should have one thing on your mind; that's how to get home. That's where you belong."

"God, help me." Isabel reached for the call button, hoping for a nurse, hoping for any way to escort her mother outside.

"What you need is family," Charlene said. "You get yourself home, and we'll take care of the rest."

"I'm blind; not helpless, Mom. You don't have to take care of me."

Isabel sank into her pillow and tuned out Charlene. Even though she agreed that going home was an appealing concept, the realities of getting healthy seemed clear.

Despite her daily pain, frustration, and confusion, she stayed confident in Stanford. The doctors here knew their jobs. They specialized in everything. Isabel had no doubt that they would get her seeing and dancing again before the end of spring semester. Any alternative would be too horrifying to imagine.

Unfortunately, that hard-earned physician trust began to crumble on a cold Tuesday morning when Dr. Linoff came to her bedside and outlined his dilemma.

"Good morning, Isabel. I just had a meeting with Dr. Felder and Dr. Wescott. The subject was your condition and where do we go from here. What it comes down to is this. Physically, your eyes are in good shape. Your corneas have no occlusions. Vitreous is clear. The IOP—the intraocular pressure—is normal. Your retinas seem to be intact; no apparent damage. The CAT scans; well, they show nothing anomalous. Now, you have had some peri-orbital swelling and cranial trauma. But I have to be honest; we can't attribute your blindness to either of those factors."

Isabel sat patiently as Linoff finally got to his point. "As far as we can tell," he said, "you have everything you need to see."

"Obviously not everything," she said. "Otherwise, we wouldn't be having this conversation."

"I wish I could point to some test result and say, 'yes, there's a problem here.' If we had that, then we would have a start. We could assign a protocol and hope for progress. But so far, we haven't a clue."

"There's always more tests. Brad had good insurance. They'll pay. I know they will."

Linoff sighed and tapped Isabel's wrist. "I want to try a different approach. There's a chance—a small chance, perhaps—that your condition, well, it could be psychosomatic."

Isabel cringed. She didn't care for Linoff's tone or his implication.

"What that means is this; because of the accident, your body has gone through a tremendous amount of stress—physical *and* emotional. I don't have to tell you that. You know what you went through. But we think that in your case, the combination of both, has, in effect, overwhelmed you. The trauma goes up and your body reacts." Linoff paused as if waiting for Isabel to finish the thought.

"Continue," she said, reluctantly.

"What I'm trying to say is this. On the night of the accident ... on that night, you saw something so horrible, so terrifying, your mind is refusing to see it ... or see anything."

Isabel scowled. "What are you trying to say? My eyes are playing tricks? Trust me, Dr. Linoff, you're sitting right in front of me, and I have no idea what you look like. Dear God, you have to believe me. I'd do anything to see again."

"Isabel, listen to me. This blindness is not that uncommon. I've seen others in the same situation, and most of them recover."

"I am not making this up. I know my own body, and I know what's wrong. I've been told that it could be vascular; Behçet's or something like that. That's also trauma related and a real possibility. Or it could be these meds you got me on; they're *aggravating* the optics, not *helping*." Isabel tried to use the same jargon that Barry and Drake had used, but she got nowhere close to sounding professional.

"Dr. Wescott will help sort it out," Linoff said. "He'll work with you from this point on. Promise me that you'll give him a chance." Linoff put away his chart and gave her a pat on the shoulder.

So that became the final diagnosis; Isabel was crazy for being blind, too stubborn to see. It sounded more like the old Stanford shuffle; if you can't find the real issue, assign one more doctor and send the patient out the door. Collect the insurance. Goodbye, Isabel Espinosa.

She pouted and grumbled for the rest of the morning. She refused to eat her boiled chicken-and-rice lunch. Later that afternoon, when Wescott wandered in and pulled up a chair, she was in no mood for frivolous opinions or medical hand waving.

"Isabel, I'm Leonard Wescott. I know we've been introduced, but this will be our first *official* meeting. Did Dr. Linoff explain the situation?"

"He certainly did," she said, touching her head. "I'm blind, I'm sick, and Linoff is bailing out. He wants you to get in here and poke around. You know, take out the short circuits and work your miracles."

"You disagree, I take it."

"Let me put it this way. I know when someone's quitting, and Linoff just threw his hands in the air and called in the psychic—the witch doctor. Whatever it takes to close out the books."

"He's still seeing you, is that true?"

"For the easy stuff," she said. "Like broken bones or whatever shows up on the X-rays."

"Sounds like you're pretty upset."

"Upset is an understatement. Truth is; I hate Dr. Linoff the same way I hate my father. Is that what you want to hear? I imagine so. Then you might as well know this; I despise my mother intensely. How's that for a start?"

"We can start any way you like," Wescott said. "There are no rules to follow—except one."

"What's that?"

"You're going to have to want this. Therapy cannot be force fed. It's not something you can just sit back, listen, and expect to work. To be honest, *you'll* be doing the work. My only job is to help you along."

Isabel felt a moment of déjà vu. Those psycho clichés sure sounded familiar. She didn't believe it with Ross, and she didn't believe it now. She sat up straight and tried to make her point. "Well, *my* job is to prove Dr. Linoff wrong. I'll do whatever it takes to show him that it's not up here." She pointed at her head. "At least psychologically. Maybe then, he'll believe me and get to the real issue."

"That's one way to approach it."

Isabel sat back and folded her arms. "Let's get this over with."

"Great. So, what's on your mind?" Wescott settled in his seat and flipped open a notebook.

"You want to hear about the accident? Everyone else does."

"Only if you feel like discussing it."

"I don't," she said.

"That's fine," he said. "Pick any subject."

"Anything?"

"Anything."

Isabel fluffed her pillow and took a deep breath. She took a sip of water and got ready to speak her mind. If Wescott was paid to listen, there was no sense wasting a dime. It was either; talk to him or listen to another episode of *Days of Our Lives*. Wescott seemed marginally better.

"I was born in San Jose," she said, smiling, "and from that point on, it got worse."

Isabel chuckled at her insight and then felt obliged to recite her biography; her schools, names and ages of family members, the books she had read, where she had spent summer vacations. Once she got started, she relaxed. It felt good to be with a man who got paid to listen. It felt refreshing to reflect on her past. She remained blind at the end of the session, but at least the tension in her back and head relented.

"My mother was wrong," she said, summing up her revelations. "She didn't pass on the family curse. I had one accident. That's not going to slow me down."

"Good for you," Wescott said. "That's a step forward."

"How about the next step?"

Wescott scribbled a few more notes and then closed up the hour. "We'll have three sessions a week for the next two months. After that, we'll see how it goes."

Isabel nodded. Talking seemed to be the one activity she could do without asking for a pain pill. She remained skeptical that therapy would open her eyes, but her head felt long-overdue for a change.

By the middle of January—with Wescott's guidance—Isabel had slowly fallen into a routine, or whatever was routine for a blind woman living in the long-term recovery wing of Stanford Hospital. She remained bitter about the accident, and when pressed, she would rail against drunks on the road. But slowly, imperceptibly, her anger and resentment faded into a quiet acceptance of her condition.

Meanwhile, Drake and Barry stopped in as much as they could. Drake came every day; Barry once a week. Both men were courteous to a fault. Isabel could still snap her fingers, and Drake would immediately jump. Barry—he also jumped, but not quite as high. A few presents, a few friends, plenty of opportunities to relax and talk.

It was not quite like the old days, but even so, it felt pretty good. She gave thanks for her true friends. She felt blessed to be at Drake and Barry's side. And she thought she had made tremendous progress; until one bitterly cold Sunday afternoon when both men became bitter disappointments.

Drake stepped to her bedside and placed a small bottle in her hand. "Here, tell me what you think."

Isabel caressed the delicate ridges and removed the cap. She gently inhaled. "Fruity," she guessed, "with a hint of roses."

"Close enough," Drake said, "It's Ysatis, direct from Paris. I picked it up last week."

"Business or pleasure?"

"I stopped by to see Jean-Paul."

"I remember," she said. "He has a new restaurant."

"Officially, he opens in March. Already, he has a two-month waiting list. Unbelievable. Everything—his entire reputation—is based on his *petit sale de canard*. One dish and they call him a genius."

"For the petite something?"

"Yeah," Drake said. "You got it."

Isabel sighed, suddenly overwhelmed by fading visions of Paris and the Champs Elysees. "Actually, Drake, what *I'm* getting is boneless turkey and rice pilaf—straight from the four-star hospital kitchen."

"I'll talk to the chef," Drake said. "We can whip up something more palatable."

"I'm sure you can, but the cook here has one big advantage."

"What's that?"

"Personally," Isabel said, "I don't care what the food looks like, as long as I can find it on the plate."

Drake sighed. "Not getting easier, is it?"

"Easier?" She laughed. "What could be easier than a room at the Stanford? Look at the servants I have. One feeds me; another drives me around. I've got a personal trainer for my arm and leg and a psychiatrist for my head. What more could I possibly want?"

"I just thought that you might be well enough in a couple months to go out for a while."

"Two months, Drake? I can't even plan for tomorrow! As far as I'm concerned, *this* is my permanent address." Isabel snapped on the TV and tried her best to forget about Paris or any place beyond the Stanford walls.

Drake stumbled halfway through his apology when Barry picked the worst possible moment to walk in.

"We've got five minutes to kickoff." Barry slid a guest chair and plopped down.

Isabel ignored him and continued to jab at the remote control.

"I think it's on channel seven," Barry said.

"What is?" she mumbled.

"The playoff."

Isabel skipped over the game on the way up to the movie channel.

"I've got five hundred bucks on this," Barry said, sternly, "and a six point spread in the first quarter."

"That's nice." Isabel paused on a musical comedy.

"How about channel seven?" Barry asked.

"I'm looking for a movie."

Barry groused about missing the first play. He stood and spun the channel on the overhead TV.

"How can you listen to that garbage?" Isabel nearly screamed. She punched the remote control to switch channels. "Don't you know how boring it is?"

"Jesus, Isabel, it's a two-hour game," Barry said. "What's the big deal?"

"It's a two-hour waste of my day, if you ask me."

"I don't get it," Drake said with an insolent tone. "You never complained before. We came to give you a taste of the old days. What's so wrong with that?"

"First off, Drake, I can't see what they're doing. And if the game's so important, why don't you go outside and watch it? You know I never liked sports."

"Well, *now* I know." Drake tapped Barry on the shoulder, and in a heartbeat they were gone.

"Why is it they always need control?" Isabel muttered as she ran up and down the channels. A minute later, she found her movie, but now the pleasure was gone. *Stupid game. I don't know why people even bother.*

She got her way, but for some reason, it didn't feel satisfying. She sat alone with only a TV and a bottle of Ysatis to keep her company. It was not satisfying by any stretch.

The next day in her therapy session, she had plenty to consider. "Dr. Wescott, I think I made a mistake."

"How's that?" Wescott pulled a chair to the bedside and opened his notepad.

"I antagonized my two best friends."

"Tell me about it," Wescott said.

"An argument over the remote control. Basically, I chased them away over a small piece of plastic. I still can't believe it. It took me half the night to figure it out. But they were gone, and I was to blame. What's the matter with me, Dr. Wescott? Am I really that selfish? Do I always have to have control?"

"You tell me."

"I don't know. Maybe so. I can hardly pick and choose friends these days. And Drake; I know I'm lucky to have him around. I don't know what I'd do without him." Isabel gave a little sigh. "Of course, I called him later and apologized."

"And?" Wescott asked.

"And he said, 'forget it.' "

"That's all?"

"Well, he asked me not to call during the game. Oh, he was polite enough, but I could tell; he was still upset."

"How does that make you feel?" Wescott asked.

"It seems that I'm disappointing a lot of folks," Isabel said. "Drake, Barry, the cops. You too, I imagine."

"How's that?"

"I understand you're trying to help. Personally, I don't think you can get my eyes back, but I know that I have other problems to work on. Many other problems. I'm not ashamed to admit it."

"Like what kind of problems?"

"You have them written down; I'm sure. I'm selfish, for one. I scare people away. I'm uncooperative ... once in a while. Nobody thinks that I'm nice anymore."

"Isabel, this is not about being nice. We understand what you've been through."

"I've decided that from now on, I won't give you any trouble. If talking will get us to move forward, then I'll talk about anything you want."

"Anything?"

"Yes," she said. "Anything. My mother, father, Drake, Barry, school, you name it. No more kidding around."

"Very good," Wescott said, shifting in his seat. "Then what can you tell me about Brad?"

Isabel grimaced. "Let me clarify. I'll talk about anyone *except* Brad. I do need to draw the line somewhere."

"I had a feeling you'd say that."

"Come on, Dr. Wescott. I admitted that I have problems. That's a good first step, would you agree?"

"Generally, yes."

Isabel settled back with a grin. "Well, okay. It looks like we made some progress."

***

Progress may have been the word of the day, but for the next two months there seemed to be little—if any—moving forward. Isabel continued to ramble on about her family, her friends, and the many jobs she never had. All topics save the most critical; Brad Thompson—the man who died in a tragic November crash. Wescott was frustrated; Isabel was well aware of that.

And she was also aware that she had grown quite comfortable in her spacious room with the flowers, the stuffed bears, and the feather pillow the size of Manhattan. She and Wescott both agreed that it was time to venture out.

Now that she could sit for hours in a wheelchair, a trip to the mental health floor seemed to be the perfect road trip. As it turned out, the change in routine—the short field trip across the Stanford building—would set the tone for the rest of her therapy.

"Don't worry," the nurse said as she pushed Isabel through the corridors, up the elevator, and down the hallway to Wescott's waiting room. "I'll be back at three to pick you up."

"Please, leave me parked outside," Isabel said. "These days, I get a little claustrophobic."

The nurse agreed and assured her, "Five minutes should do it. His one o'clock is never late."

That sounded straightforward enough. But when the nurse closed the elevator door at the end of the hall, Isabel began to have second thoughts about being dumped in the middle of nowhere. Here she was; a young and beautiful woman, blind, and utterly defenseless. Her only weapon was a five-pound cast on her left arm. Her only tactic if assaulted in the psychiatric ward—scream as loud as she could. She maneuvered her chair closer to the waiting room door. Believing it safer inside than out, she felt for the knob and wrangled her position.

Too late for anything but regrets and a muted curse, she heard heavy footsteps coming up fast.

"Isabel?" Some person called her by name.

Isabel groaned when she recognized the harsh, grating voice. It belonged to Ross Hutten; the man who had stolen her heart, promised her the perfect marriage, and then spoiled it all by sleeping with another woman. The nightmare returned stronger than ever.

"Wow, what happened?" Ross stood in front of her like a truck, blocking the easy escape.

She spun her wheelchair, trying to keep her distance, trying to keep her leg cast between her and Ross. "Seems I had an accident a few months ago." She put on a happy face and refused to greet Ross by his name. "Got real banged up, you might say."

"Yeah, I can see that. Hope no one else got hurt."

Isabel winced at the two reminders of her situation; Ross could see, and she couldn't. And yes, somebody died.

"There was someone else in the car," she said, offering minimal disclosure. She bit her lip. Even that single admission made her ill.

Despite Ross's curiosity, there was no way that Isabel would turn the accident into a conversation. She had no desire to share another word. Suddenly, she felt desperate to change the topic. Fortunately, she had a surefire way of doing it. She brought up the subject of Ross himself.

"I heard that you finished your residency," she said, forcing a smile. "Officially, you are a psychiatrist."

"Finally, yes," he said. "Looking back, it's unbelievable how much work I put in. But in the long-run, it's worth it. I have my patients now and my classes—teaching, that is. At Stanford, of course."

"Congratulations."

"What can I say; I have a new department and a few more responsibilities. You know how it goes." Ross paused as if checking out Isabel from head to heel. "So, how long has it been?"

"A long time," she said. *Not long enough*, she thought.

"I expect we have some catching up to do."

Catching up? Isabel recoiled at the notion. Who did Ross think he was talking to; some long-lost friend? One of his old buddies from school? Ross must've been blind himself not to see the hatred rise to her eyes. Dear Lord, she caught him in the sack with a Stanford nurse. She had enough emotional trauma from that one incident to last a lifetime, and she had no desire to relive it.

At this point, it was clear that Ross didn't realize that his ex-fiancée was blind. She had no intention of correcting him. As soon as Wescott's patient walked out, Isabel caught the door and rolled in. She faced away from Ross.

"I'd love to catch up, Ross, but I am totally booked. What with physical therapy, counseling, and piano lessons; there's no way I could squeeze you in."

"I sense a bit of sarcasm. Maybe deserved, perhaps not."

"Excuse me," she snapped. "I have an appointment."

"Sorry," Ross said, "that didn't come out right. Let me rephrase it. Hopefully, I'll see you around."

Isabel shot him a quick smile then slammed the door behind. She grimaced and squirmed and clawed the plastic arms of her wheelchair. She wished that she could throttle Ross's neck in her one good hand.

"You want to talk about it?" Wescott asked in his typically casual manner.

Isabel spun around to Wescott's direction and raised her voice. "I can't believe he said that."

"Who?"

"It's been over two years, and he hasn't changed one bit."

"Who's that?" Wescott asked.

"My ex-fiancée; that's who. What a creep. I mean, talk about your recurring disease, it's impossible to get rid of this guy."

"Tell me about—"

"As if it wasn't bad enough," she said, "he still treats me like a child. What do I have to do to get any respect around here?"

"Around here?" Wescott said, a bit startled.

"I'm going to tell you this now, and it's not to leave this room. I know about confidentiality, and if you break it; the State Board's going to find out."

"Isabel, whatever you say—"

"Do you believe it; I thought I was in love. I was so stupid back then. Marry Ross? I must've been out of my mind."

"Who was that?"

"Ross Hutten, you know—the antichrist."

"I *do* know a Dr. Ross Hutten," Wescott said, wavering. "Is there any relation?"

Isabel clarified the best she could. "I never told you about him, did I? Yeah, well, if there was any one man who taught me how to hate, that had to be Ross. He got caught, plain and clear. You know what I mean; he had his train going through the wrong tunnel. Oh, I wanted to kill him on the spot. Instead, I told him to get out of my life. I never wanted to see him again. But Jesus Christ, no one listens to me."

Wescott swallowed hard. He was obviously thinking hard. He was no doubt wrangling with the new gossip and pleased that his patient was opening up with more of her personal situation.

Isabel softened her tone but gave Wescott a stern warning. "Don't you ever leave me alone out there. If that man comes up again, I'll scream. I don't care what he says. I am so tired of men like him. They think they know everything, but they really know squat. Exactly like my old man. And to make it easier for you, Dr. Wescott, I'll jump to the Freudian connection."

Isabel took a long, deep breath. She had a lot on her mind, and she was just getting warmed up. "I'll tell you this; I cannot stand my father. Arrogant, selfish, pig-headed, old man. How dare he call himself a human being? But hey, why should I stop there? You know how much I hated my mother and my sister. And the way I feel now, the whole world could screw itself."

She made a fist and began to sob. Try as she might, there was no way to hold back the tears that flowed.

Wescott passed her a tissue and tried to get to the heart of the matter. "Just say whatever comes to mind."

She held the tissue to her eyes and tried to wipe away the pain and frustration. "How could I ever forget Brad? Why did I do it? For three days, I never asked about him. All I could do was think about myself. Brad loved me. He really did. He would've done anything for me. How could I let him die like that and not even remember? He left me. Brad left me, and I never told him that I loved him. Dear God, I hate myself worst of all."

Isabel lifted her palm to her face and cried. She begged to be taken back to her room. She cried for the next hour and most of the afternoon. She cried for the sake of a forgotten man and for the three words that could've made a difference. "I love you" didn't seem to matter now that Brad was little more than a burning memory.

She felt incredibly sad and angry that day at Wescott's office. Isabel never realized at the time, but she had successfully passed through step one of her recovery program; recognize the guilt. Congratulations. Dr. Wescott was no doubt pleased with her progress and unavoidably pleased with himself. Finally, it seemed, he had earned his pay.

Chapter 19

THE FAINT SCENT of leather, the crisp snap of a freshly starched uniform, a thick tension in the air. Isabel knew that her morning was getting off to a rough start.

"Officer Grissom?" she said, only half-guessing.

"Good morning, ma'am," Grissom said, unsurprised. "I hope you don't mind me dropping in on you and Dr. Wescott. But it's been a while; I thought an update was in order." He moved closer to Isabel.

"By update," she said, "do you mean for me or you?"

"It works both ways," he said. "It's been five months since the accident. Some things have changed. Some have not. One goal that has *not* changed is this; we both want the driver convicted. Manslaughter, no bargain, straight-up guilty. We both want him to pay for what he did."

"Agreed," Isabel said. "But whether it's five months ago or today, sorry to say, *my* update is the same; I don't remember the accident. Dr. Wescott could've said that on the phone. He could've saved you a visit."

"Yes," Wescott said. "As I explained to Officer Grissom; therapy—the professional kind—is like peeling the layers on an onion. It takes time and tears to get to the core. It's *not* an overnight process."

"I understand," Grissom said. "But something we need to keep in mind is that we have several goals here, not necessarily overlapping."

"And those are?" Wescott asked.

"Getting Isabel healthy is obviously the top priority," Grissom said.

"Healthy enough to testify," she said.

"Essentially, yes—which gets us to our stance on the case. Our focus—the DA's focus—is extremely narrow."

"Come out and say it," Wescott said.

"Not to be crass," Grissom said, "but Isabel, as a witness, it's not required that you can see. You don't need your vision restored. The *only* thing we do need is a statement of the traffic light. At the moment of the impact, was it red or green? If it was green, we go to trial. That's it."

"I've said this before," Wescott said, sternly, "and I'll reiterate. We're not running a production line here. We don't use sodium amytal, and we don't do shock treatments. If and when Isabel sees again—or recalls anything—it will be on her schedule. Not yours. Not mine."

"Meanwhile," Grissom said, "for the second part of our update. Ma'am, you have to know that Huffnagle is back at work, practicing medicine, and expanding his practice."

"Like nothing ever happened," Isabel said softly.

Grissom lightly tapped her wrist. "Let me know when you get well."

***

Isabel had no clue when she would get well. She could only grasp a small sliver of optimism that some days were better than others.

Physically, she was improving. Emotionally, she teetered on the point of diminishing returns. As she made her twentieth trip to Wescott's office, she wondered if it was worth the effort and pain.

"What's been on your mind this week?" Wescott began the session and reached for a pen.

Isabel ignored the question and asked one of her own. "Tell me, Dr. Wescott; when did you start wearing a mustache?"

"Since Friday." He scraped his fingers along the whiskers and seemed rather pleased.

"Let me guess. Graying temples, glasses, salt and pepper mustache. Very distinguished, I assume."

It was hardly a guess. Every sound in that office had become familiar. Reading glasses; off the desk at the start of the session, back down when their time was up. A grumbling stomach when he skipped lunch. A short session if his mind was on food. He rocked back in his chair when he was bored, forward when Isabel spoke her mind. Today, she didn't care where he sat.

"They told me that I was beautiful," she said, trying to find a comfortable spot in the office chair.

"Who did?" Wescott asked.

"The men I dated. And a few others."

"Uh huh."

"Do you?" Isabel asked. "Do *you* think I'm beautiful?"

Wescott leaned forward and cleared his throat.

"Come on, Dr. Wescott; you can tell me. I know you look at me; my hair, my skin. How do you feel? What do you think?"

"Now, Isabel, this is *your* session. We're here to talk about *you*."

"You do." She giggled. "You do think I'm beautiful. You know, so did Ross. Of course, he also thought that I was a tease. I'm not so sure about that. I mean, I never thought I was. Or if I was, it was never intentional."

She took a sip of water. She nodded then went on, "I was just doing whatever seemed natural. I thought that Ross had the problem. I don't think that I ever teased Drake. I was a lot more careful after Ross. Much more careful. And Drake was different. I probably just used him."

"How's that?"

"First, let me tell you that I was never out for his money; not a single dime. But if a trinket happened to appear, well, I didn't ask questions. Drake, bless his heart, he'd go out and fetch me a ring, or a purse, or a new car, whatever. After a while, I got used to it."

"How did that make you feel?"

"Feel? Happy, I suppose. He proved that he loved me. It wasn't like he was trying to buy sex, if you know what I mean. He had respect for me, and I loved him for that. He would've been perfect, except for that one little trait."

"And that would be?" Wescott opened his pad to a new page.

"Jealousy. Drake was consumed by it. I couldn't go anywhere alone. He watched over me nonstop. I told him never to follow, but he never listened."

She fell silent as Wescott scribbled on a new page. He caught up and urged her forward. "Tell me more about that."

Isabel frowned then twitched her thumbs.

"If it's on your mind, Isabel, I want you to say it out loud."

She faced away.

"Out loud," Wescott said, firmly.

Isabel squirmed in her chair. Why admit to something that everyone else already knew? She pouted then began with a halting whisper. "You know, the only reason I went out with Brad was to get even with Drake. Of course, I knew back then that it was wrong. I didn't care. Drake had it coming. I'm sorry that Brad got caught in the middle. It wasn't his fault. I was … I was just using him to get back at Drake."

She faced away from Wescott and began to weep. "Brad, I'm sorry. I never meant to hurt you. I really didn't."

Wescott wrote his notes and nodded his head. One more step down the road, one more peel of the onion.

Chapter 20

THE CAMINO CENTER for the Blind. These people never promised miracles, but they did offer something that Isabel had sorely lacked for so many months; hope and the expectations that came with it. They had first appeared in the middle of winter; young volunteers, both sighted and non. They started slowly and then came on strong.

Isabel had made it clear that she had two priorities; the first was to see again, the second was to put more food in her mouth than on her lap. Losing her sight was bad enough, but nowadays, eating had become an unbearable chore. For her, there was no satisfaction in getting mashed potatoes up her nose or clamping down on a cold, empty fork. But which was worse; having the nurse feed her like an infant or going hungry from the wasted food?

While Wescott explored his psychological theories, Isabel went back to the basics. She learned to cope. The volunteers taught her two rules of survival. First; make your surroundings as predictable as possible then don't be surprised when they're not. Within weeks, she learned the fundamental skill of eating with a knife and fork. She learned how to smell the food before tasting it. She learned—on her own—to judge the difference in weight between one pea and two. Some said otherwise, but she found it true; her four remaining senses began to compensate for the loss of one.

Fortunately, she became a quick study. Soon, she began to eat and walk and laugh with the best of the blind. The black and blue shins didn't slow down her down. By mid-April, she roamed the halls on crutches and entertained anyone who passed her way. Being blind was no less a calamity, but after a while, she grudgingly accepted what seemed to be her inevitable fate.

But God, how she wanted to read again; just to sit back on a lazy Sunday morning and browse through the *Mercury News* or drag out an old Harlequin romance. Having Drake stop by and read the latest issue of *Fortune* was simply not the same experience.

When she began to learn Braille, she stepped into a world that she truly loved. Reading had always been her passion and her ultimate escape. Now, when she ran her fingers over the small bumps on the plastic tape, slowly—unbearably slowly—the words appeared. She persisted, and soon she read a paragraph a day, then a chapter a day, then a novel a day. Not so hard considering that she had little else to keep her occupied.

By the middle of May, even Isabel had to admit that she was making progress. Even though she remained blind, she felt a whole lot better and a tad more confident. The arm and leg casts were gone. It was a big relief in more ways than one. She could walk without crutches and walk with little pain. As long as she had a white cane and a little patience, she could wander through the east wing of the Medical Center or down to the cafeteria and back. Life had become downright boring, and that was certainly a welcome change. Slowly, she put the accident behind her.

***

She looked forward to a summer of hope. Her horoscope predicted a season of new beginnings. And that beginning—to her surprise—came on a warm Thursday night when a new visitor arrived.

Isabel had just finished her cream corn and whitefish dinner. She looked forward to a pleasant evening with Drake. Yesterday, he had read from an old mystery novel. Tonight, he promised a romance. Not likely, Isabel surmised. Drake would never stoop so low to read what others thought of romance. She fluffed her pillow, laughed at herself, and got ready for her typical hospital date.

Everything went according to plan until she heard an unexpected voice from the open door. Oh Lord, it was Charlene. Why did she arrive on a Thursday night? Why didn't she call? Drake was due any minute, and the last thing Isabel wanted was for those two to meet head on.

"Will you hurry up?" Charlene called out, barely above a whisper.

"I told you to slow down," Leo said. "You know I can't run with it."

Now that signaled a bad omen; both parents on the same night. For sure, there was either a death in the family or a problem with Leo's job.

"What's going on?" Isabel asked impatiently.

"Come on, before someone sees you," Charlene snapped at Leo. Then she turned and moved closer to Isabel. "We brought you a present, *Mija*."

A present. Why didn't they say that in the first place? She was always in the mood for new toys. Suddenly, her mind veered off Drake and onto the surprise. It could be that tape player she wanted, or a new cotton blouse, or a box of chocolates, or an Agatha Christie novel in Braille.

Charlene stuttered like a nervous thief. "Leo, gimme the box. Go stand by the door. Make sure no one comes."

Stand by the door? What kind of present was this? And whom did Leo have to keep out? Isabel changed her mind. This surprise had disaster written in bold letters.

"Here, open it." Charlene plopped a box onto Isabel's lap.

The box was about the size of a toaster oven, but it sure didn't feel like one. Isabel popped off the lid and nearly jumped. Something moved inside.

"Keep your voice down," Charlene said.

"Oh my God. It's a puppy!" Isabel squealed.

"Shh. Come on. Somebody's going to hear you."

"Oh, don't tell me. She's my Saint Bernard, isn't she?" Isabel took a wild guess as the little dog bounded up and licked her face.

Leo called from the doorway. "That's enough. Let's go. Let's go."

"Sorry, *Mija*. Your father's having a fit. We just stopped by to show you."

"Candy," she said, hugging the puppy. "That's it. I'm going to call my Bernard, Candy."

"That's a good name," Charlene said. "You can play with Candy when you come home—which will be any day now, yes?"

"Sooner, I hope."

***

Isabel couldn't believe how much she looked forward to going home. Seven months ago, she had tried to purge her mind of any thoughts of San Jose. Her goal back then; get away from the city and keep on running. In a surprise turnabout, she couldn't wait to get back to the Espinosa family; back to her old room and a new Saint Bernard. Considering her present accommodations, San Jose seemed a pretty sweet deal.

From the sound of it, she was also going home to a brand new mother. This one seemed compassionate and much more understanding. Perhaps living in San Jose would be less of a nightmare and more of a sunrise.

A few days later, Dr. Linoff stopped by and gave another helping of encouraging news. "Eight weeks," he said. "In eight weeks you'll be checking out."

"Could be worse, I suppose."

"We're playing it safe. Physical therapy, rest, and good nutrition; you need as much as you can get. But in two months, you'll be an outpatient. That's something to look forward to."

"Except that I can't see, everything is fine."

"We haven't given up," Linoff said.

"So you tell me."

Linoff sighed then switched to an upbeat tone. "I understand you have a job."

"Starting tomorrow," Isabel said. "Two hours a day at the Blind Center."

"Pretty good start."

She walked to her closet and sifted through her new work clothes; color coordinated and tagged with the help of her mother and sister. "It doesn't pay much, but there is plenty of job satisfaction from what I've heard."

"You'll do fine, I'm sure," Linoff said.

Isabel heard his assurance but tempered her enthusiasm. She realized that this would be her first honest to goodness job where she would work with real people and a real boss, who, for two hours a day, expected results. Trepidation aside, she felt jitters of excitement as she stepped into a genuine career.

Starting the next day and continuing for the next two months, she caught the shuttle to the Blind Center and worked hard for her minimum wage. She taught clients—mostly macular degeneration patients and accident victims—to walk and read and get along in a near-normal life. She talked to them, trained them, and convinced them that total independence was the only way to go.

She urged them to set aside the self-pity and guilt. She told them to deal with the reality at hand. And the more she taught her clients, the more she believed it herself. After eight months of emotional and physical turmoil, Isabel felt genuinely happy. Helping others gave her a warm glow and made her consider therapy as a real career.

"I can do this," she said. "This is one job where I can make a difference."

By mid-July, Isabel had convinced herself on the concept of true independence. She got ready to pack her bags, check out of the hospital, and say "so long" to Stanford and everyone there. She walked into Wescott's office for what she believed was their last visit. She wished him the best of luck.

"I'll let you know," she told him, "when I can start back with our sessions. However, for the time being, I'll be living at home."

Wescott let out a deep sigh. "Isabel, it's more important now than ever to keep your appointments. I don't want you to quit."

"End of the road," she said. "I am past the blame. I am past the accusations. I am long past the guilt. I've learned to accept fate for what it is, and I'm ready to move on. With your help and Dr. Linoff's, I've got myself a job. God willing, I might make it a living. Thank you, Dr. Wescott; it was fun while it lasted."

"You know, there's only one reason not to quit."

"What's that?" she asked.

"Your blindness. I'm still convinced that we have a chance."

"A chance for what? Frustration, aggravation, more reminders of what I'm missing? At least Dr. Linoff was pragmatic. He told me to my face that he didn't have a clue what the real issue is. I understand.

We have our limits. Medical science and I; well, we do not see eye to eye on this. And honestly, as of now, I am no longer using visual metaphors. I am officially blind … and I can live with it."

"I admire your courage," Wescott said. "And I agree; you should move on. How about a compromise?"

"Like what?" Isabel asked, remaining skeptical.

Wescott leaned forward. "I'll recommend you for immediate release, pending—"

"Pending a few more strings?"

"If you agree to one visit a week, I'll sign you out in the morning. Isabel, even if the chance of seeing again is one in a million, you have to take it."

Isabel heard 'immediate release' and lost track of anything else. "I can get out of this place tomorrow?"

"I'll double-check with Dr. Linoff, but I don't expect a problem."

She smiled. "Dr. Wescott, sign me up for the next week, because tomorrow, I'm going home."

Chapter *21*

RELAPSE. They said it was possible, but Isabel didn't believe it—until she blacked out on the way to the Stanford Hospital cafeteria and fell flat on her butt. Four hours before discharge; she lay in her bed, wondering what had happened.

Shock was part of the problem. Her blood pressure had dropped to near zero, and that was way too low to keep her on her feet. The doctors proffered a dozen theories on what went wrong; internal bleeding, electrolyte imbalance, anemia, stress—a dozen theories and not one decent explanation.

Isabel had one question; why didn't they find the problem before? Why didn't they know that her pancreas was inflamed? And who was monitoring her blood count? The doctors had watched her every day; how could they have missed such a basic issue?

Now, because of that mishap, she began to wonder again; could it be that they also misdiagnosed her blindness? Could it be that the physical trauma was the real culprit after all? Could it be that the six and a half months of psychotherapy was merely a false hope for a lost cause? If those doctors had done their jobs properly, perhaps she would be seeing by now.

Instead of a genuine apology, she got the same old mantra; "Sorry, Isabel, you can't go home until we find the real problem. We'll write you a new release ... when it's appropriate."

It took a week for Isabel to regain her strength. Antibiotics, anti-inflammatory meds, and plenty of water; she took anything to get on her feet again. When she got to the point where she could walk—or stagger—down the hallway, she held fast to one goal; meet with Dr. Wescott and give him a resounding, "I told you so."

She struggled to Wescott's office and then sat down for her usual appointment. In her mind, there was only one way to get well; she would have to heal herself.

"I don't understand," she said to Wescott. "I've been meeting you for over six months now, and I still can't see. I mean, isn't that the reason that I'm here? Why do I have to sit here week after week like I'm going to a lousy confessional? I get so tired of hearing myself talk! And I've told you everything. As far as I'm concerned, *this* is my last appointment."

Wescott remained unmoved. He seemed annoyingly casual about her final decision. "Last session, you talked about your mother. Is there still a problem there?"

"No, there's no problem there. I don't care what I said before. I was wrong. My mother loves me. I know that for a fact; and nobody's going to tell me otherwise. And I'll tell you this; I was wrong about Ross. I have no doubt about it; the man's a jerk. To think I ever felt guilty. I never teased him. That was all in his mind. I promised my life to him and how does he treat me? The minute I turn my back, he's poking his needle in some nurse. He makes me want to scream!"

"I've never seen you this angry," Wescott said.

"Angry? No, I'm not angry. I'm tired. You put me through six months of guilt here, and I don't think I deserved it. I shouldn't feel guilty about nobody. Not Ross, not Drake, not even Brad."

"Brad?"

"Yeah, especially, Brad. I was so mad at myself. I know I used him. I used him to get even with Drake. And you got me to feel guilty about that. But you know what; Brad knew the situation. He knew all about Drake, and he proposed to me anyway. I loved Brad. I might not have told him so, but I really did. Why should I be ashamed? I know the kind of person I am, and if they didn't like it, well, that's tough."

Isabel took a long breath and summed up her psychotherapy, "I'm sorry, Dr. Wescott, our session is over."

She closed the door on Wescott and trudged to her room. She fumed about her dilemma. If the cause of her blindness was some obscure brain lesion, how could she trust the doctors to find it? How could she trust them to operate? Or in the worst possible case; what if they said it was inoperable, and the blindness—as she had predicted—was truly permanent?

Isabel held firm to one belief; the only person she truly trusted was herself. Perhaps Drake could offer long-term love and financial support. Perhaps Barry would become a real doctor someday and get to the root cause. But for now, she had to take care of herself. That was her bottom-line therapy.

So she made plans. She made plans to work at the Blind Center full time, plans to live nearby, plans to find a workable commute. She had hope of regaining her vision someday, but for now, reality sufficed. Isabel sensed a long road ahead, but with her reborn spirit—a rekindled confidence—she knew that she could navigate it. By herself if need be.

Only one detail remained; sign the release form and head on home. Isabel packed her bags and made the rounds to say, "Thanks and so long."

With one last stop, she would be good to go. Dr. Wescott would provide the final signature then it would be home sweet home.

Unfortunately, Wescott—stubborn and manipulative as always—had his own terms and conditions to apply. He would sign the release—only after a final therapy session. Instinctively, Isabel sensed a trap. She dreaded another long hour ahead.

"I can sign the paperwork in my room," she told him at his office. "This is a long walk for a short goodbye."

"You should know that I have ulterior motives," Wescott said, "if you've learned anything about me."

"I've learned that you've canceled my next week's appointments. That means you're taking me seriously."

"I've always taken you seriously. Today is no different."

"But?"

Wescott chuckled. "But yes, I do have one last offer."

Isabel shook her head. "Best and *final* offer? I hope so, because I am so ready to book out of this town."

"My plan is this," Wescott said. "If—after our session today—you determine that you've made no progress, then we shake hands and go our separate ways. We'll keep in touch. But as you said, it is best to move on."

Isabel crossed her arms and squirmed in her chair. "What's so different about today?"

"Today," he said with a shaky breath, "is a different tack; unorthodox, in a way. Unlike our last sessions, I want to make you relaxed. Then step by step, we talk about the events leading to the accident."

"I'm already relaxed," Isabel said sternly.

"Do you know much about hypnosis?"

"Hypnosis?" She snickered. "Yeah, I tried it once. I thought it would help me study. At least the therapist told me it would."

"And?"

"I almost failed economics."

"This will be different," he said. "Our first goal is to put your mind at ease. No fear, no distractions. Then we work minute by minute, starting with the morning of the accident."

"And how is hypnosis going to work?" Isabel asked, shaking her head. "I can't even see your spinning crystals."

"There's no hand waving," he said. "I use words and images. Images that you can see yourself. Words that relax you."

"If it's so good, how come you haven't done it before?"

"Isabel, you're finally at the point where you can talk about Brad. I know it's still upsetting, but recently—especially recently—you've been open and honest about your feelings. That's what we need for the treatment."

Isabel shrugged. The hour had already been paid for, and arguing now would only up her agitation. Plus, a one in a million shot at getting her vision restored seemed better than no chance at all.

"Sure, why not?" she said with a familiar sigh. "Let's give it a try."

Wescott urged her to his office recliner. Then he lowered the window shades, mostly for his own benefit. He sat in his usual chair and began at the top of the script.

"First, I want you to settle back and rest your hands on your lap ... That's it. Now I want you to think of a place. Someplace you go to escape. A favorite place. Calm ... peaceful ... you're by yourself. No one else around to bother you."

That seemed easy enough. After all, Isabel did spend most of her waking hours in some kind of daydream or some kind of escape. Finally, she mused, a treatment to relate to. She had her place, and with a single breath she was halfway there.

"Do you see it now?" Wescott asked.

"It's a beach in Carmel." She relaxed with a tiny smile. "Yeah, that's it. A couple years ago, the guys and me went down for a drive. They went out for a beer, and I went for a walk."

"Tell me how you feel."

Another deep breath and Isabel went on, "I remember the sun and how warm it felt. A cool breeze once in a while. I remember the waves and the gulls. It's strange; I can still see the ocean."

Wescott raised the shades until the subdued sunlight splashed on her face. "That's good. The ocean's going to be your home for the next hour. If you feel any pain, go to your beach. Feel the warm sun. Let the breeze cool you. Relax."

Wescott's voice faded into a deep, soft monotone. If he was new at this, it certainly didn't show. For the first session in six and a half months of emotional therapy, Isabel almost enjoyed the session. Soon, she became totally limp. Her arms dangled. Her face became that of a sleeping angel; so innocent, totally trusting.

"Now," he said, "I'll count to ten. Slowly. With each count, you'll feel the stress leave your body. No worries, no problems. Just you and your beach ... One ... Start with your eyes and relax. Two."

Wescott flipped his notes as if reading a script. "Ten," he said. "Now your stress is totally gone. How do you feel?"

She drifted to a near-sleep. She barely heard his voice.

"Isabel," Wescott spoke louder.

"What?" she said in her best do-not-disturb tone.

"Good. Now, I'll count to three. When I reach three, you'll be awake. But when you wake up, it won't be today. It'll be a cool Saturday in November; the morning *after* your Italian dinner with Brad." Wescott shifted in his chair and leaned forward. "Let's begin. One ... Two ... Three. Tell me how you feel."

"Leave me alone. I want to go back to sleep," she growled.

Wescott cleared his throat. He closed his book and waited.

Then Isabel spoke. "Who's calling at this hour?" She twitched her hand and rolled her head. "Yes, Brad. What do you want now?"

"Talk to him, Isabel. Tell me what he wants."

"Of course, I had fun. But call me again when I wake up." She rubbed her eyes, trying to get the sleep out.

"Tell me what he says."

"He wants to have lunch. I told him I couldn't make it."

"Why? Why can't you make it?"

"Don't know," Isabel said, faltering. "I can't remember. I can't—"

"That's fine. Just tell me what happened next."

Isabel paused to gather her strength. She forced herself to move forward. "I told him I was hungry. I wanted some waffles." She laughed. "I said 'bye' and went back to sleep."

She ran her fingers across her temples to hold back the surge of another migraine. The throbbing continued.

"Slow down," Wescott said. "No need to rush. We'll head back to the beach. Remember how relaxing it felt. Listen to the waves."

Isabel went to her safe place. She breathed in the ocean air and let her arms drop. She took on the face of a sleeping babe, and then Wescott yanked her back to that day in November.

"Tell me what happened next."

"I had breakfast, of course. And my mother yelled at me, of course. Same old story. She accused me of staying out too late and sleeping around. Why does she always do that? Why didn't she ever believe me? I just had to get out; get in my car and drive away."

Wescott pushed the same routine. When Isabel got excited, he would calm her down at her beach. Step by step, they walked through the minutes of that forgotten day. Gradually and painfully, her memories returned; the trip to the mall, lunch by herself at McDonald's, shopping at Macy's, coming home and talking to Brad.

"He told me to get my pretty butt over there. He said to dress warm and bring a scarf. Now, what was he up to? When I got to his apartment, he showed me; two tickets to the Stanford game. So what's the big deal? It's just a football game. I mean, who cares about that? He almost had to push me out. No way did I want to go."

Once again, she stood at the edge. Her lips quivered with every new word. She couldn't do it. She couldn't take another step.

"No, Brad. Please. Don't open the door. I can't get in. Don't make me do it." Isabel shook her hand and waved at her make-believe van. She fought with all the strength she had. She snapped her eyes open as if the van and Brad had appeared in front of her. But she saw nothing more than her memories.

Wescott leaned in front of her face, but she never blinked. No question about it; the situation had become out of control. "Close the door and step away. Move back. Now! Move back. Don't look at the van." Wescott's voice trembled more than hers as he pleaded for a safe return.

"Isabel, listen to me. Brad's not there anymore. You have your hand on the door. Don't open it until you're ready."

"I can't. I can't."

"Okay, we've gone far enough. I want you to relax as I bring you back home; home to your beach, home to your safe place." Dr. Wescott—the world's most careful psychiatrist—squirmed in his chair, seeming more nervous than his patient. He ended the day's session flustered and breathless—but not before Isabel added her own summary.

She woke from the trance in a cold sweat. She couldn't wait to try it again. "I saw him!" she nearly cried. "I swear I saw him! He was standing right in front of me. It was Brad. I know it was Brad."

"Yes, I believe you. And if you believe me, then trust me. Realize that our session is over for today. Rest. Take care of yourself and come back tomorrow. Okay?"

"Yes," she said. "Definitely, I will be here."

They both rested for one full day and night then they reconvened. This was it. Wescott canceled his morning appointments and penciled in Isabel for as long as she needed. For this session, there would be no stopping, no turning back, no hiding from the pain.

With barely a nudge, Isabel fell deep into a trance. She knew that she could trust her doctor. She also knew that this was her last and most desperate chance. Once again, she stepped through the day, getting so far as to climb into the van with Brad. They rode to the Stanford game. Then she smiled.

"He was like a kid again," she said. "His team was winning. He was yelling. Yeah, him and twenty thousand others. What a mob. I was so afraid I'd get lost. When the game ended, I held on tight to Brad's hand. I wasn't about to lose him. All those people pushing, shoving. Brad; he loved every minute of it. I could see it in his eyes. Not just the game, it was the excitement and the noise he loved. And me at his side. I honestly believe that Brad was happy. Then I told him. I told him that I loved him. He turned to me and smiled."

Isabel cried a tear and went silent.

"Go on. What happened next?"

"We got to the van," she whispered, out of breath. Like a marathon runner, she forced out each word, syllable by syllable.

"Don't think of the van," Wescott said. "Tell me how you feel."

She fell quiet. Then she laughed. "I felt like a high school kid. I felt nervous. Jitters. It was a good feeling though. I couldn't stop laughing. I don't know why."

She paused to catch her breath and then skipped forward. "I can see the traffic. Cars are moving but not too fast. We got to Middlefield Road, and we talked about a late snack. No cars now, but the lights are all red. Who cares? It was another chance to fool around. Whenever we stopped, Brad would lean over and give me a kiss. It was fun. I couldn't help but laugh.

"The radio, yeah, the radio was playing a Creedence song. *Down on the Corner*. That was it. I tried to sing. I couldn't remember half the words. The light was red, so he kissed me a good, long kiss. I saw the light change. I told him that we'd better get moving. He smiled and kissed me again."

Isabel stopped. For her, it was the end of the story. She remained deep in a trance, blocked by the nightmare that lay ahead. One more step to the end of the road. It became Wescott's job to push her forward.

"Then what happened?" he asked but got no response. "Don't think of it. Move forward and tell me what you see."

Tears began to fall. Now, every agonizing memory surfaced and played for Isabel like a slow-motion film. There was no way around it. She stepped into the van again and got ready to crash. She snapped her head up and froze in panic. Filtered sunlight splashed on her face. She didn't squint and didn't look away. She couldn't move; couldn't stop the tears.

"I'm looking right at him," she cried. "But I can't see. He's only a shadow. I can't see his face. God, that light! It can't be a train! It can't. Brad, please. Please get out of the way. He's looking straight at me, but he doesn't hear. I can't scream. Nothing's coming out. Oh God, the explosion! Can't breathe." Her eyes darted in a frantic beat. She didn't know where to turn, where to hide.

Wescott pushed her on. "Don't stop, Isabel. Tell me what you see."

"Then the light moved. Now I can see him. I see his face. Oh dear God, he looks so scared. I can't help you, Brad. I'm sorry. I'm so sorry."

Isabel cried. She waved her hands at the sunlight; if only she could chase it away. It was no use. She buried her face in her palms, and the tears kept coming. She dropped her hands and turned to the doctor.

"I saw it all," she cried. "I saw the van. I saw Brad. And I saw him die in front of my eyes. Oh dear Lord, what did I do wrong?"

Wescott looked at her. "It wasn't your fault, Isabel," he said. "There wasn't a thing you could do." He moved closer and grabbed her hands. "Isabel, did you hear me? It was not your fault."

"Yes, yes. I heard you. And God forgive me, Brad; I can see again."

Chapter *22*

IN THE CORNER stood a white cane. When Isabel saw it, she vowed never to touch it; or look at it again. This was one part of her life that she would rather forget. Eight months at the hospital, eight months of unbearable torture. Up to this point, she had never been sure if Dr. Wescott was part of the problem or the ultimate solution. The continued probing and digging into her mind was as painful as any compound fracture.

But here sat the man who had just given her sight. She looked at his face. Where were the deep Freudian eyes of a psychological master? Where was the awesome, overwhelming figure of a man that Isabel had always imagined? Instead, Wescott patiently sat there with an honest smile and the hint of a tear forming in his baby blue eyes. Apparently, being a savior was all in a day's work.

Isabel cried for the longest time in his office that day. She felt totally split between the terrifying vision of Brad's last moments and the beautiful sight of an old coffee cup on the walnut desk. After a while, she stood, walked around the office, and forced herself to appreciate the view in front of her eyes. For months, she could only smell the reference books on the back shelf, the dust on the window sill, the Hazelnut coffee scent that permeated the room.

Now, every shape and shadow burst out with a new excitement; the curves of a leather sofa, the exquisite rainbows from a Waterford lamp, the delicate leaves of a ficus in the corner. She looked around for the first and last time. "I think I want to go home."

"Isabel, listen to me. This is not something we can rush. You have to let your eyes—and your head—get accustomed."

"What do you mean?"

"You just relived the worst trauma of your life. Believe it or not, you're still unstable. You can see now, but you could have a relapse. You've come a long way, and I don't want you to fall back."

"Don't worry. I have no intentions of looking back." She reached for the door. "Oh, and by the way, Dr. Wescott, I came here by myself, and I intend to leave the same way."

"You mean?"

"Yes, I'm going back to my room, and I don't want you or your secretary to follow."

Despite Wescott's objections, Isabel left the office by herself and spent the next hour strolling through the hospital corridors. She got lost more than once on the way to her room. After making so many trips in the dark, her vision had become a total distraction, a beautiful distraction at that. No complaints in the least.

She walked outside to a patio garden and knelt beside a bed of dazzling red marigolds. It was her first visit outdoors without her dark glasses; her first visit to a garden where she could do more than sniff the flowers.

She lifted a marigold and held it close. To see this again—to see anything in the Stanford courtyard—seemed an answer to her prayers. Isabel sighed. The fragrance and the sight made her think of Marie's garden. It reminded her of flowering vines of clematis, lemonade at a backyard table, and long, friendly talks with Brad and Marie. It reminded her of a wedding that they had planned. She felt sorry that things had to change.

This was the saddest—and the happiest—day of Isabel's life at the Medical Center. Her memory had returned, and now she vowed to leave it behind. God had given her a second chance, and she felt determined not to waste it by dwelling on the past and fretting over things she couldn't control.

When she got back to her room, she hung up a calendar and counted the days to her final release. Of course, that release took another two months of physical therapy, twenty hours of emotional counseling, two dozen X-rays, a million blood tests, and just for good luck—a CAT scan and visual acuity test.

"Any chance for a relapse?" Isabel asked.

"In a few weeks," Dr. Linoff said, "you'll be as good as new—if you take it slow."

"Except for a few nightmares and this pain in my leg."

"Give it time," Linoff said. "You'll get back to normal."

Isabel sighed. *Back to normal;* what did that mean for someone like her? Sure, her mother had become a changed woman; despite a few more gray hairs and more creases on her forehead. Charlene beamed continuous smiles on the drive home from the hospital. That was a welcome sight. It felt so different from a year ago today. But would it be the same old house, same old father, same old boyfriend? Isabel felt desperate for change, and after that purgatory at Stanford, she refused to settle for the status quo.

She arrived home and immediately saw her next miracle. As they pulled into the driveway, Leo stood next to the open hood of the Capri; a wrench in one hand, a greasy rag in the other. The blade of a screwdriver peeked out from his rear pocket.

He walked to Isabel and told her, "I got the oil changed, and your tune-up's almost done." He kicked his tool box closer to the car and moved closer to Isabel for a welcome home hug. At the last second, he noticed a grease smear on his hands. "Sorry, we'll save it for later."

Isabel understood but hugged him nevertheless. "It feels good to be home." Her sense of smell was still working overtime. Somewhere on the old man, she picked up the scent of dime-store aftershave and the pungent aroma of vinegar and water. "You cleaned my windows?"

"And waxed your car with Carnauba." Leo showed her the can. He moved to the trunk and wiped off a spot.

Isabel yanked open the door. The new-car smell had long-ago vanished. It was more like coming home to an old friend. *Thank-you Drake for continuing the payments.* She sat on the soft vinyl seat and slid her hand along the steering wheel. She fought a fragment of memory that took her to a dark November road in Palo Alto. So many mixed feelings. Would she ever have the courage to drive again? Would she ever be able to face the onslaught of rush hour traffic or the headlights of oncoming cars?

She dropped her hand to the gear shift and gradually felt the resurgence of a long-lost freedom and independence. After almost a year in a cramped hospital room, she felt eager to reach out and explore a world that had teased her. Isabel knew that it would take a while to get used to driving again, but there was no question in her mind; once she got on the road, there would be no turning back.

Isabel stepped out of her car. She heard the screen door open and heavy feet coming on fast. She spun just in time to catch a glance of a hundred-pound Saint Bernard puppy. The dog headed straight for her hips. Too late to dodge, no time to beg for mercy, she braced herself as Candy nudged her against the side of the Capri.

"So help me, my next Bernard's going to be a dry mouth." She leaned over and hugged Candy's neck.

Charlene preferred to express her welcome home affections in a more private moment later in the week. On a quiet Thursday afternoon, she coaxed Isabel into the kitchen for a pitcher of raspberry lemonade and a long-overdue lesson on how to make the perfect Mexican sweet bread. Coils, braids, turtles, and fish. According to Charlene, "Every shape tastes a bit different; each bread is for a different occasion."

Isabel wondered what kind of shape was appropriate for an occasion like this; mother and daughter, cooking and chatting like the best of friends. They shared a piece of bread, love, and hope for tomorrow. Some surprises could be good.

Even Isabel had to admit that home had become better. But unfortunately for her, work was getting worse. Every day, she faithfully drove herself to the Center for the Blind. She trained the older people with macular degeneration and younger patients with ocular trauma. She loved the feeling she got when her clients learned how to read, eat, and live independently.

It was tough at times. Occasionally, she would flash back to her own blindness and to the circumstances that led up to it. But whenever that happened, she would try to recall the many doctors, staff, and volunteers who had helped her when she was down. They helped her, and now, in her own small way, she could return the favor.

She went to the Center and tried to work the best she could, but lately, she didn't feel part of the club. Coping with blindness was commendable, but recovering her sight—totally—led to coworker confusion, misunderstanding, and a fair amount of jealousy. Isabel left the Blind Center—forever—with a few parting words.

"I will never apologize for recovering. I've got perfect eyes now and not one speck of guilt. And *that* I can live with."

***

With her old career fading to black, she picked up the pieces and fashioned together a new direction with seemingly endless possibilities. With Drake's steadfast support and with only a few minor changes, Isabel, bit by bit, eased herself into a high-gear lifestyle that reminded her of the better days. Thankfully, Drake had tempered his ambitions with patience and understanding. Likewise, Isabel had new ambitions but plenty of impatience. They seemed to balance.

She kicked off the first of the new changes in Drake's life when she went to his house in Palo Alto. She stepped into his custom van and immediately ordered some new decor.

"The stereo, leather seats, and footrest can stay," she said. "But the wet bar and the radar detector—they're gone."

"No problem," Drake said. "Anything else?"

"Yeah. Where's the roadster?" She pointed at a red Mercedes-Benz 450 coupe.

"How do you mean?"

"When I last saw it, the Benz was silver."

"Sorry," Drake said. "I loaned it to Ben, and he wrapped it around a tree. It was last year's model; so no loss."

Isabel cringed. "Slow down and be safe." She glared at Drake and Barry as they helped her settle into her seat. "Because I am not going to tell you again."

Drake nodded then drove them straight to the auto shop to fix up the van.

Slow down became her motto for the road, but everywhere else it seemed that she had a lot of catching up to do. In the months that followed—with Drake and Barry at her side—Isabel drifted a million miles from her tragic memories. She vowed to replace the old with the new. She looked forward to filling her journal with long-overdue adventure.

She preferred gentle excursions at first; sailing the Monterey Bay, leisurely flights to Tahoe, dining at Fisherman's Wharf. Then slowly—and gratefully—the elegant life returned. Croissants in Paris, designer dresses in Milan, competitive skydiving in Sao Paulo, Brazil. Isabel embraced anything that could put distance between her and her past. The road to healing seemed to be any road that led her down a new path.

She counted her recent blessings; a temporary job in Silicon Valley, loving, less controlling parents at home, a playful dog for the backyard, and a man to cater every whim. She had every right to move forward and never look back. She had a chance for a fresh start and a clean break from her past. New beginnings. A renaissance of sorts. But she knew that—eventually—the call would come. And she knew exactly how she would answer.

Isabel checked into her room at the Hotel Vancouver in British Columbia, Canada and found a message waiting. She shivered as the reality took hold. The stunning views of downtown Vancouver and the Pacific Coast Range could not assuage her near-overwhelming anxiety as she read the jarring and to-the-point note; *Call Officer Grissom. Trial about to begin.*

Suddenly, her head swarmed with nagging images; a defense attorney pointing an accusing finger, court reporters straining to hear every word, a black-robed judge urging her to get to the point, a defendant taking on the face of the devil himself. She saw a dozen overwhelming images and only one logical solution.

"I have to go back," she told Drake. "Without me, there's no testimony, no trial, no justice. I knew that it would come to this, and I knew that I couldn't run forever. I'm not going to use the word 'closure,' because for me, there's no such thing. Brad will be with me forever. I'm sorry, Drake, that's how it is. But the sooner we have the trial, the sooner I can move on; move on to whatever is next."

"I've seen plenty of trials," Drake said. "I know what attorneys can do to people."

"You don't have to remind me of that," Isabel said with a smirk. "I've dated one off and on for what, over two years now?"

"Point is; this is a turning point and purely *your* decision. But if you do decide to go ahead, I'll be beside you every step of the way."

"I wouldn't expect anything less. And yes, I've already decided; I *will* go ahead, and we will go to trial."

Isabel stood firm. She chose to set aside the cross country runs and the luxurious vacations ...for now. She made up her mind to focus on her one and only mission; get ready for court and stand for the truth. It felt long overdue.

She got home and set up her meetings with Officer Grissom, the DA, the assistant DA, and each of the Stanford doctors who had helped her through her medical and emotional situations. They had a lot of meetings to plan and a ton of details to organize. Isabel did her best to cooperate.

Unfortunately, one detail had been critically overlooked. She had mentioned the upcoming trial to Charlene and quickly realized her first mistake; don't expect support or constructive advice from someone who was afraid to talk to the white bagger at the neighborhood grocery store.

"They'll laugh at you," Charlene said. "If not in front of your face, then behind your back. They'll make it sound like it was your fault; or that you lied and made everything up. In the end, nothing will matter. Nothing will change. They only real difference; you'll feel miserable."

"I honestly don't know what's going to happen, Mom. Maybe they'll laugh at me, maybe they'll listen. The only thing I can say for certain is that if I say nothing—if I *do* nothing—then I *will* feel miserable. Probably for the rest of my life. At the very least, I have to try. I owe that to Brad. I owe his family. I owe everyone who's helped me and believed in me. I suppose I owe it to myself to get a hint of justice for what I've been through."

Isabel sighed. She had a feeling; what she had been through was simply the start of what was to come.

A month before the trial, the depositions began. Now, when Isabel talked about the accident, she didn't have a warm, comfortable, private office to relax in. She sat in the open, with every move being watched and every word transcribed. She lived a recurring nightmare. Every visit to the past became another stab to the heart. Brad; that poor man. How often could she sit and watch him die? For the attorneys, it seemed more of a sport. How did she know Brad? How did they spend the day? What did he have to drink? How fast did he drive? The questions—and the answers—seemed equally brutal.

Half the time, she answered the questions. Half the time she demanded the attorneys to quit. Throughout the entire round of depositions, Wescott stood beside her; guiding her, consoling her, and helping her to survive.

That was fine for a deposition. But soon enough, Isabel would have to walk to the witness stand, and who would help her then? Not Wescott, not Drake, not the prosecuting attorney. Once she raised her hand and took that solemn oath; she would have no one to rely on except herself. It was a scary thought, but it had to be done.

With the trial scheduled a week away, the DA had one last piece of advice; "Don't try to impress anyone. Just say what's on your mind, and there's no way we can lose."

Isabel laughed. "Can't lose? Come on, you can do better than that."

She knew that those lawyers could rip her apart. She knew how they could use their perverted logic and twist every one of her syllables into words that she would never recognize. And how did she know? She had dated one of them for many frustrating years. And Drake—the one attorney that she truly trusted—knew exactly how to win the case.

"Leave the witness alone. Let Isabel tell her story. Let the jury listen. Coach her all you want, but in the end, she'll wind up telling it her way."

The DA told her to expect a two-day trial. Isabel wasn't sure if that was a good strategy or bad. The defense might have been confident; two days for a trial, acquittal, then the defendant heads back to work. The prosecuting attorney might have been confident. The basic truth, when boiled down to the fundamentals, could have been told in an hour or less. Either way, Isabel expected that the two days would seem like forever.

On the morning of the trial, she faced her first challenge. She stood in front of her closet, sorted through her clothes, and picked out an appropriate ensemble. Her dark blue cotton dress seemed the best choice. It stopped at the knees and had a Sunday School neckline to show off a delicate strand of J.C. Penny pearls. She slipped on a silver bracelet from Macy's. To complete the image, she stepped into her dark blue hose and half-inch heels. Isabel showed herself to be no less than stunning. But was she believable? In a couple hours, she and everyone else would find out.

She drove herself to Drake's house. From there, they headed straight for the courthouse. Charlene, Leo, and the rest of the family were never told of the trial date. This fight was between Isabel and the drunk. And no man, woman, or child could distract her from the task ahead.

Drake led her to the courtroom door and then fell behind. Isabel took a deep breath and moved forward, no hesitation. She stepped through the doors, and everyone faced her way. The courtroom hushed. No question about it; she exuded confidence, charm, and poise. With her one moment in the spotlight, she sparkled like a jewel.

She walked up and took a seat directly behind the DA. Next to her sat Wescott. His job was to keep the medical situation under control and assure that his patient was not blindly pushed over the edge. Behind Isabel, sat the Thompsons—Ed and Marie. Their job was to offer much-appreciated moral support and later sue the defendant for every cent he had.

Barry sat next to Drake in the back row. From there, they could keep notes on anything or anyone that spoke, moved, or looked the least bit suspicious. Isabel believed it more than a small comfort to know that they were there. She felt nervous enough; surrounded by unfamiliar faces. Friendly eyes in a sea of strangers went a long way to balancing the view.

Then she glanced to the left and got a perfect view of the defense. What a frightening sight they were. That had to be Huffnagle in the middle. Even though Isabel had never seen him or a picture of him, she knew the face of a killer. He sat there; stoic and proud, in his best pillar of the community, pinstripe Italian suit. Thinning gray hair, loose jowls, bushy eyebrows; this man cast a dark shadow. He turned and glared over his nose.

"Don't look at him," the DA said. "You'll turn to stone."

"Don't worry," she said. One glance was enough for a lifetime.

After a while, the jury marched in. Isabel made a quick count; six men—two black, the rest white. Six women—one Hispanic, the rest white. She wondered; whom or what did these people worship—physicians, God, or justice? And could they understand the difference?

"What about me?" Isabel asked. "When do I testify?"

"You come this afternoon. I want the jury to think about you overnight."

Isabel nodded.

By mid-morning, the trial got seriously underway. First came the facts. The prosecutor stepped up and presented his case, including; Officer Grissom's description of the accident scene, the blood alcohol report, cause of death of the victim. After lunch, the Petersons arrived as key witnesses for the prosecution. In less than an hour, they had corroborated the police version of the events and set the stage for the final prosecution witness.

When the bailiff called Isabel's name, her heart skipped a beat. Her hands trembled as she unsteadily rose to her feet. Finally, the months of anticipation culminated in a him-versus-her battle for the hearts and respect of the jurors. A tragic November event had to be distilled into a few believable words. Somehow, she had to convey the total sense of loss and despair that she felt. All eyes in the courtroom turned her way.

She took her oath, sat down, and cleared her mind. She told her story straight from her soul. In a matter of minutes, she calmly worked her way to the final scene, revealing the truth to a dead quiet courtroom.

"The game ended, and we began to drive home or to a snack— we couldn't decide. I was in no hurry; I wanted to spend every second that I could with Brad. We stopped at the light. I remember the music and I remember holding his hand. He kissed me once and teased me about the wedding. Brad; he was so sweet. He couldn't help but smile. Then I looked up when the light turned green. I thought there was a car behind us, so I told him he'd better move. You know, before the light turned red again. He glanced ahead, and we started a left turn.

"Then I saw the light. Oh God, they were coming so fast. I didn't know what to do. I couldn't scream. Didn't have time to—" Isabel looked at Wescott and then at the jury. She cried and told them with a wavering voice, "He hit us. He came through the van and hit us. I didn't know what was happening. I heard the bang—loud like an explosion. I saw the flying glass. I saw the steering wheel crush Brad's chest. I saw his head slam against the collapsing door. Then I saw nothing. I swear, as long as I live, I will never forget what I saw that night. The man that I loved—the man I had promised to marry—he was gone in a second. Dead. And there was not a thing I could do. Brad never ... *we* never had a chance."

Long faces hung on the jury with barely a dry eye. Isabel's account would stay with them for the rest of the night and most of the next morning. Who knew what they were thinking. Who could tell if the feeling would last. But Isabel had told her story the best way she could, and no one laughed at her. No one chased her away. If nothing else came from this trial, her story would count as a small token of victory and vindication.

By mid-morning of the second day, it became the defendant's turn to speak his mind. Huffnagle moved to center stage, and Isabel finally saw what she was up against.

The defense attorney rose from his seat. "State your name and occupation."

"Robert Huffnagle. Physician. Orthopedics."

"Where do you practice?"

"In a Palo Alto clinic, affiliated with the Stanford Medical Center. But I should add that I'm also actively involved in the Senior Health Care Alliance, the Camino Center for Etiological studies, and I've also acted as an advisor to the university Board of Trustees."

Now the jury knew; to keep this man away from his job—for a single day—would be a great disservice to the community, a disaster for his patients. The many years of experience, years of education and specialized knowledge—an entire career—in jeopardy because of this unwarranted distraction. To listen to Huffnagle, it would appear that *he* was the innocent victim, *he* was the one who had suffered.

"I had two drinks after work," he said, "which is my personal limit. After the second one, I looked at my watch. It was about a quarter to twelve, so I knew I had to get home. My wife gets a little jealous, if you know what I mean." He chuckled, looked at the guys in the jury then got serious.

"I don't know exactly how fast I was going. I knew the traffic was light, and I could see a half-mile ahead. It could've been five or six miles over the limit at the most. I've been down that street almost every week for the past year. I know every light by heart. I have each one memorized. I got to Middlefield Road, and the light in front of me was green, changing to yellow. I never gave it a second thought. I never thought that anyone would do that. Then from nowhere, this van jumped the light and cut in front of me. I swear; I never had a chance to slam on the brakes. It happened so fast."

Huffnagle hung his head and covered his face as if he had rehearsed every careful word, every subtle move. Shortly, Huffnagle stepped down from the stand. He shuffled to his seat and listened quietly as his attorney whispered in his ear.

Isabel could almost hear a "Well done."

Following Huffnagle, came a merry band of supporting witnesses; mostly from his night at the bar, mostly corroborating his story. No doubt, they had driven home drunk themselves.

Closing arguments came shortly after lunch, but it was hard to say if the jury listened. They adjourned to the deliberation room, and less than two hours later, they returned to the courtroom with a verdict. Isabel had barely finished her lemonade when she was asked, once again, to take her place behind the DA.

"Toss of the dice," the DA said. "After years of working with juries, I have yet to develop a knack to read their faces."

Isabel shared the ambivalence. She gave the jurors a glance, half-hoping for a smile, half-fearing a frown. When she saw no response, she closed her eyes and faced forward. Favorable outcome or not, the decision seemed brutally swift. The judge ordered the defendant to rise and asked the jury foreman to read the verdict.

The foreman rose. Looking directly at the judge, he spoke clearly and concisely. "On the count of driving under the influence, we the jury, find the defendant, Robert Huffnagle; guilty. On the count of manslaughter, we find the defendant; guilty."

And that was it. The foreman took his seat, and the judge made a note. Otherwise, there was no courtroom chatter, applause, or griping about injustice. Short, sweet, and to the point. The judge thanked the members of the jury, dismissed them, and stated that the defendant could remain free until sentencing in two weeks. The proceeding was closed. There was a sigh of relief on the prosecution side and a somber mood for the defense.

Now Robert Huffnagle had officially become a convicted felon. Unofficially, he was a remorseless killer. He sat stone-faced and frozen, barely a blink from his deadpan eyes. His wife sat by his side. Her eyes grew wide and wet, no doubt totally unprepared for a verdict like this.

Even if her husband got off with probation or a suspended sentence, a felony conviction was impossible to erase—a heavy anchor for any professional man and a risk for his medical license. Not to mention the gossip at the bridge club and embarrassment at the yacht club. Both Huffnagle and his wife were bound to suffer.

Two weeks passed, and the same players appeared in court. Huffnagle and his flock of attorneys begged for leniency and implored the judge to consider the patients who would be adversely affected and severely distressed.

"The defendant," the defense attorney said, "is a respected physician and community leader. To lose his services for any duration would be a detriment to those in need. Dr. Huffnagle has acquired years of specialized education and experience; skills he has put to use in treating a diverse group.

"From patients, like Mrs. Wagner; an elderly lady who could be anyone's grandmother. He treated her fractured hip and allowed her to walk again; independently and without pain. There's also Manuel Rodriguez; a seven-year-old boy from Honduras. He arrived at the clinic with calcium deficiency. Dr. Huffnagle has treated him at no cost to Manuel's family. Now Manuel can walk again—and play— with other boys his age.

"Your Honor, Dr. Huffnagle has learned his lesson. He admits to his mistakes. Question is; how do we proceed? An alcohol treatment program—yes, I think we can agree. Or community service. The city had a crying need for medical assistance to the poor and disadvantaged. Dr. Huffnagle is willing to expand his role and apply his skills. This is a fine man, your Honor. He helps people, and he wants to continue helping ... unabated. Let us not punish ourselves—our community—while we struggle to move forward."

And with that impassioned plea, the defense rested the defendant's fate on the mercy of the court.

Now it became Isabel's turn. As one of the victims in the case, she was entitled to make a personal statement before sentence was pronounced. She, of course, had her own definition of justice. Twenty years in prison or a lifetime behind bars—whichever was longer—might have been a good start. She crammed her notes into her handbag, glanced at the witnesses in the courtroom, and then faced the judge. With a trembling start, she said what had to be said.

"Your Honor, I've had a long time to think about this. What would I do, what would I say if I ever got to this point? How could I explain the feelings I've built up for almost a year and a half? I'm not sure if I can explain anything. I think about the accident, and I think about justice. Somehow, I can never get the two to match. I don't know. It still doesn't make sense. No matter what happens, how can anything be fair?

"I lost a year of my life. That's one year that I'll never get back. While my friends went to school, I got to know every doctor in the ICU of Stanford. How could I think about economics or accounting? I was laid up in a cast and confined to a bed.

"Yes, I had opportunities to read. I had plenty of books; from novels to California history. Problem was; I couldn't see a single one—for no other reason than an avoidable crash in the middle of the night. It was horrible to be blind. It took my entire strength simply to survive. Eat and survive. That was it. That was the extent of what I did. No school, no job, no traveling, no nothing. An entire year—gone because of that man.

"I'll have nightmares from now on. Whenever I step into a car, I can't help but remember the crash. I see the windshield, and I feel my head moving toward it. No matter what happens, your Honor, I will *never* forget.

"But I am alive. And for that, I thank God. But what about Brad? His dreams, his ambitions, and his life were gone in a flash. My fiancée died that night. I'll never see him again. I'll never hold his hand or walk by his side. If I live to be a hundred, I will never forget the love I should've had. I don't know about justice, your Honor, but please, whatever you do, keep that man from killing again."

Huffnagle remained unmoved. He had stopped listening when Isabel had begun talking. To him, there was only one opinion that truly counted. And that opinion came straight from the judge; the fifty-year-old, university-educated, conservative, white man on the bench.

Professional courtesy aside, the judge quickly got to his point. He barely acknowledged Isabel and looked directly at Huffnagle. "In sentencing, I consider several factors. I look at the defendant's record, his willingness to change, and any show of remorse. I evaluate the overall threat—the danger—to the community. However, standing in the professional community is *not* a factor, nor is history of meritorious service.

"Regrettably in this case, you, Dr. Huffnagle, have shown no willingness to change. This was not your first alcohol-related offense. It has been almost a year and a half since the accident; that is more than adequate time to enlist a treatment program. It is well beyond the limit to seek professional help. I find no evidence of reformation. Contrary to your claims, I see no signs of remorse. That means I have no choice in the matter."

The judge paused to catch his breath and to make a note. Then he went straight to the bottom line. "The defendant is hereby sentenced to ten years in the California State Corrections; sentence to commence immediately upon the close of this hearing. Prisoner to be remanded to the custody of the bailiff."

The judge pounded his gavel, stood, and promptly exited the courtroom.

Huffnagle sat like a rock. No suspended sentence. No probation. No chance to head out and party. Huffnagle froze as if the words failed to sink in, as if the judge was bound to return with a "just kidding, you are free to leave."

When it became clear that the judge was not returning, Huffnagle's wife began to understand—and react. She cried, louder and louder, until her sobs filled every nook of the courtroom.

Huffnagle, the rock, turned a deep shade of crimson and began to shake. He stared straight ahead.

Isabel breathed a heavy sigh of relief as a transient joy swept through her body. She flashed an uneasy smile at the DA for a job well done. The moment passed. There was no closure here and no lasting sense of joy. After what had happened to Brad and Isabel, today's sentence became merely one step out of the abyss. No apology, jail time, or public outrage could ever compensate for her sense of loss.

When the gavel pounded, she simply heard, "move on and do the best you can." Perhaps today's sentence could allow her to do that. The DA offered her a warm handshake as he ushered her away from the beleaguered defense team and toward the courtroom exit. Isabel turned her back on Huffnagle, eager to put distance between her and him.

Then bam! Huffnagle slammed his fist on the table in front of him. He turned toward Isabel and growled like an old, beaten dog. "Jesus Christ! You lousy, lying wetback! Don't think this is the end of it. It's not even close. You watch your back, girl, 'cause you're gonna get yours. I don't care if it takes ten years or twenty—you're gonna regret crossing me. I'll tell ya this—you got away with nothing. You hear me—nothing!"

Huffnagle flailed his arms and glared at Isabel until the bailiff restrained him and dragged him down the hall to the holding cell.

Case closed? Apparently not.

Chapter **23**

"IT'S OVER," Marie Thompson said. "Trust me, he'll be locked away until he's too old to drive anything but a wheelchair."

"Did you see that look in his eyes?" Isabel asked. "He meant every word."

"Doesn't matter. After we get through with him, he won't have a dime to his name. That means you can forget about the appeals. By the time he gets out, he'll be a sixty-five-year-old felon. Who's going to listen to him then?"

Isabel and Marie sat at a café in downtown Palo Alto. When last they were there, they had cause to celebrate. Brad and Isabel had just become engaged, and there were wedding plans to be made; church, wedding dress, flowers, photographers, honeymoon, and happiness thereafter. The good old days, they both agreed.

Now, for what it was worth, they celebrated again. It was a small victory to be sure; sending that man to jail seemed only partial retribution for the crime committed. These days, they hungered for any hint of optimism. They drank and talked and reminisced for as long as they could. They talked about Brad, his father, his family, and a marriage that could've been. It was all harmless speculation for two women who would probably never meet again.

Too bad, Isabel thought. *Too bad that things couldn't have been different.* Marie would've made a great mother-in-law or a good friend. Now, when she saw Marie, she couldn't help but think about her son. And that, she was sorry, was no way to stay healthy. Isabel topped her iced tea with two spoons of sugar. She took a last sip then stood to leave. She hugged Marie; then it was "goodbye and wish you the best of luck." A minute later they walked apart and closed the door behind.

"It's over," Isabel said to Charlene as they brought out the supper dishes. The scent of salsa and corn chips filled the kitchen and once again reminded her that it was good to be home. "The trial ended two weeks ago. The sentencing today."

"Guilty?" Charlene asked, raising an eyebrow.

"Beyond a reasonable doubt. With jail time—and plenty of it. I wasn't sure if it would happen, but now that it has, well, I'm a totally relieved."

"I'm glad you're not disappointed." Charlene scooped out a ladle of refried beans. She plopped it onto Leo's plate as Leo washed up in the bathroom. "I know that some people can be mean. I know that some people can't see what's inside of you. But I know that you have a good heart, *Mija*. I don't want you to think I was ever mean. If I say things—if I do things—it's only because I want to protect you; whether you need it or not."

"I know, Mom. And it's okay. It's okay if you see me as your little girl. I can live with that ... for now." Isabel smiled. "Someday, you'll see me grown up. Someday, I won't need protection. I'll come across mean people, and I'll handle them on my own. But if you tell me that you'll *love* me forever then I can't ask for much more than that. How does that sound, Mom?"

"You know you don't have to ask," Charlene said. "You know how I feel."

***

Lately, even the simplest of chores in San Jose left Isabel with some of her fondest memories. A trip to the neighborhood *carniceria*—far from Harrods of London—allowed her to fill each of her five senses with a special treat. The pungent scent of pico de gallo, the floppy feel of corn tortillas, the bright pinks of Mexican sweet bread, the crunch of tortilla chips mixed with mouthwatering guacamole.

At the store, she collected each of those for her mother, plus the usual gallon of whole milk, whole grain cereal, and a dozen eggs. Shopping seemed less of a chore and more of an opportunity to rebuild a new life based on the simplest of pleasures.

Isabel had no complaints, especially when the butcher, Carlos, carved his *carne asada* with a smile. Of course, occasionally even the simplest events left her with mixed memories that were bound to remain with her for a lifetime.

In the checkout line of the *carniceria*, Isabel noticed a vaguely familiar shape. From behind, the woman reminded her of Colette; same figure, height, and brunette hair color. She eased to the woman's side then wavered. The woman had Colette's height, but her slouch made her appear frail. She had Colette's face but had way too many wrinkles. With dark sunglasses and long bangs of split ends, Isabel had to ask to be sure.

"Colette?" she asked, cautiously.

Colette turned unsteadily to face Isabel. Her face suddenly flushed as if she had been surprised or embarrassed.

"Isabel?" Colette said, her mouth gaping. Almost instinctively, she slid a box of Cheerios next to her six pack of Coors on the checkout belt. "Wow, I did not expect to see you here."

"Some things change," Isabel said. "Some do not. And yes, I am still living at home and still shopping the same stores, including this one." She slid her Gucci purse between her elbow and ribs so that the designer brand couldn't be seen.

"How's your mom?" Colette asked, her breath hinting of cigarettes, her crooked teeth splotched in yellow.

"Same situation; part of her has changed, part has not. So, that would be better, I suppose. How about yourself, Colette? It's been, well, it's been a while since you saw you last."

"Johnny and me, we keep busy. Yeah, we got stuff going on. This and that, you know."

"Johnny—he's your ...?"

"Boyfriend. Roommate. Well, so far. We'll see." Colette pushed a loaf of white bread against her Cheerios and backed it up with her basket. She fidgeted and furtively glanced at the exit door.

No doubt, Colette wished to make a quick exit and disappear with little more than a parting word. Caught off guard and out of her element, she seemed more like a frightened rabbit than a long-lost friend.

Isabel felt inclined to leave her with the parting words, *Well, it was good to see you, Colette. I'll tell Mom that I bumped into you.*

Other than a box of cereal and a bag of tortillas, what did she and Colette have in common now? They had obviously followed widely separate paths, but for some reason, those separate paths had momentarily crossed. Coincidence, destiny, or a meaningless encounter; Isabel nonetheless sensed a friend in need; a straggler at the side of the road.

"Colette, what would you say to a cup of coffee?"

Colette grimaced. She glanced at Isabel then slid her cash and food stamps to the clerk. "Sounds good," she said, "but my carton of milk is going to spoil. Maybe a rain check?"

"Not good enough," Isabel said. "I'll get ice—for your milk and my *carne asada*. Trust me, your milk will be fine, and Johnny won't go stale for a half-hour. We'll cross the street and have a donut. How's that?"

Colette stared at the donut shop. "You don't know Johnny like I do. Warm beer makes for a cold heart."

"That's why we have ice. We'll keep the beer—and Johnny—chilled for a while."

Colette grinned, although it seemed more forced than natural. Of course, with the creases on her cheeks and forehead, very little about her seemed natural anymore.

As the clerk dropped groceries into Colette's paper bag and passed her the change, she nodded. "Sure. Why not? One donut will not head for my hips."

"Great." Isabel bought the ice and split it between her bags and Colette's. They dropped the groceries in their cars and crossed the street for coffee and a cinnamon twist.

As they sat down in a booth, Isabel forced her own smile. The overhead fluorescent lights cast a harsh pallor to Colette's face. Her mousy brown hair seemed dry and ragged. Her eyes darted. Her hands struggled to stay steady. Disheveled and frumpy, Colette appeared barely a step up from homeless. She stubbornly wore her oversized sunglasses and nervously arranged the bangs on her forehead.

At that point, Isabel's intuition easily kicked in. "Tell me about Johnny. Is he the one, the only, the best man you've ever met?"

"He is cute," Colette said. "I'll start there. Tall and trim, I suppose. And a mustache, kind of. He's still working on that." She smirked.

"And for a job, what's he working on there?"

"Transportation mostly," Colette said. "For a company."

"Sounds like my father—the truck driver. But if it's a steady job, it should keep you guys happy. What I mean to say; if Johnny is *not* like my father, you're off to a good start."

"Honey, Johnny is like no one else I know. We balance each other. Ying, yang, so to speak. I'm up, and he's down. When I'm down, he cheers me up. I got flowers this morning and breakfast in bed. Now you tell me; how many men would do that?"

Isabel expected a "for someone like me" tag, but Colette left it hanging. Isabel had certainly seen her share of flowers, often with note attached; "Sorry for last night." She wondered if the black eye behind the sunglasses had been Johnny's motive to buy the flowers or to provide breakfast in bed. The streaks of mascara that peeked below the glasses certainly told part of the true story.

Isabel flashed through a long list of questions. How did Colette ever get into this mess? How could she ever get out? Did she want to get out? Or had she—at a very young age—accepted her station in life? Was a black eye the rock bottom of a life, or were the flowers the symbol of a new beginning?

"How often does he give you flowers?" she asked.

"I know what you're getting at." Colette picked at her cinnamon twist and followed it with a sip of decaf. "But nobody's perfect. I make mistakes. Likewise Johnny. Point is, we're always there for each other."

Isabel doubted that, and she doubted that Colette—over a single cup of coffee—would reveal much more than, "We're doing fine." Even so, she thought it worthwhile to prompt her to consider a path beyond a six pack, to consider the big picture made from little choices.

"Another point being," Isabel said, chomping down on her donut, "where would you like to be in five years? If you could sketch your own future, what would I see?" She opened her palms.

"Five years from now? I'm already worried about the beer getting warm. I know what Johnny and me have planned for the weekend. And that's it."

"I understand, Colette. I know that plans can change in a heartbeat. I can tell stories about that, for sure. Lots of stories. But those are my stories, not yours."

Isabel pushed aside her donut, sipped her coffee, and tried to focus on Colette's shifting gaze. She wondered what kind of trauma, what kind of heartache would pile on the stress on a young woman like her. Nervous twitch, blotchy skin, crow's-feet by her eyes. No one deserved that.

"Then forget about the future and tell me this. You and Johnny; looking back, can you tell me about the good memories? I mean, that's what it comes down to. In the end, that's all we have left; family, friends, and memories. You and Johnny have what?"

Colette froze as if composing an essay for a college exam. She appeared deep in thought; no picking at the cinnamon twist, no stirring of coffee with the plastic spoon. She kept her eyes low and appeared to be searching for an answer. She took on a faraway look.

In a low voice, she finally said, "I have nothing. I've been with Johnny almost a year now, and honestly, I don't have a single happy memory. From the time he got out of jail to what, this morning—a year of nothing." Colette sighed. "And the flowers, they don't even come close to covering this."

She lifted her sunglasses and confirmed the black eye.

Isabel gently touched her hand, and from that point on, Colette seemed to open up like an old friend with a lot of new pains. She spoke slowly and quietly at first. Then she gathered courage to share the highlights and the low points of her recent history.

Although she jumped from one topic to another—work, family, friends they used to know, the apartment where she lived now—she invariably returned to the topic of Johnny. And when she did, her eyes glazed over, and she stuttered through a lot of I-don't-knows. Again, she lowered her hands to her lap and glanced at the exit door.

Isabel sensed that Colette had become stuck in a dead-end, both in her romance and her conversation at the donut shop. She sensed that now was the time for some blunt advice.

"Honestly, Colette, Johnny's not going to change. Not now. Not never. You know that. Odds are; neither will you. Change, that is."

Colette kept her gaze low and quietly nodded.

"But," Isabel said, "if you can't change who you are, you might be able to change *where* you are."

"I don't understand."

"How about this; I'll tell you where I lived last year, and you tell me if you see a connection."

Again, Colette nodded.

"First thing, erase any assumptions about where you think I've been. It's not even close to Paris, or Rome, or even Saratoga. Think the opposite. Think small. Think cramped and boring. If it helps, close your eyes and picture it, because where I lived was not a pretty sight.

"What I used to call home was a one-room place on the peninsula. Of course, calling it a room would be a compliment. A closet was more like it. I had a bed and side chair, and that was about it. No lights and no view. I barely had TV. No wine, Pepsi, or chips. Definitely no cinnamon twist. Essentially, if I didn't need it to survive, I didn't get it. The truth is, I felt miserable so many times at that place, I lost count. But I survived. For ten months, I stayed there; for reasons I'd rather not discuss. But it could've been worse, I suppose.

"While I was there, I felt safe. I trusted the people around me, and they gave me support. They helped me to get back on the right path. That was probably the key. That was probably why I don't regret it now. In the long run, it turned out for the best. I made some new friends and rediscovered some old. It took the longest while, but eventually, yeah, I got back on my feet. Nowadays, it's totally different. *I'm* totally different. *Carne asada* makes me happy. My boyfriend makes me happy. And you, Colette, you can make me happy."

"How so?"

Isabel grabbed a pen and paper from her handbag and wrote down a cross-street and address. She passed the note to Colette. "It's a safe place for women like you. I've never stopped in, but I know it's there. I see women there, exactly in your situation. I see them come and go. And I'm guessing that there is only one difference between them and you."

Colette lifted her eyes.

"They've taken the first step. I'd say the hardest step. I can guarantee that no one there is worried about the milk—or the beer—getting warm. And I have a hunch, Colette; us meeting here, it's not a chance thing. There's got to be more. At least I'm hoping there's more. Fate is, oh, what's the word? Capricious. That's a big word meaning that we met today for a reason."

Isabel left it at that. If she had to explain the reason, then surely the reason would've been lost.

"I hear ya," Colette said, barely out loud. She slowly rose from her seat then gave Isabel a hug. "I have to go."

Isabel stood then pressed the address of the women's shelter into Colette's palm. Again they hugged. "No more flowers, okay?"

Colette nodded a reluctant goodbye then trudged to her car. Isabel lagged behind, half because she wanted Colette to take the lead and half she wanted to know which direction Colette would choose. The road to the left led to the shelter. The road to the right led to

Johnny's apartment. As Colette got into her car and merged into traffic, Isabel watched closely.

As she watched, Isabel arrived at her own turning point of sorts. It had crossed her mind before, but now she felt certain. Her new mission, career, or calling—whatever the label—suddenly made sense. Her helping others. Isabel decided that she could feel good about herself by doing good for others. Once again, she vowed to become a therapist, even if it took the next five or ten years.

She grinned. A donut shop and a women's shelter seemed a strange way to make a life choice, but perhaps that was fate. Colette herself may or may not have been a lost cause, but so many others were waiting to be helped. Isabel had taken her first step to making a difference.

She squinted as she watched Colette reach the end of the road. Isabel knew that there was more than a metaphor at stake. Colette's life, her true future, hung in the balance. It came down to the simple spin of the steering wheel. As it was, Colette tapped her brakes, hesitated, and then hung a left toward the direction that led to the women's shelter.

Isabel smiled. Fate may have had a partner that day.

Chapter *24*

FROM A SMALL *carniceria* in San Jose to quaint *tiendas*—gift shops—on the Baja California peninsula in Mexico, Isabel felt another change in direction coming. And that direction, she believed, would be totally opposite from a cramped women's shelter near a strip mall and bank, a hundred and eighty degrees from an abusive alcoholic fresh out of jail.

Yesterday, Drake, Barry, and Isabel had taken a commercial flight to La Paz, near the southern tip of Baja. From there, they rode with Drake's friends up the highway to the fishing village of Loreto. Once there, they settled into a three-star hotel—one of the finest by the water's edge.

They had planned on a long weekend on the coast to be followed by a brisk drive up Highway 1 to Santa Rosalia. Typical of most of Drake's travels, he had promised to stay with friends or to make new friends along the way. Loreto, as he had said, would be no exception. That was fine by Isabel. For this trip, Drake had his agenda, and she had hers.

While Drake and Barry socialized with the locals and sampled the Baja cervezas, Isabel wandered off to take in the surrounding ambience. After grabbing nachos for lunch at a taco stand, she popped into each of the shops along Salvatierra Boulevard. She fingered the seashell necklaces, studied at the framed art, and haggled over the price of a Talavera pot. The only Spanish she knew, *muy caro*—very expensive—served her well with her negotiations. She walked away with a paper mâché angel for pesos.

She took her time as she wandered from store to store. She bought nothing more but touched all that was hanging on racks or stacked on shelves. It felt good to be out and about by herself. The sun, the clean air, the friendly people; so far, the weekend seemed ideal. The village seemed to be a slice of paradise. Eventually, she made her way to the marina and took her place on a rock near a cluster of fishing boats.

She couldn't help but smile as she gazed at the palm trees and shimmering water. Despite being miles from home—essentially in the middle of nowhere—she felt totally safe, independent, and secure. Such a strange feeling. A year ago, she felt lucky simply to walk without crutches. Two years ago, she felt lucky to walk anywhere without Drake standing guard.

Inevitably, she thought back to her time in the hospital. She was amazed that one year could make such a huge difference in how she felt and how Drake behaved. As she told Colette, living in a small room and cutting her requirements to the bone was no doubt the main reason.

While at Stanford, Isabel proved to Drake that she didn't need a fancy house or grand hotel to live in. For ten months, all she had was a bed with no view and a hallway with no lights. She proved that she didn't need elegant restaurants and haute cuisine. A tray of pork chops and green beans suited her purpose just fine. She didn't need the ballet or opera in San Francisco when *Days of Our Lives* and *Happy Days* came on the TV in Palo Alto.

While at Stanford, she proved that she didn't need Drake for transportation, employment, education, or entertainment. Looking back; fundamentally, she didn't need Drake for anything.

Drake seemed to understand the situation. He accepted his place in the picture. These days, he gave Isabel freedom; freedom to set her own schedule and freedom to walk anywhere and go anywhere by herself. She had no chaperone on her elbow and no time cards to punch. There was no doubt in Isabel's mind; she was at the peak of her independence, the height of her happiness. Now her plan was to keep it that way.

It seemed ironic; the more that Drake trusted her and the more independence he gave her, the more she wanted him around. Isabel finally understood the difference between need and want. And at this moment, in this remote and quiet village, she wanted more than ever for Drake to be at her side and stay at her side. She had a hunch that Drake would share the feeling.

She looked around and began to make sense of it all. Romantic beach, azure blue water, exotic location, and a warm breeze to ignite the passion; Loreto seemed custom-fit for a marriage proposal. The timing seemed to make perfect sense.

Lately, Drake had been hinting of a more permanent relationship. He had been dropping subtle reminders of how great they looked as a couple. He had asked about dream vacation spots. He didn't exactly say "honeymoon," but Isabel knew what he meant.

Drake had also begun compiling a somewhat discreet list of upcoming choices. Where were the best homes in Saratoga and Atherton? Which schools had the best psychology programs? Which baby names were the cutest? Which is better; family or career, both or none? And the most ominous clue about his wish for a wedding; he had once again asked to meet the parents. Isabel politely told him 'no' on a visit to the parents, and 'yes' to the Bahamas or Fiji.

Last week, she had discreetly written her own priority list in her journal. Would she spend six years or ten years in school? Would she help in a women's shelter or become a counselor in a cancer ward? Would she have kids sooner, later, or never?

She wrote down the tough questions but couldn't think of a single answer ... yet. Eventually, she got down to more immediate concerns and scribbled the most pressing question on her list; when would Drake propose and where?

She wondered; would this be the weekend? Would this beach be the spot? Would she stand by the palm trees and again say 'yes' to the one man who could offer the full package; provide, protect, love, and laugh? For a man like Drake, whose mission in life was to make memories, Loreto seemed the perfect setting for holding hands and slipping on an engagement ring.

The only snag in the plan; Drake was nowhere near. At the moment, that seemed to be a minor problem at best. For once, she knew exactly where he was, and for once, he had no idea where she was. Yet another reason to smile. Isabel got up from her rock on the beach and slowly made her way to the restaurant near the hotel. With perfect timing, she dropped into El Corazón del Mar just as Drake and Barry sat down for dinner at the table for twelve.

Regrettably, the noise, the commotion, the half-English, half-Spanish conversations knocked away her sense of serenity. Isabel pulled up a seat next to Drake but doubted that she would stay for the main course. She wasn't hungry because she had nibbled on nachos for lunch and as a late afternoon snack. And she couldn't join the discussions on cervezas or the debates over which car would be faster on Highway 1; a Mercedes coupe or a Corvette? She had no interest in horsepower and no expertise on beer. Despite her afternoon wish for a lifetime together, Isabel suddenly felt alone in a crowd.

"This is not what I expected," she muttered. She hoped that Drake would promise a moonlight stroll on the beach or a private table in the corner. But no such luck. At the moment, Drake seemed immersed in his own special world.

Isabel sipped her sangria and tried to cope. She shook her head as Drake and Barry held another belching contest with the locals. Now she doubted her instincts; was Drake was setting up the weekend for a proposal or lining up another frat party? Everlasting love and the promise of protection; how about a moment of civility and the promise of a quiet night for sleep?

Barry pushed a bowl of food in front of Isabel's face. "Come on," he said. "Give it a whirl. We've got ceviche, chilaquiles, and huitlacoche enchiladas. Best food south of the border."

"No, thanks," she said. "I don't eat anything I can't pronounce."

"Suit yourself." Barry poured on the molcajete sauce. "There's plenty more where this came from."

Isabel grumbled. Drake's flair for dramatic wedding proposals and lasting memories seemed a back-burner issue while he and Barry devoured the pork carnitas and cerveza. She politely bowed out from the scent of cabbage and grease.

"Enough fun for one day," she said. "My bed is calling me."

"So soon?" Drake said. "We're barely getting warmed up."

"I can tell. Thanks, but no."

Drake frowned but obliged. He stood, pulled out her chair, and gave her a goodnight kiss. "*Buenas noches, cariño.* We'll see you in the morning."

Isabel waved a half-hearted goodbye to Drake and the others. She walked up the street and climbed the stairs to her room on the hotel's second floor. Suddenly, she felt tired and disheartened.

She had misgivings about the dinner feast but tried to stay optimistic. They had one more day on their trip and one more chance for a fairytale ending. Isabel curled up in bed with a romance novel and figured her own final chapter was just about due; hopefully before the drive to Santa Rosalia, hopefully at sunrise on the beach. She fluffed her pillow, stretched out her legs, and propped her paper mâché angel on the nightstand. Guardian of the night, she called her little trinket.

She read her book for a while but set it aside when old aches and pains uncomfortably intruded. Slowly, but definitely, the long day— the long weekend—was catching up. The symptoms began gently then came on stronger. A throbbing headache, cold shivers in her arms and legs, stomach pains that persisted. She tried to ignore it. She told herself to enjoy the ambience. She told herself to look forward to tomorrow.

Isabel unsteadily walked to the window balcony and gazed at a sandy moonlit beach. Isla Carmen in the dark background; a gentle surf nearby; a lone mariachi. It was a perfect night for new beginnings and a great way to forget about the past.

Even so, she couldn't shake the nagging feeling of old apprehensions. She couldn't help but flash back to her groggy, unstable nights in the hospital. She refused to say, "relapse." But when the blood slowly drained from her head, she tried hard to stay on her feet. The symptoms seemed painfully familiar.

She held tightly to the balcony railing, feeling light-headed and nauseous. Then she wobbled, almost teetering on the verge of collapse. Quickly, her déjà vu went into overdrive, and she easily recognized the precursor to a medical nightmare.

Unclear of what was happening; Isabel ran her fingers across her forehead. Sure enough, she felt a fever. She confirmed what she had already suspected; she was now officially and acutely ill. It was a bad way to end the night. It was no way to encourage a proposal.

Trying to clear her mind and settle her stomach, she took in a deep breath of the fresh sea air. Bad mistake. The nausea swept over her like a tidal wave and drowned her in gut-wrenching pain. Forget about romance, forget about love. Only one thought leapt into her head; get to the bathroom and throw up her guts.

The mysterious nagging pain she had felt since she had climbed the stairs of the hotel came on with a vengeance as it burned from her stomach to her throat. Tossing her lunch into the toilet didn't help. She flushed away the bitter taste of nachos, but the fire inside—and the nausea—simply doubled.

Dear God, what's happening? Isabel dragged herself to the bed as the pain spread along her spine and throbbed in sync with her pulse. She flopped onto the bed covers and drew her knees to her chest. It didn't help. Violent cramps grabbed her body, and she found it near impossible to catch her breath.

Dr. Linoff had warned her about the possibility of relapse from the trauma of the accident. He had warned her to take it slow and easy during her long, long recovery. Isabel never paid him much mind. She thought that she knew her body better than anyone else. She thought she knew how to pace herself. Now, she wasn't sure. Now, with her body fighting her, she worried that her dark prophesy might finally be coming true. She worried that tonight was a sign that she could never escape her past.

Isabel shuddered from pain and fear. How could she switch from a healthy, starry-eyed woman one minute to a desperate victim the next? Medically, something had gone dreadfully wrong. Psychologically, an evil had appeared on her doorstep.

As the room faded in and out, she thought the worse. Was she going to die in some obscure Mexican village on a street she could barely pronounce? Would Drake look for her now or wait until morning? Would she be flown home in a coffin or buried on-site? Of the hundred thoughts that popped into her mind, one frightful image troubled her the most; what would Charlene say when she got word of her daughter's demise? Would Charlene be sad, angry, fearful, or simply say, "I told you so."

And who would give Charlene the news; Drake, Barry, or some nameless official of the San Jose Health Department? The reality of Isabel's double life had abruptly caught up. As far as Charlene knew, her daughter was simply cross-town, visiting friends or relatives, or staying at a spiritual retreat. Now Drake would have to meet the parents the hard way. He would have to explain himself, his life, and a second horrible incident. Isabel's worst nightmare was about to manifest.

She winced from the stabbing pain and reached long to the nightstand. She fumbled the phone, called the front desk, and begged the clerk to find Drake at the restaurant. Then she let the receiver drop to the floor and let her arm slump over the side of the bed. She had no energy to say another word.

Most of what happened next came to her in fragments of blurred images and distorted sounds. She struggled to remain conscience. She hoped to stay alive.

In a short while, her room door swung open and slammed against the wall with a bang. As the hotel clerk stepped aside, Drake pushed his way forward. From that point on, Drake did what he did best; he gave orders to everyone he saw.

"Barry, get over here and check her out. Luis, get the manager and the phone number of the clinic. Isabel, open your eyes, talk to me."

"Drake," she moaned, "I don't feel so good."

"You'll be fine," he said. "Barry's here. A doctor's on the way. Between us, we'll get you on your feet."

She looked up to Drake, then to Barry, and then closed her eyes.

"What's wrong, Barry? She was fine an hour ago."

Barry moved in and checked the vitals. "Pulse rate—a hundred twenty. Feverish. Probably vomiting. She's definitely sick."

"Yeah, we know."

"What do you want me to say? She's got the stomach flu? An intestinal virus? It could be anything." Barry scowled at Drake then snagged a desk lamp for a clearer look. "Okay, her pupils respond. Her throat's red, a bit dry. Respiration looks okay. What did she have for breakfast?"

"How would I know?" Drake said. "She spent the morning in town and the afternoon by herself." He leaned over Isabel and gently spoke. "What did you have for breakfast?"

Isabel simply shook her head and moaned.

"What about last night?" Barry asked.

"*That* I can tell you," Drake said. "She had prime rib; the same as you and me. Remember?"

Barry nodded. "If it's staphylococcus, I'd say give her a day, and she'll be fine. But ..."

"But what?"

Barry looked at Drake then at Isabel. "I'm sorry, Isabel, you are not a normal woman. And I mean that in the most generous sense. Those injuries you got last year; they may be showing up now. Plus complications." He turned to Drake. "Bottom line, she needs a hospital. They have to run lab tests, and we have to get the results fast!"

Drake cooled her forehead with a damp cloth then paced the floor between the balcony and the hallway door. "How far is the clinic?"

"Luis called for an ambulance."

"Where's the cook? I want a word with him."

Isabel shook her head 'no' and barely caught Drake's fading words.

If anything happens to her," Drake said, "I swear—"

Then Isabel faded. Her light head made it impossible to focus. The pain in her gut forced her to one thought only; *Am I going to die today? Is this my punishment for pushing too hard?*

She passed out, only to wake up later to strange Spanish voices. She felt delirious, and her stomach pain would not let up.

"*No esta aqui*," a man said. "*Esta enfermo.*"

"You mean we have no driver?" Barry said furiously. "And no ambulance?"

"*Si, por este noche.*"

"*You're* the doctor," Drake said loudly to the Spanish man. "How did *you* get here?"

"I walked," the doctor said, "from home."

"Where's your sphygmomanometer?" Barry said, as loud as Drake.

"*Que?*"

"Your blood pressure gauge."

"At the clinic," the doctor said.

"Antibiotics? IV fluids?"

"*Lo mismo.*"

"She has a temperature of a hundred and five," Barry said to the doctor. "What do you suggest?"

The doctor shrugged. "Drive her to the clinic. *Maybe* we can help."

Isabel glanced at the clock on the wall. 2:02 a.m. She looked at Drake then mumbled, "I love you, Drake. Whatever happens, please don't leave me."

"Don't worry," Drake said. "I will never leave you again."

Isabel closed her eyes again and passed out again—her last feeling was one of pain, dread, and doom. Her last thought was one of a beautiful life crashing hard.

In a short while, she woke up to more voices and pushing hands. The agony in her stomach and the confusion in her head seemed relentless. She didn't know where she was—other than the middle of trouble. She opened her eyes and looked up.

"Okay, darling," Drake said, "you'll have to walk a little and ride a lot. If you can get to the jet, we'll take it from there."

"Jet?" Isabel asked.

"I asked my father to send down the Lear, and it's landing as we speak. Forget Loreto. We're going home."

Isabel bobbed her head. The first part of her prayer had been answered; she had heard the word 'home.' The second part of her prayer—getting healthy again—remained problematic.

With one hand on her stomach and the other on the bed, Isabel swung her feet over the edge. With Drake's help, she unsteadily stood. She looped her purse around her neck and stuffed her paper mâché angel into her purse. That small token gave her courage to move and to keep on moving. She hobbled to the room door and down the hotel stairs, desperately trying to stay conscience and stay on her feet.

From the hotel and on their way to the airport, she took in snippets of sights and sounds; headlights, taillights, odd voices, rumbling cars, Drake yelling commands. Isabel clutched her angel as the old Ford sped around curves and dodged oncoming traffic. The fear of a crash crossed her mind. The terror of a Mexican hospital seemed real.

Finally, after a bumpy, twisting ride to the nearby airport, she whiffed the scent of jet exhaust on the tarmac. She felt a little better. Then, when Drake leaned closer and caressed her cheek, she took in his exotic—but now familiar—fragrance. Suddenly, she felt much better. Then she closed her eyes and passed out.

When she opened her eyes again—still in a haze—she incredulously stared at an array of heart monitors, IV tubes, and oxygen bottles. She swiveled her head left and saw Dr. Linoff checking his charts and glancing at her over the rim of his glasses. Drake and Barry stood at the foot of her bed. Dr. Wescott peeked in from the doorway.

"This must be Stanford," Isabel said, half in relief, half in distress as old memories resurfaced.

"I thought I had sent you home," Linoff said, "with a one-way ticket."

"Sorry," Isabel squeaked.

"Nevertheless, welcome back, so to speak. In case you're curious, here's a small list of what brought you here; dehydration, staph infection, exhaustion, stress, anemia. Shall I go on?"

Isabel shook her head 'no.'

"I would add stubbornness, but instead I'll phrase it like this; you, young lady, were very lucky to get here when you did."

Isabel sighed. Despite the long list of underlying causes, she felt pretty good. Despite being called stubborn, she knew that she had done nothing wrong. Despite the fuzziness in her head, she came close to smiling.

With Drake and Barry nearby, Dr. Linoff with his charts, and Dr. Wescott at the ready, she couldn't have asked for a better team. She couldn't have found a more caring group. She realized that once in a while, she really did *need* someone. She was not totally independent all the time. And that was okay. Good friends and people she could trust; it was a good feeling to know that they were there—if she ever needed.

She gazed lovingly at Drake. She knew that Drake's vow to love and protect could span miles and time to make it so. Now, without a doubt, she knew that she would get better, much better.

"Luck didn't have much to do with it," she told Linoff while smiling at Drake. "If you know what I mean."

Linoff looked at Drake then nodded. "Yes, I know exactly what you mean."

Isabel rested and recuperated almost a week at Stanford. A paper mâché angel on her nightstand, a real angel—Drake—at her side. Despite the limited visiting hours, Drake spent every possible moment at her side, offering comfort and talking about a healthy and happy future that they both so richly deserved.

Then soon, like a cutaway shot from a Hollywood movie, Drake held her hand and asked her to close her eyes. When Isabel figuratively opened them again, she took in the view of another pristine, sandy beach. No dream, no delusion, no worries about doctors or hospitals.

The big difference from Loreto; this beach, near Helen's condo on Maui, felt so much safer. Trained medical staff nearby, health codes on the pineapple and poi, plus Drake at her side; Isabel had no fear of a repeat episode. She had no expectations other than a pleasant memory to be made.

Doubly nice, there was no one else in sight. No Barry, no bikers, no cabbies, no shopkeepers hustling their pots and pans. All she saw; wide beaches, lava rocks, palm and Kiawe trees. All she heard was a rolling surf that played like music in paradise. A warm breeze passed through to Isabel's heart as she gently held onto Drake's hand.

They gazed at the setting sun as though they were teenagers on a first date. And much like their years-ago true first date, Drake seemed perfectly styled in his tan slacks and white linen shirt. Casual, elegant, sophisticated, handsome. Not one hair out of place. No hint of disarray.

Isabel herself, expecting a night to remember, had slipped into her favorite blue jeans and lavender cotton top. It was cool and comfortable and much less revealing than a Stanford hospital gown. She felt ready to hear whatever Drake had to say. She felt open to any advice he had to share. So she listened.

"I'd like to ask your opinion," Drake said softly, "about a promise I made years ago; to protect, respect, and totally love you. A promise I made on the first day we met. And a promise that will be there tomorrow; if you can tell me this."

"Go on," Isabel said, feeling a touch of elation.

"You can tell me if second, or third, or so many missed chances are real. You can tell me the answer to a last-chance question."

"I promise a good answer."

Drake took a deep breath, gazed at Isabel, and gently held her hand. "Will you give me a chance to prove myself now and for as long as we live? Will you allow me to love you as long as I can? What I'm asking is; will you marry me? Will you marry me and love me for the rest of your life?"

He reached into his pocket and withdrew a small ring box. There it was; the flash of a diamond to remind her of his promise to stay by her side. It was a larger ring than the ones before—from a gentler, more compassionate man than anyone before.

Isabel slid on the ring as she turned to Drake and smiled.

"Yes," she said. "Yes, I will, Drake. I will marry you and love you the rest of my life. And you should know me by now; there was *no* chance that I would say anything else."

THE END